Dark Tides

Dark Tides

KIMBERLY VALE

KINGDOM OF BONES BOOK 2

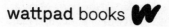

wattpad books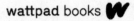

An imprint of Wattpad WEBTOON Book Group

Copyright© 2022 Kimberly Vale

Content warning: violence, mentions of abuse, death, abortion, gore and blood, grief

Published in Canada by Wattpad WEBTOON Book Group, a division of Wattpad Corp.

36 Wellington Street E., Suite 200, Toronto, ON M5E 1C7 Canada

www.wattpad.com

First Wattpad Books edition: October 2022

ISBN 978-1-99025-931-9 (Hardcover original)

ISBN 978-1-99025-932-6 (eBook edition)

Library and Archives Canada Cataloguing in Publication information is available upon request.

Printed and bound in Canada

1 3 5 7 9 10 8 6 4 2

Cover design by Laura Mensinga
Images © vasssaa, © Georgii Boronin, © radist777 via iStock

For Derek, my heart, my anchor

THE
KINGDOMS
OF FOUR

VENTYS

MACAYA

INCENDIA

BRONZE SEA

THE
LOST ISLE

N

CROSSBONES

THE
FROZEN GAP

INCENDIA

PORT
BARLOW

BALTESSA

SILVER SEA

CERULIA

RAVANA

OLD SEA

SARVA

TERRAN

The Ash Wastes

West Incendia
Early Frostfall

Jaron Thorne was afraid of neither man nor monster.

From the time his parents had left him and his little brother in the care of their uncle, he'd faced each morning with a brave heart and a steady mind. Ready to carry on like his mother and father hadn't left a gaping hole in his chest. When he left the small harbor town he called home, he didn't look back, even though his absence caused holes of his own making. Even when he'd been lined up against the wall at the training grounds of the Incendian Navy, he'd stood strong as stone, waiting his turn to face an emberblood and hoping to the gods that his flesh would heal soon after.

But now, as he stood in front of a monstrous volcano, fear took root in his heart, spreading through his veins like weeds. Smoke billowed from its top, the air surrounding him reeking of sulfur, a clear sign of imminent explosion. He'd die from the fumes or magma, whichever got him first.

He should be far away from West Incendia, searching Cerulia for the pirates who'd pillaged his harbor home years ago, but the whispers, always creeping along the edges of his mind, told him to come to this barren wasteland instead. Jaron cursed himself every moment he spent sailing through the Frozen Gap and riding horseback across the Ash Wastes. He tried to ignore the whispers completely, but they were there, scratching at the back of his mind with rusty nails.

Dig.

The whisper was so sudden it nearly made him jump out of the thick cloak he wore. He looked around, taking in the remains of what used to be a forest, thin spikes of bone-white wood jutting up from the pale, cracked dirt. The whisper had first come to him during the loneliest of nights, when a leap from the nearest cliff seemed better than facing another day, when there was nothing left for him to live for.

And they'd offered him *everything*.

Dig.

Firmer this time, a command. He questioned the voices: *Dig? Here?*

The whispered command repeated again and Jaron dropped the satchel from his back with a clunk and unbuttoned the collar of his cloak, removing it from his shoulders so that he could roll up his sleeves. The broad end of the shovel he'd brought with him all this way gleamed in the occasional flashes of light from the sun hidden behind the clouds and smoke. If the whispers wanted him to dig, then he'd dig. Maybe then they would leave his head for good.

Whoever or whatever the whispers belonged to, they didn't stop, even when his shovel broke earth. They continued their cadence, becoming a song that mirrored the rhythm of his strokes.

Dig. Dig. Dig.

He was knee-deep in a hole when the words became his own thoughts, a part of his every breath.

Dig. Dig. Dig.

When the height of the dirt walls reached his shoulders, his blistering hands went numb and the whisper became his own. "Dig," Jaron grunted as he threw each scoop of earth above him. "Dig. Dig."

The wretched whisper screamed back at him, an echo only Jaron could hear.

The sun had disappeared and the moon had taken its place when he discarded his shovel at the top and began digging through the raw earth with bare hands like a crazed animal, losing more of himself than he ever knew he had within him. Blood mixed with dirt on his palms, skin peeling away from his fingers with each strike of his hands into the ground. The bone forest above had been quiet before, but now it seemed that even the volcano had ceased its grumbling to watch him fall apart, his grunts and yells filling the silence, darkening the area even as the dawn of the next morning tried to peek through the clouds.

Dig. Dig. D—

Jaron's fingers scraped against something hard, and he stilled. For a flicker of a moment, he wondered if it was only a rock. Then he started digging even faster than before, brushing away the dirt until the outline of a long ebony box emerged.

Take it.

The sudden change of lyrics in the whisper's song took him

aback. He'd thought of the whispers in his head as blind ambition or sheer insanity, or maybe the echo of some tale he'd heard that had brought him to this dark place. But perhaps the voice was more after all. Perhaps his losses hadn't riddled his mind the way the other Scouts claimed as they'd jeered at him.

He stayed in the hole he'd dug and laid the box on the unsettled ground in front of him. Across the wood were etchings that mirrored tendrils of flame, an ebony as vast as he'd ever seen. Bottomless. Threatening to swallow him if he stared too long. His mutilated hands remained at his sides, quivering.

Why aren't you taking it? It'sss what you came here for.

A shadow grew around the edges of the box, blossoming from beneath as if it were awakening from a deep sleep. A piece of him—maybe the sliver of him he'd left behind in Port Hullscar—knew he should be scrambling out of the hole, but he only leaned closer, drawn in by the allure of the treasure he'd dug up.

I can give you everything you want. Everything you need.

Power. Strength. Revenge.

Jaron traced his bloody fingers over the box, mumbling his lost brother's name and promising to find him as his voice cracked like the broken man he was.

Wield the Flame and the Torch. Be my champion. Do what othersss before you could not, and you will have it all.

No longer hesitating, he curled his fingers around the box and for the first time in his life, he took something for himself.

PART ONE

LOST TREASURE

CHAPTER ONE
KANE

Death's Cove
Late Frostfall

Death's Cove takes no prisoners.

Words Kane Blackwater had heard his father say many times when the *Iron Jewel* would sail too close to the ship trap. It was a treacherous place he'd never been to, but one that had haunted his dreams as a child. Yet even though the thought made his spine go rigid, the *Iron Jewel* sailed straight toward its dark waters.

Kane stood at the helm of his ship, one hand gripping the smooth blackened-oak handle of the wheel, the other holding a spyglass to his eye, as he searched for a safe spot to enter. The clouds above were as gloomy as his mood, growing darker by the moment. Death's Cove was a splotch on the map of anyone who sailed the Sister Seas. It lurked on the tail of the Silver Sea like a silent predator waiting for its prey.

Jagged sea-stacks sprouted up from the waves like daggers,

sharp enough to rip straight through any ship that dared to venture close. Kane was used to sailing through the deep turquoise waves of the Sister Seas. From Crossbones, all the way to Sarva, the waters were the clearest and most beautiful of any he'd sailed. The sea surrounding Death's Cove was nearly the black of kraken's ink. *It's only because of the weather,* he lied to himself.

"Death's Cove takes no prisoners," said a voice very different from the slurred rasp of Kane's father. Kane pulled away from the lens of his spyglass and glanced to his right. Flynn Gunnison leaned against the railing, the wild sea wind blowing stray pieces of his sand-colored hair out of its tie and across his face. Two seasons ago, Kane would've decked Flynn for standing too close, but today, he was glad to not be alone. Today, he was glad to have a friend. Typically, Flynn would've been manning his own ship on this search mission, but the *Anaphine* remained docked in Baltessa, receiving much-needed repairs after a skirmish with a small Incendian fleet. Kane needed all the help he could get.

"We won't be anyone's prisoners," Kane replied, collapsing the barrels of the spyglass with a clap. "Not today or any other day."

Flynn slapped Kane on the back and chuckled. "Those sound like famous last words, Blackwater." The crooked smile slipped from his face for a moment. "I would rather not die today though. No offense, mate, but I'd much rather have Csilla's face be the last thing I see. Not your ugly mug." Csilla Abado was the newly crowned Queen of Bones. She was back in Baltessa, the capital of the island kingdom of Cerulia, along with the Maidens and Lorelei Storm—whose face was one that Kane found himself missing as the days and nights at sea blurred together.

"Remind me again why I brought you here?" Kane asked, pocketing the spyglass and grabbing the wheel with both hands.

"It's become apparent that it wasn't to help man the ship, as you're up here and not with the rest of the crew."

"You brought me to help search for Rove because there's a chance you might need my impeccable shot." As a reminder, Flynn drew one of his pistols from his belt and spun it over his fingers. The barrel came to a stop in front of his pursed lips and he puffed once like he was blowing out the wick of a candle. "Besides, is there *really* a need for me to break my back over some sails? Your crew has beefed up pretty nicely over the past few moons. Plus, Arius and Borne are down there, so I'd say we're faring well."

"You say faring well, I say barely cutting it."

"You *have* always been the flask-half-empty type."

Kane was about to attempt a comeback when something white caught the corner of his attention. He turned to his left just as the shouts from the men on the deck reached his ears. From behind one of the largest sea-stacks emerged the white sails of a fully stocked brig. It slid out from behind its hiding place like it had been waiting for them all along. Kane didn't have to pull out his spyglass to see the flag waving in the wind atop the brig's highest mast, or the emblem of flame and sword imprinted on the fabric.

"Incendians!" Kane yelled down to his crew. "Man your posts! Prepare for evasive maneuvers!"

His crew burst into action, some disappearing belowdecks while others prepared the ropes and pulleys for sail adjustments. Kane wasn't afraid to take on a brig. He'd sunk more than one with fewer men on his ship, but this was the worst possible time. He couldn't waste his energy and resources on these Incendians when he was so close to Death's Cove and the answers he sought in its shadows.

Kane was about to tell his men to drop the sails so that they could sail full course through the sea of stone daggers when a burst of light arced over the deck of the *Iron Jewel*, followed by the scream of flames. Kane witnessed the ball of fire before it hit the sea with an angry hiss. Waves from the impact washed up onto the deck, coating the wood and making it even slicker.

"They have an emberblood on board," Flynn said, breathless.

Kane had forgotten that Flynn was standing next to him. "It would seem that way," Kane grunted as he gripped the wheel harder, trying to keep his balance as the ship rocked from the sudden waves.

"If you can get us close enough, then I can take him out." Flynn was already staring down the barrel of his pistol, watching, waiting for his moment.

"There's no way you could—"

"You must've not been there when I shot a nectarine off Arius's head."

"I could do that."

"While blindfolded."

Kane huffed. He could get Flynn close enough for a clear shot, there was no question about it, but there wasn't time to ponder as a second Incendian brig emerged from behind a sea-stack on the starboard side of the ship.

Shit.

He'd been following leads for two moons about Rove and where he might've been hiding since his disappearance from Crossbones. The harbor gossip had led Kane straight to Death's Cove, but it seemed those rumors had also reached the ears of the Incendians, who were getting bolder by the day.

A burst of flame erupted from the second brig and arced over the sea toward the *Iron Jewel*. The shot nicked the top of the ship with a crash and crackle of fire, taking the eagle's nest with it. Scraps of singed wood rained down on them. Another ember-blood. They didn't stand a chance. They had to evade.

"We'll have to test your impeccable shot another day," Kane told Flynn as he spun the wheel, changing the angle of the masts.

The ship rocked to the right as the wind filled the sails and took the *Iron Jewel's* course to the southwest, narrowly dodging a sprouted sea-stack. This move, however, put them in line with the second brig, the wind pushing them straight toward the Incendians. Another burst of flame sliced through the air toward his ship, cutting close enough on the starboard side for Kane to feel the heat of the blaze. Two out of three shots from the ember-bloods missed, but how many did they truly need in order to sink a wooden ship? Kane wasn't going to find out.

Turning the sails again would bring them too close to the brig, close enough for the emberblood to cause catastrophic damage to the *Iron Jewel*. He had to turn faster, *much* faster.

"Take the wheel!" Kane yelled to Flynn, who shoved his pistol back into its holster and took hold of the handles. "We're club-hauling!" Kane leapt away from the wheel and down the flight of stairs leading to the lower deck.

"Don't rip a hole in your ship!" Flynn's yell was barely audible as another ball of flame arced over them.

This time the attack came from behind, where the first brig chased them, both the brigs beginning to trap them in. Kane shoved past the men who scrambled in front of him with ropes in their hands and ran forward, his boots slipping through the sea-slick as he raced toward the fore of the ship.

Taking two steps at a time up the stairs, he reached the fo'c'sle deck and ran to the portside. A knotted rope sat on a wooden hook, holding one of the portside anchors up on the side of the ship. Sea spray whipped at his face, stinging his skin, but with one heave, he lifted the knot and threw it over the side of the ship, dropping the anchor down into the sea with it. He only had a moment to withdraw his sword before the rope tightened and the anchor hit the sea floor. The ship jerked like a plaything, sending men flying onto the deck, as it made a sharp turn away from the incoming brig.

Kane gained his balance and sliced through the anchor's rope in one clean sweep of his sword. As soon as they were untethered, Kane spun and leapt back down the stairs.

"Drop the sails!" he yelled as he raced back to the helm of his ship. "Full sails! Full sails!"

His men brushed themselves off and heaved at the ropes, sending them sailing at full mast. Kane wove through them, hoping to the Sea Sisters that Flynn could stay away from at least one sea-stack until Kane returned to the wheel. The wind was on their side, pushing them quickly against the angry currents surrounding Death's Cove.

Kane bounded up the steps to the poop deck and quickly pivoted back to the helm. Flynn stepped aside and swept his wild hair away from his face. Kane watched as the two brigs raced toward each other now, the current of the sea and the wind in their sails pushing them until they crashed together in the middle. A sight that made the storm inside Kane settle just a smidge.

"Quick thinking," Flynn said, giving Kane a pat on the back. "You really outdid yourself there. I mean, the sheer brilliance of—"

"Will you shut up?" Kane growled, not needing any of Flynn's distractions. He had to get this ship into Death's Cove in one piece. If he had any hopes of finding Rove or learning what the man had planned next, this is where he would find answers. Kane squinted at the two dark peaks in the distance and the shadowed crevice between, the place where ships went to die, taking with them the secrets they held. Secrets that Kane was hell-bent on uncovering.

The closer the *Iron Jewel* sailed to Death's Cove, the fiercer the wind whipped at the black sails. Kane feared they might not hold up and they'd have to be pulled back. Doing so, however, would leave the ship at the mercy of the dark and restless waters. Sea-stacks would destroy the ship in no time at all.

Despite his instincts and the ghost of his father's voice telling him to turn back toward safe waters, Kane kept them sailing to the nearing shadowed sliver of the cove, weaving his ship between sea-stacks like a snake between rocks in its path.

When they miraculously reached the foot of the two mountainous peaks, a shadow loomed over the ship, casting the deck in darkness. The coolness of the shade pricked Kane's skin, making each hair stand on end. He should've felt some inkling of fear, yet there was nothing in him but the fire of determination.

"Aye," mused Flynn, looking up toward the peaks. "I just got chills."

"Pull up your bootstraps," Kane told him, stepping away from the wheel. Flynn followed close behind.

"What's next?" Flynn asked. "We raid the cove of all valuables? Imagine the treasures that've been trapped in there for lifetimes."

Kane stopped and whipped back around to Flynn, unamused. "No distractions. We're here for one reason: to find Rove." As the two descended the stairs together, Kane yelled to Doan, one of his longest-serving and most loyal crewmates. "Doan! Take the wheel! Navigate us into the cove while I prepare a scouting crew."

Two pirates met Kane and Flynn at the bottom of the stairs. Arius Pavel smiled at them both, dimples in his light-brown cheeks, his curly, sun-kissed hair cut since half of it had been singed off at Crossbones. Borne, a clear calm to Arius's wild storm, stood nearly a head shorter than Arius. The witchblood's golden eyes were now faded to brown, his magic diminished after giving it up to save Lorelei from her fate a season ago. Freckles were scattered over the bridge of his nose, and his auburn hair blew in the wind like the flames of a brushfire.

"I don't know what we'll find in there," Kane said, his vision surveying across the deck and to the nearing cove, "but a reliable trader in Ravana said that this was where a Bonedog ship was headed."

"Why though?" Arius asked, confusion twisting his brow. "Death's Cove is a no-man's-land."

Borne shifted his weight. "There may be no men, but there are secrets to be told."

"Did your mother tell you that one too?" Arius teased, giving Borne a light nudge.

"Why are you speaking of my mother?" Borne turned on him. If Borne's eyes had still been gold like his mother's, Arius probably wouldn't be so brave.

"Gentlemen, gentlemen," Flynn said, interrupting their squabble. "Time is of the essence here. Let's not make the Blackwater mad now." Flynn glanced back at Kane with a devious smile that Kane wanted to smack off his face.

"Are you lot having a good time listening to yourselves?" Kane lifted one brow.

"Oh, he has jokes now." Arius laughed. "We must be rubbin' off on him, mates."

Kane rolled his eyes. "Borne is right. We could very well find no Bonedogs, but a lost ship of theirs could hold the knowledge that we need about Rove's whereabouts."

The *Iron Jewel* entered the shadow of Death's Cove. Smooth obsidian walls rose up on either side of the ship, stretching so far up, most of the sparse sunlight was blocked, leaving the ship cloaked in cool darkness.

"Light the lanterns!" Kane shouted to his crew. There was some scrambling across the deck and several moments later, lanterns lit up one by one, casting the ship in an eerie glow. Sharp shadows cut through the light.

A rustling sound came from the left and Kane quickly spun toward it, his hand resting at his sword hilt, always ready for a fight. Nothing was there. Light crept along the wall as the ship sailed forward. More rustling. The others must have heard it too as they turned in the same direction as Kane. He pulled at his sword now, sliding the top inch from its sheath.

Then Kane saw it. Sitting in a nest built in a hollowed portion of the wall was a seabird unlike any he had seen before. It had a long, skinny neck like an egret, a black beak narrow and sharp like a dagger, and feathers that were glossy like they'd been dipped in ink. Its brilliant cerulean eyes stared right at Kane, unblinking. A chill swept up his spine.

"Comoras." Borne's whisper cut through the quiet like a knife. "I've only seen paintings in one of my mother's books."

As the *Iron Jewel* sailed farther into the cove, more nests and comoras filled the crevices of the wall, pair after pair of mesmerizing eyes falling on the ship, long necks craning to watch them. Something twisted inside Kane, making him feel unsteady.

"Never seen them before," Flynn said quietly with his hands

at his pistols. He must have felt the same uneasiness as Kane. "Definitely never heard of them."

"Because they're not supposed to be here," Borne explained.

"Then where are they supposed to be?"

"In Limbo."

The words made the breath whoosh out of Kane. If these birds were supposed to be trapped in another realm like the fire god Magnus and other monsters and creatures, then there had to be a good reason for it. Kane wasn't sure he wanted to find out what it was.

"Look at their eyes. They're nearly hypnotizing," Arius mused. Arius took a step forward toward the deck railing. "They're like little drops of seawater. Why would someone put such pretty birds in Limbo?"

The comora nearest to Arius spread its wings, its wingspan wider than Kane stood tall. Leaving its nest, it flew the short distance to the *Iron Jewel*, perching on the railing, big enough to be brow level with Arius. Arius reached toward the seabird, his fingers splayed. The comora stretched its neck forward, its head tilting as if observing Arius curiously, its ruffled black feathers falling smoothly back into place. Then it opened its beak, letting out a horrid, scratchy shriek. Row after row of sharp teeth glittered at them. Arius stumbled back, falling onto the deck.

"What do they eat?" Kane asked, unsheathing his sword fully.

"Anything that moves," Borne answered, matter-of-factly. "But they have a particular liking for human flesh."

Arius stood up quickly and dusted off his pants. "You know, Borne, you could have mentioned that before I tried to pet the thing."

As if on cue, a chorus of shrieks blasted through the shadowed cove, echoing off the cove's walls and right into Kane's core. He nearly froze, knees buckling, but instead, he burst into action, yelling at his crew to prepare to fight. Everyone scrambled, some grabbing weapons they didn't have before.

It wasn't long before the first comora swooped down, its toothed beak wide open, ready to snatch someone up. It missed and circled back around toward a crew member in the middle of the deck who didn't see it coming. This time the bird found its target, its claws ripping into the man's shoulders from behind. He screamed and Kane raced forward to help him, but it was too late as the comora's beak unhinged and cut off the man's scream with a quick bite.

The sound made Kane seasick. He stumbled back as the bird flew off with the man's head, leaving the rest of his body to collapse, blood spilling freely onto the deck. Black spots filled Kane's vision as his face went cold.

He couldn't die today. There was still so much to do, so many frayed ends that needed to be tied. Lorelei's face flashed in his mind, the soft blush that often rosed her pale cheeks, the delicate curve of her nose, the shocking blue of her eyes with her dark hair blown by the sea wind. He'd promised her on the docks that he'd come back to Baltessa. He never broke his promises, and he wasn't going to start now.

Kane barely had a moment to compose himself before another comora swooped toward him, talons reaching. But he was ready. He held his sword back and waited. When the bird was close enough to rip into him, he spun out of the way and severed the comora's head with one heavy swing.

The rattling shrieks of the comoras and the screams of his men began to blend together as the attack continued. A shot rang out to Kane's left and a comora came crashing onto the deck, ramming into a lantern on its way down, making the shadows on the ship sharpen. Kane found Flynn holding his pistol and looking very pleased with himself. Arius and Borne stood back-to-back: Arius with pistols of his own, Borne with the short dual-swords Kane had had his blacksmith make for him.

"I thought I told you I didn't want to die today!" Flynn yelled to Kane. He cocked his pistol and aimed at the sky again. His bullet found its mark, and he stepped out of the way of the free-falling comora.

"Keep shooting like that and you won't!" Kane shouted in return, stepping forward to slash the back of a nearby comora. Its shriek split his ears as it took off, its flight wobbly.

The fight continued as comora after comora swept in, some finding victims in his men, but most dying at the end of a blade or pistol. As soon as it began, it came to a stop, the shrieks falling silent, the beating of wings the only sound remaining in the quiet of the cove.

Arius laughed at the sky. "We were too much for 'em, mates!" A chorus of cheers rose up from the crew, but Kane remained stoic, curious.

"Perhaps they've eaten recently," Kane suggested. If a Bonedog ship had been through here first, then the comoras could very well be full from their last meal. "Someone relight the lanterns. Tend to the wounded and prepare the dead for a proper funeral when we return to sea."

Through all this, the *Iron Jewel* continued through the cove, the walls on either side of the ship beginning to widen. The fallen lanterns were lit again, revealing the carnage on the deck. More

comoras than men lay scattered, the wood slick with the black
blood oozing from their bodies.

"So . . ." Flynn's voice trailed off. "Anyone have any ideas why
those birds are here and not in Limbo?"

Arius shrugged and wiped the sweat from his brow. "Your
guess is as good as mine."

"There must be a crack in Limbo," Borne said, his voice soft
but clear. He held more wisdom than the three of them, and at a
younger age. "An opening left behind by Lorelei."

Lorelei had died in Kane's arms back in Skull Cave. He'd felt the
warmth leave her body, guilt staining his soul like her blood on
his clothes. She'd spent her stolen moments in Limbo until Borne
was able to reverse what Rhoda Abado's dagger had done. Kane
could never get her to tell him what had happened while she'd
been in the realm between realms, but Borne had mentioned that
she might not return to the realm of the living as the same girl she
had been. Kane hadn't seen a sign of this yet, but he often found
himself lying awake at night, staring up at the ceiling, wondering
what Borne had meant and what future it foretold.

"Let me get this straight," Flynn said, his unkempt hair falling
from its tie again. "You're saying that when Lorelei came back
through Limbo, she left the door open behind her?"

"In a way, yes," Borne answered. "Possibly more than one."

If the comoras can slip through, Kane wondered, *what else can?*

"And Magnus?" Kane asked aloud. "Could he pass through as
well?"

"I do not know," Borne replied, hanging his head. "Only time
will tell."

"Captain!" yelled Doan from behind them at the helm.
"Shipwrecks ahead!"

On the starboard side of the ship, light from the lanterns crept over the shapes hidden in shadow. Kane could make out the stretch of masts and tarnished sails. Ships split in two; others untouched but as empty as Arius's flask.

"It's a shipyard," Arius said.

"Imagine the loot . . ." Flynn said.

"If we could just have an hour . . ."

"Focus!" Kane snapped. Flynn and Arius stood straighter. It was then that he saw it sitting on the farthest edge of the shipyard. He wasn't sure at first, but as the *Iron Jewel* sailed closer, it became clear. The light from the lanterns reflected off the gold engravings and railings on the ship.

A Bonedog ship. Kane couldn't believe it. He'd actually found one of Rove's boats.

Kane directed Doan to sail the ship toward the *Bonedog* while Arius and Borne prepared a dinghy for their scouting group to board. While they worked, Flynn turned to Kane.

"Are you certain about this, Blackwater?" he asked. "This doesn't feel right."

Kane straightened the collar of his black overcoat and tried to ignore the pit forming in his stomach. "We didn't come this far for nothing."

—

Stepping onto the deck of the *Bonedog* was like stepping into a bad memory. Dominic Rove had once owned the most ships in the pirate fleet, until he disappeared with them all after betraying Cerulia at Crossbones. This particular ship might not have been the one Kane visited to make deals with Rove in exchange for gold to fix the *Iron Jewel*, but that didn't change the unease that swam in his veins. He had to finish this and get off the ship before he lost his mind completely.

He tried his best to focus on the echo of his boots on the deck and the task at hand, not on the dark memories threatening to cloud his mind. Everywhere he looked, he saw the past, the faces of the men he'd once silenced for Rove—in the grooves of the wooden planks, in the shadows cast by the lantern Borne carried, everywhere. Kane blinked, attempting to be rid of them all.

Rotting bodies of the *Bonedog* crew were scattered over the deck. Old bloodstains streaked across the wood. Claw marks slashed the brown sails above into ribbons. Just as Kane had suspected.

"Looks like the comoras got them first," Flynn said, fingers under his nose, trying to block the stench that filled the air. "How long do you think they've been here?"

Kane crouched down by the dead Bonedogs nearest to him, angling himself so that the light from Borne's lantern shone on the dead man's hollowed cheeks. The man was bloated and gray, splotches of green and black stretching over his skin. His eyes were sunken in and the white fuzz of fungi had begun to grow below his nostrils and around the edges of his mouth. "About two weeks or so," Kane answered before standing again.

Anything of importance would be in the captain's cabin, so that was where Kane headed, his crew following behind him. He grabbed the golden handles of the doors to the cabin and swung them open. The stench of the dead exploded out of the room, making him stumble back. Behind him, Arius heaved. Kane put his sleeve to his nose and stepped inside.

The lantern light set the room in an eerie glow, illuminating gold ornaments and woven tapestries hanging from the walls. He'd expected a mess inside, but the room was untouched aside from a chair knocked to the ground. A body sat slumped against the far wall, but Kane could tell from its clothes and lack of feathered hat that it wasn't Rove. It was very possible that he hadn't even been on this ship when it had sailed to Death's Cove.

Kane took the lantern from Borne's hand and went to the desk near the decomposing body. Scrolls, maps, and pieces of gold were scattered across the oaken desk. Kane fumbled through them, brushing scribbled papers and quills to the side. *Nothing.* There was nothing here. Kane slammed his fist on the desk and swept his arm across its surface, sending nearly everything to the floor.

He cursed under his breath and was about to walk away when he noticed a scroll left behind from his outburst. It was more tattered than the rest, frayed and torn at the edges and having lost its color. One word on the paper stood out among the rest.

LIMBO.

He held the lantern closer to the smudged words as he tried to make out the print.

"What does it say?" Flynn asked.

"It's a scroll about Limbo," Kane said, his voice echoing in the quiet room. "How it was closed after the Old War and how to open it again . . ."

Flynn's mouth opened in reply, but nothing came out. Kane heard movement behind him and spun around.

The slouched-over dead man was now on his feet, sword in his hand, shuffling toward Kane. Kane had only a moment to dodge out of the way, but he wasn't quick enough as the dead man stabbed the tender flesh where Kane's chest met his left shoulder.

Kane grunted through his teeth and kicked the dead man away with a boot to the chest, sending him stumbling back into the wall, the tip of his sword coated with Kane's blood.

Before the dead man could attack again, Kane put the lantern on the desk and swiftly unsheathed his sword. One smooth slash sent the dead man's rotting head flying through the air. Since it was a corpse, Kane didn't expect any blood, but he also didn't expect the body to continue its attack. The dead man swung his sword again, narrowly missing Kane's face. He quickly rounded the desk and shoved it forward until it pinned the now headless dead man to the wall, his sword swinging aimlessly.

"What in Goddess's name?" Flynn asked quietly.

"Half-souls," Borne replied. "Part of their souls have remained in their bodies, while the rest remains trapped in Limbo. It's the crack in the realms. It's worse than I'd thought."

"Do you think the rest of the Bonedogs are—"

Bootsteps echoing across the main deck outside the cabin answered Flynn's wonderings. Kane glanced back at the dead man still trying to attack while pinned to the wall. "There's no use in fighting them," he said. "It seems our swords do nothing to end them. Jump ship, get to the dinghy, and head back to the *Iron Jewel*. Then we set sail straight for Baltessa. We have to warn them about Limbo as soon as possible."

The crew nodded and drew their weapons, facing the cabin door. Kane followed behind them, rolling his left shoulder and wincing at the pain that shot through his arm and chest. It had only been the tip of the dead man's sword that had gotten him, yet he felt it deep in his bones.

Just a scratch, he told himself. *It's only a scratch.*

CHAPTER TWO
CSILLA

Baltessa

Early Rainrise

Sleep didn't come often for Csilla Abado, and when it did, it was riddled with dreams she didn't want. They were a plague that she couldn't be rid of, reminding her of everything she'd lost and couldn't get back. There was no cure for dreams in this world, but if there was, she'd gladly take it.

Anything to keep her from revisiting her sister's death over and over again.

Csilla's mind was in a fog as she sat slouched on the golden throne. She could hardly stay awake as she held court, listening to the troubles of the people of Cerulia, most specifically the ones who dwelled on the capital island of Baltessa. She'd heard the woes of a merchant whose ship had sunk during a violent storm. Two brothers squabbled over who should receive the inn that their family owned after their father had passed away. A farmer and his wife from Macaya shared that their crops were dying and they couldn't figure out why. Another man had lost his son to Incendian Scouts and hadn't seen him since. Csilla promised to help each of them, as a good queen would do.

It was still odd to think of herself as that—a queen. The weight of the Bone Crown on her head was a constant reminder of the responsibility that rested on her shoulders.

As she waited for the next civilian to come and be heard, she surveyed the throne room she had grown accustomed to. The room stood taller than the masts of the *Scarlet Maiden*; golden chandeliers lit with candles hung down from the roof. The floor was marbled with one red-and-gold woven rug stretching down the very middle from her throne to the doors at the end. She remembered visiting the throne room when she was younger and back then, the windows lining the walls had always been closed. On Csilla's first day on the throne, she requested that they all remain open, letting the sea breeze roll in and help her feel a little more at home.

Crown officials were seated in rows before her in their black robes. They'd never held a sword, but their weapon was knowledge. They were men and women who'd spent their lives learning the history and ways of the world, who knew the workings of a queendom and were there to provide their knowledge or guidance if Csilla so needed. Csilla didn't know most of them by name, but she did know the man who sat off on his own, polishing the handle of his whip—General Lockhart, who wasn't a crown official, but more of a counselor, and one with whom she didn't always agree.

Tapestries depicting the flags of the pirate fleet hung down on either side of the room. Her ship, the *Scarlet Maiden*, had a crimson flag, woven with a skull with roses in its empty sockets. Beside it was a black flag for the *Iron Jewel*, the fabric complete with a skull and two crossed blades. On the other side was the flag for the *Anaphine*, faded blue with smoking pistols, and lastly, the *Wavecutter*, its flag gray with a sword between two curling waves. The brown flag of the *Bonedog* had also once hung from the rafter, but since Dominic Rove's betrayal, it had been torn down and tossed into the sea.

Csilla's attention kept falling back to the *Anaphine*'s flag, her thoughts trailing to the captain of the ship, her heart sinking each time. She hadn't seen Flynn in nearly two moons since he'd left with Kane to try to find Dominic Rove. Truth be told, she missed his crooked smile and his sand-colored hair that he had trouble keeping tied back. She missed his touches on cold nights and his kisses under the warm sun. She missed him like she missed the sea.

"Do you need to take a break?" Nara asked, placing her hand on Csilla's shoulder. Nara was always there—during court, during training, during her darkest moments when Flynn wasn't there, and when the terrible dreams had started a moon cycle ago. Csilla wasn't sure what she'd do without her first mate, her dearest of friends. Nara's voice was quiet enough so that none of the crown officials overheard. "You look like you need a break."

Csilla sat up straight on the golden throne and rubbed her face. "No," she answered. "I'm fine. I just had trouble sleeping."

"Again?" Nara stepped slightly in front of the throne and turned to Csilla, concern curving her brow and narrowing her smoky eyes. A strand of her silky black hair fell in front of her face and she smoothed it back into place. "This is the third time this week."

"It's the dreams," Csilla admitted. Just the thought of them pricked Csilla's spine. "They always start differently, but end the same—with my sword in Rhoda's gut. This time, she started to flake away, like she was burning from the inside out, until nothing was left but her bones."

"Csilla"—Nara took a step forward, quieting her voice—"you feel guilty about what happened to your sister, but you have to know it wasn't your fault. She wasn't herself. She was consumed by Magnus's whispers. In actuality, you helped set her free."

Csilla turned back to the flag of the *Scarlet Maiden*. Wasn't it her fault though? Their grandmother had appointed Csilla as captain instead of Rhoda. Would she be proud of what Csilla had done? Was this the legacy her grandmother had hoped for? Now, because of Csilla's sword, there was only one Abado left to carry on the name.

"Summon the next speaker," Csilla said. If she'd still worn her red scarf over her white eye, she would've pulled at the edges, making sure her imperfection was covered, but she hadn't covered her blind eye since her return from Crossbones. Her fingers went to her gold rings instead, spinning one absently on her pointer finger.

"Are you sure?" Nara asked, noticing Csilla's fidgeting. "I'm certain the people wouldn't mind if—"

"Please." Csilla stopped her. "Let me think of something else for the moment."

"I understand," Nara said, stepping back to Csilla's side. "Let the next speaker in."

The guards at the end of the throne room opened the doors, allowing a man to step through. He slowly hobbled forward with his cane. The silver hair on his head was cropped short, but his braided beard stretched down his chest. Silver rings lined his ears and black tattoos peeked through the holes on the sleeves of his brown shirt. He looked to have surely sailed the seas with the fleet in his younger years.

"Queen of Bones," the man greeted her, his voice raspy. He came to a stop before the steps of the throne, his back to the crown officials behind him. "I am honored." He bowed his head and moved to lower himself to his knees, his cane wobbling.

"Please stand," Csilla said, unable to watch the man struggle for the sake of ridiculous formalities. "Tell me, did you once sail with the pirate fleet?"

The man stood a little straighter, though he still hunched forward, his weight on his cane. "I did," he said, pride strengthening his voice. "My name is Cenius Smyth and I was once a Son of Anaphine. I believe I knew the father of your betrothed before we lost him during a kraken attack."

"Oh." Csilla almost choked on her words. "Flynn Gunnison and I . . . we are not betrothed."

"My apologies for assuming," Cenius said, casting his gaze to the floor.

"There is nothing to apologize for," Csilla told him, softening her voice. "What has brought you here today? What can I do to help you?"

"Well, you see . . ." Cenius rubbed the back of his neck, seemingly nervous. "It's my wife. We lost our son, Samuel, to an illness many, many years ago when he was just a boy."

"I'm so sorry to hear about your loss," Csilla said. "I've lost my mother . . . and my sister, but I cannot imagine the pain of losing a child."

"Thank you. Although the loss nearly tore us apart, we have

healed some over time. But recently, my wife became plagued by these dreams of him." Cenius glanced around as if trying to find the right words. "She says they're the most vivid nightmares she's ever had and it has gotten to the point where she is afraid to go to sleep at night."

At the mention of the dreams, Csilla's spine went rigid. "These dreams, when did they start?"

"Around early frostfall. She often jolts awake in the night, screaming our boy's name." His pale face grew paler then. "One night, a week ago, I woke up to her sobbing in her sleep. When I rolled over in our bed to comfort her, I couldn't move because of what I saw."

"What did you see?" Csilla leaned forward, elbows on her knees. She fiddled with one of the gold rings on her finger.

Cenius gripped the knob of his cane so tightly that his knuckles turned white. His voice trembled. "At first, I thought a man had broken into our home, but then I realized this was no man. It hovered over my wife, a black hooded cloak waving even though there was no wind. Looking at it, I'd never felt so . . . hollow inside. Like someone had snatched my hopes and wishes right out of me."

Csilla shook her head. She'd thought that maybe hearing this man's story would somehow give her an answer to her own dreams, but it seemed that he was having wild dreams of his own. "Cenius, you and your wife have been through—"

"I know what it sounds like," Cenius interrupted. He quickly put his fingers to his mouth and cleared his throat. "But I swear to the Sea Sisters that I saw a dreamwraith stealing my wife's soul as she slept. I'm afraid if this continues, I'll lose her completely."

Csilla shook her head. *Impossible.* The crown officials behind

Cenius turned and whispered to each other. General Lockhart suddenly stopped polishing the handle of his whip and tucked it into his belt. Dreamwraiths were locked away in Limbo with other nightmarish creatures—where they should be. Unless . . .

Csilla remembered the night before the coronation, when she'd found Lorelei out on one of the palace balconies. Lorelei had been terrified of a power that she believed rested within her, but never showed any clues to its existence aside from a flash of gold sparks in her lightning-blue irises when she'd awoken from her death. Since then, Limbo had been on Csilla's mind—what had happened while Lorelei was there and what were the consequences of bringing her back through?

Was this one of them?

"Thank you, Mr. Smyth," General Lockhart said, rising from his chair. "I promise you that a group of crown officials will look further into your claims."

"But my wife," Cenius said, his voice quivering. "What about my wife?"

"I'm afraid that we cannot help with your wife," Lockhart said. "There are more pressing matters the queen must attend to than myths."

Cenius nodded solemnly, defeat sagging his shoulders as he turned to hobble back to the doors of the throne room.

"Wait," Csilla called out to him. He slowly turned back to face her. "You served Cerulia, so it's only right that we try to help you. Please, let one of the guards know where we can find your home, and I will personally send some officials to witness your wife's dreamwraith."

Surprise lit the man's features before his lips curled into a smile. "Thank you, Queen Csilla. Your grace knows no bounds."

He turned back toward the doors as Lockhart ascended the steps to the throne.

"You shouldn't give in to fantasies," he reprimanded her, his face stern beneath his salt-and-pepper hair. "You'll waste your time trying to please every citizen, instead of focusing on what really matters, like those damned Incendians."

"General," Csilla said from her throne, craning her head to look up at Lockhart with a cynical expression. "Did you forget that last redwind, Magnus narrowly escaped Limbo? Investigating this man's claims isn't too far-fetched, I would assume. Unless you have a good reason why we should not help a man who once served the fleet, I see no problem in using the resources we have available to try to provide him with a solution."

Lockhart clasped his hands behind his back and gave her a curt nod. "As you wish, my queen. I was only trying to keep you from possible distractions. Cerulian traders are reporting higher numbers of Incendian brigs encroaching on our waters. It's only a matter of time before they launch a full-scale attack. With all of Rove's extra ships now gone, we would surely be outnumbered, even with the royal fleet at our command."

"Then we will need more ships."

"But constructing one ship alone can take two years and we need at least ten more. We don't have that kind of time."

Csilla motioned over a scribe, a tall woman with long honey-blond hair. "I need the scribes to create a pamphlet to be distributed among the Coin District stating that any merchant willing to give their ship to the fleet will be rewarded handsomely with gold, and their landlords paid off in full." The scribe's quill flitted across the scroll she held. "We will stock their ships with guns, cannons, chain-shots, and stronger sails. Should they want to join the fleet and sail their own ship, they will be welcomed indefinitely."

"With an offer like that," Nara said from beside Csilla, "we might obtain more ships than needed."

"Is there anything you'd like to add, General Lockhart?" Csilla cocked one brow at him.

He cleared his throat. "N-no, I think you covered it well."

"In that case," Csilla said, rising from the throne, "I'd like to head to the training grounds and check on our recruits. I've heard that we have some truly talented prospects—"

Suddenly, the doors at the end of the throne room burst open. Csilla's heart climbed up her throat. Perhaps the attack against Cerulia had come early, or someone had brought terrible and urgent news with them. She was able to breathe a sigh of relief when she recognized the ragtag group that walked in. Her favorite face was among them and even from the distance, his crooked smile sent her stomach fluttering.

"Aye," he said, his sight set only on her as he left the group behind to cross the throne room. "You're here."

"Flynn," Csilla said. She couldn't help the smile that tugged at her lips. "You've made it back in one piece, I see."

He bounded up the steps, his sea eyes sparkling at her, his sandy hair coming out of its tie like he'd run all the way to the palace to see her. The collar of his cream-colored shirt was unbuttoned and his vest had seen better days. He was a mess, but a mess that she'd come to adore. Just how much, she wasn't sure she'd ever tell him.

Flynn stopped a pace away from her. "Did you miss me?" he asked, smirking as if he already knew the answer.

Yes, she wanted to say.

"I've been terribly busy." Csilla glanced away from him,

watching as the crown officials began to disperse. Perhaps if she seemed distracted, he wouldn't see through her and straight to the way her heart raced at the sight of him.

He stepped closer then, his hand lightly touching her waist, his fingers lingering on her belt. "Strapped and ready for a fight, even with a crown on your head."

"A pirate should be ready for anything," she replied, taking another step closer until her leathers brushed against him. She was so close now that she could smell the sea on him.

"Aye." His voice was almost a whisper. "I've missed you."

"I—" Csilla stopped herself, heat rising to her cheeks. "What's brought you all back so soon? You weren't due to return until mid-rainrise."

The smile from Flynn's face fell and Csilla's heart fell with it. She should've returned his sentiment. She should've said *something* instead of changing the subject.

"We ran into a bit of a revelation," Flynn said. "I'll let Kane fill you in on what we sailed upon."

Csilla glanced away from Flynn and at Kane, who was making his way up the steps to the throne. His black hair framed his face, his eyes darker than Csilla had remembered. He didn't glance her way and instead looked around the room as if searching for something or someone.

He asked one simple question, but his voice sounded strange, a slight panic to his tone. "Where's Lorelei?"

CHAPTER THREE

LORELEI

Baltessa

Early Rainrise

The sea breeze in Cerulia was a stark difference to the bitter wind of Incendia.

When Lorelei stood on one of the many balconies of the palace in the Cerulian capital, the warm wind played with strands of her long dark hair. Even during frostfall, the breeze was kissed by the sun. But in Incendia, the wind always seemed to hold a bite, the skies a never-ending dull gray. Living in Cerulia was like living in a whole new world—a world she'd seen only through her mother's stories.

Now she was living them.

Back then, she'd thought she was just one stalk of wheat in an endless sea of crops. Because of her mother's omission, Lorelei hadn't known the vital importance of the blood in her veins. Since the truth had come to light, Lorelei was typically flanked by guards who watched her every move throughout the palace grounds. She knew it was for her protection, but that didn't make her feel any less caged. She was a bird that needed to spread her wings, and when her guards weren't looking, she would take flight.

Today, she'd escaped to the Coin District, navigating through the bustling crowds perusing the rows of market stalls. The navy-colored cloak she wore masked her identity, the hood she'd pulled up over her hair casting the top half of her face in shadow. She'd stopped by many stalls already, emptying her pockets of gold, her satchel growing with the trinkets she'd found. No one questioned if she was the Storm. No guards ushered her back to the palace. She felt like she was back in Port Barlow again, just a harbor girl of no importance, except to her mother and her old friend, Luis.

She wondered what they would both think now, their Lorelei brought back from the dead, living in the city she never thought she'd see. But now her mother was gone, lost to her because of Dominic Rove, who still sailed free on the seas, and the trapped fire god, Magnus, whose whispered promises had caused the pirate to do his bidding.

She also didn't know if she'd ever see Luis, the butcher's boy with whom she used to race down the slippery docks of Port Barlow when they were children, again. Their last conversation concerned him leaving for the Incendian capital to train for the navy, despite what Lorelei had to say about it. Though she'd been angry with him, and they often argued over his view of Cerulia and pirates, she still missed his too-loud laugh and the scent of embers he'd brought with him from his father's smokehouse.

Lorelei let herself get lost among the market stalls, pretending that she was just the ordinary girl that her mother and Luis knew, even though she was anything but ordinary. The magic swimming through her veins promised that much. The power of the Storm she'd used while fighting Magnus in Limbo didn't fade like she'd thought it would when she returned.

Thinking about the magic made her skin buzz. It was an unwanted presence, resting under her skin, waiting for its moment to be unleashed. But Lorelei kept it bottled tightly, terrified of what might happen, who she might hurt if she didn't. The prickling sensation started in her core, sprouting through her chest and trickling down her arms like raindrops.

Control it, she told herself. Losing it in the middle of the Coin District on a market day wasn't an option. *Think about anything else besides magic.*

A face she hadn't seen in many moons flashed in her mind. The more days that blurred past, the more she found herself longing to see the captain of the *Iron Jewel* again. Facing the trials of Crossbones had ignited a connection between them, one that Lorelei was still trying to figure out. She remembered when the Trials had ended and she was lying in the bed in Kane's quarters, broken and tired from returning from the dead. He rarely left her side, and with each day that had passed at sea, his gunmetal gaze softened to inky pools that watched her with what she'd hoped was something more than camaraderie. Had their time apart squashed the blooming possibility of them?

A glint of light to Lorelei's right caught her attention. The sun reflected off the trinkets lining the merchant's table, glittering with each step she took toward it. Wind chimes of tubed silver and golden-dipped bones and shells hung from the frame of the stall, their tinkering songs drifting on the wind. She reached out and gave one of the tubes a tap, listening as it started a new tune.

"You like the wind chimes," said the woman working the stall. She stood shorter than Lorelei, her white hair twisted into a knot on top of her head. Rings with different colored gems lined her fingers. She tapped one on her chin as she watched Lorelei curiously.

"They're beautiful," Lorelei answered. She pulled the hood farther over her hair, making sure that her face was still cast in shadow.

The merchant pointed out the larger, more detailed wind chimes to her left. "Which one would you like? I can package it up real nicely for you. The wind chimes make an excellent gift for a sister or mother."

"Oh . . ." Lorelei's voice trailed off. Her mother's lifeless body on the floor of their little cabin flickered in her mind. The blood that pooled around her mother grew in size each time Lorelei thought of it. Soon, red might be the only thing she saw. Her cheeks pricked as she felt the color leave her face. Her stomach turned over on itself, but she couldn't fall apart here. Not now. "I—I'm not buying for my mother today."

"Ah." The merchant nodded her head. "Are you searching for yourself today then, or is there someone else in mind?"

"It's for someone else, but I'm not sure he'd like the wind chimes as much as I do."

"For your lover then?" The woman waggled her thin brows at Lorelei, giving her a quick wink and knowing smile.

"A dear friend," Lorelei corrected, glad that her blushing face was hidden. She glanced down at the table and over the array of sculpted goblets, jewelry, and pocket watches, until she finally stopped on a silver compass at the end of the table.

When Lorelei had first met Kane, his father's compass was his anchor. He'd always pull the rusted gold thing out and search its face, as if the wobbling arrow would give him the answers he searched for. When he lost the thing to the depths of a mermaid lagoon on Crossbones, he was torn apart, but Lorelei was there to pick up the pieces. Maybe a new compass would help make him whole again.

Lorelei grabbed the silver compass, letting the chain dangle between her fingers. It didn't look like Kane's old compass, but perhaps he would still like it. Lorelei gave the merchant some gold pieces and thanked her, then carefully slipped the silver compass into her satchel. Stepping away from the stall, she merged back into the crowd and fell into step with the current of people. She should go back to the palace before her guards noticed she was missing—if they hadn't realized already. *Just a little bit longer.* One more moment of freedom for the day before she was locked back up in her cage.

The glint of gold helmets peeked through the crowd, stifling her hopes before they could reach too far. It seemed the guards knew exactly where she'd be. She quickly turned on her heel and retreated in the opposite direction, weaving through the mass of people, keeping her face cast down.

Her heart raced up her throat, her nerves making her magic bubble even further. Fingers twitching, she gripped the strap of her satchel, as if holding on might settle the storm inside her.

Sidestepping those in her way proved more difficult as she neared the middle of the Coin District where the crowd came to a standstill. On an elevated stage, a small band played a familiar shanty. Children ran across the stones at their feet, playing and dancing together, while the rest of the crowd stood, bodies swaying and bouncing to the tune, some singing along as they held their flasks in the air.

Lorelei took a shaky breath and continued forward, but more slowly, mumbling apologies and excusing herself as she brushed through. She dared a glance over her shoulder, damning herself when she did. The guards were closer and she was sure the one in the front noticed her as he pointed in her direction.

She wouldn't let them drag her back to the palace this time. She'd return on her own terms.

Suddenly, she slammed into a wall, stopping her in her tracks. No, not a wall. Lorelei had been looking at the ground, so the first thing she saw was a pair of black boots. Her gaze slowly trailed upward, taking in black pants with an ornate skull belt, and a loose half-tucked white shirt. The edge of a familiar jagged scar peeked through the unbuttoned collar. A little farther and she recognized the angled jaw, tied-back raven hair, and the charcoal eyes that she often saw in her dreams.

Kane. He's back.

The storm inside her settled.

They stood frozen for a moment, watching each other, their toes nearly touching. Lorelei didn't hesitate a moment longer and threw her arms around his neck, pulling him to her. The scent of the sea engulfed her. He stiffened for a moment in her embrace, as if surprised, then she felt him shift, his arms wrapping tightly around her waist. She could've sworn she heard him sigh.

"You're here!" she said, leaning back to look up at his face. "I can't believe it!" Faint black stubble grew along his jawline and chin from his days at sea. A new look for him, but one that she liked. She wanted to reach out and trace her finger along his jaw—*No. Stop it, Lorelei. You're only friends.* She retreated from his embrace and straightened the hood on her head.

Kane's arms fell back at his side. He looked at her curiously. "Why are you . . . hiding?" He looked past her and must've noticed the palace guards coming toward them. "On the run from someone again, I take it?"

"I just needed a bit of fresh air," Lorelei answered, shrugging her shoulders. "The guards follow me like protective little ducklings, but the life-sucking kind."

Kane chuckled, a deep rumble that warmed her cheeks. "Do you ever stay out of trouble?"

"Do you want me to answer that honestly?"

Another small smile from Kane. She must've been blessed by the Sea Sisters today.

The clomping of the guards' boots drew near. Kane held up his hand and the guards came to a stop behind Lorelei. She didn't turn around, but she didn't have to as Kane addressed them.

"I'll walk back with her," Kane told them.

"Captain Blackwater," the guard closest to her said. "We are under strict orders to protect Miss Storm."

"And she will be under my protection as I walk with her," Kane answered. "Do you think me inadequate?"

"Oh. N-no, sir. My apologies. You're free to do as you wish. We will keep our distance."

Kane nodded, then looked down at Lorelei. He reached toward her and she thought he might touch her face, but instead he flicked away her hood. *Great*, she thought. *Now he'll be able to see me blush.*

"There you are," he said, making her heart do wild things as he looked at her under the light of the sun. Maybe the blooming possibility of them *hadn't* been squashed in the moons apart.

"Here I am," she replied, a smile curving at her lips.

"Shall we, then?"

Kane reached out his arm to her and she took it, holding on to the crook of his elbow as he led her through the crowd. Had it really been that long since she'd hugged him goodbye on the docks? Now that he was here, it felt like it was just yesterday. He was as familiar to her as the wind.

They walked in silence for a moment before she spoke. "You weren't due back until mid-rainrise. What's brought you home sooner?" She hadn't meant to say *home*. The word sounded intimate somehow.

Kane hesitated. "Something has come to light, but I don't want to worry you here. Let's talk about that when we're back at the palace with everyone else." He said *here*, like he would let her worry someplace secluded and not in the middle of the Coin District, which gave her even more reason to worry.

She didn't reply, not quite knowing how to respond to that.

"We docked and went straight to the palace," he continued, "but you weren't there, and no one knew where you'd run off to. You know the guards are for your protection, right?"

Of course she knew that. Their hovering presence didn't make it any less smothering. "Is there really a need for them to follow me everywhere though? Aren't I safe here in Baltessa?"

"It's the safest place for you. We just can't take our chances."

"I know, I know. The whole fate-of-the-world-resting-on-my-shoulders thing." She sighed deeply, magic tingling at her fingertips again. She wished it would just go away and leave her alone. "Don't remind me."

Kane stopped then, and turned to face her. "Lorelei." It was the first time she'd heard him say her name since he'd left. She hadn't realized how much she'd missed that.

Goddess, she thought. *How deep in am I? When did this happen?*

She glanced away from him. He lightly grabbed her chin and turned her face to him, tilting her head back to look at him.

"Are you okay?" he asked, concern knitting his brow. "You seem distracted. Like something is bothering you."

Little bursts traveled up her fingers, her skin buzzing. She curled her hands into fists, digging her fingernails into her palms, trying to bury the sparks before they could erupt.

"You've just taken me by surprise," she lied, plastering a fake smile on her face. She looped her arm through his again and pulled him along. "Now let's get back before we miss too much. I'm sure Flynn's already rattling on."

Kane mumbled something about Flynn never shutting his trap, but she couldn't really hear him over the whirring in her ears. The storm inside her promised to unleash itself; it was only a matter of when.

—

Flynn was in the middle of telling a story when they walked into the War Room. He stood in a fighting stance, his fingers forming a pistol as he pretended to shoot something in front of him. Familiar faces stood around a large round table in the room that Lorelei had been in only once before when exploring the palace.

"One comora!" Flynn exclaimed, shooting at the air with his finger pistol. "Two comoras! They were everywhere!"

Kane cleared his throat as they took an open spot around the table with a map of the realm covering its face. The Kingdoms of Four were so sprawling that one could live a hundred years and not see their entirety. Little ships and other figurines scattered across the map—playing pieces in a deadly game.

"Comora?" Lorelei asked, cocking her head. "What's a comora?"

"Well, hello there, Little Storm," Arius teased from across the table. A dimple dipped in his cheek. "Glad to see you haven't gotten yourself killed yet."

"Sadly, I can't say the same about you," Lorelei teased right back, making Arius chuckle. The truth was she'd missed all of them. Their absence made the palace a very quiet place.

"Comoras are hungry, beastly creatures," Kane said gruffly, crossing his arms over his chest. She'd forgotten she'd even asked the question. "They were supposed to be locked up in Limbo, but we encountered a horde of them in Death's Cove. Among other things, but no Dominic Rove."

"Limbo?" Csilla asked from the right side of the table. Nara stood next to her with the twins Serafina and Rosalina close behind. All four of them wore crimson sashes from their belts. "I thought we'd sealed the realm when Borne pulled Lorelei back through."

Lorelei glanced at Borne on the other side of the table. If it wasn't for him, she wouldn't be standing there with them. His eyes would still be golden; his magic wouldn't be coursing through her veins, amplifying her own. Most importantly, Magnus would've broken free of Limbo and the world would be in ashes.

"Limbo was disturbed," Borne said. "Nothing has returned from there since the gods and goddesses created it. When we brought Lorelei back, we must've thinned the layer between the realms."

"If the comoras and these other things you said you saw—"

"Half-souls," Flynn informed her. "Borne, the walking archive, informed us of these. They were dead men brought back to life—rotting, mindless, tricky to kill. Kane was stabbed by one of them."

Lorelei whipped to face Kane, grabbing his arm. "What? Why didn't you tell me before?" Her fingertips prickled and she yanked her hands away from him. It was a good thing he hadn't said anything when she was coming unwound in the market. "Are you okay?"

Kane looked down at her. "I'm fine," he said. She couldn't tell if he was lying or not. He turned his attention back to the conversation. "Can we please focus? The problem is that we don't know what else is slipping through the realm. If Magnus were to escape . . ."

"Then there would already be cities in flame," Lorelei answered. "He made that very clear when I faced him in Limbo."

"What else did he say, Lorelei?" Csilla asked, both hands on the table as she leaned forward. "You haven't told us much. What should we expect?"

Magnus promised destruction, vengeance against the Sea Sisters who helped lock him away. He'd revealed how his whispers had recruited Dominic Rove and Rhoda Abado to do his bidding in the mortal realm, and had failed to coerce Kane into his plans. She remembered what he'd said about the captain of the *Iron Jewel*, her thoughts often lingering on his words in the middle of the night.

Heroes don't commit terrible acts for the price of gold.

"He promised vengeance and destruction," she told them. "If he were released, we would know."

CHAPTER FOUR
JARON

Icehaven—The Frozen Gap
Early Rainrise

Jaron thought he was used to the cold. Surviving the frostfalls of Incendia had prepared him for the chill of Icehaven. Even though it was the start of the rainrise season and the thin layer of ice surrounding this island was giving away, the cold still clung like morning frost, fogging his breath as he walked the streets of the failed trading harbor. Once a bustling port between Ventys and the other kingdoms, now it was nearly abandoned.

The only people who came to this place were those who wanted to be ghosts.

Rows of short wood-crafted structures stood on either side of him as he walked. Doors were closed tight, windows shut, tattered flags waving solemnly in the wind. The street was empty of any life, the falling snow filling any footprints that might've been there before. In all the trading harbors he'd seen along the coast of Incendia, there was always the scent of roasted birds or something being fried in a massive skillet and the sounds of traders and merchants arguing and haggling over silver. The only thing he could hear now was the frigid wind and the snow crunching under his boots with each step he took. What had happened here?

Doubt crept into Jaron's gut. Perhaps he'd come to the wrong place.

Do you not trussst me?

He had no reason not to. The whispers had only brought him greatness so far. They belonged to a god he'd worshiped his entire life, and Magnus had given him more than anyone else ever had. He'd never felt more powerful than when he'd left West Incendia with the obsidian sword he'd dug up. Not only was it an indestructible weapon, it magnified the ember magic in his blood.

Jaron continued on through the ghost harbor, burying his doubts where Magnus couldn't hear them. Movement flashed to his left. He stopped in his tracks, whipping his head to catch a glimpse. A curtain at a window fell back into place. He was being watched.

Snow crunched from behind.

He turned just in time to see a man barreling toward him with his sword in the air. Jaron stepped aside, dodging the blade as it swung down. He withdrew his own sword from his belt, the ebony blade stark against the white snow. The man stumbled to a stop and turned to face Jaron, his breath fogging in the air as he glanced down at Jaron's sword.

"Leave this place," the man said, gripping the handle of his blade with two fists. His brown coat was riddled with holes and the wool hat he wore barely covered his ears. "*Incendian.*"

Flames ignited inside Jaron. How had the man known where

he was from? "I mean you no harm," Jaron told the man. He slowly raised one empty hand, the other still attached to his sword at the ready.

"How could I believe anyone who wields a sword like that?" The man glanced at Jaron's sword again like he knew exactly where it had come from.

"I'm only here to find someone and was told he'd be here in Icehaven," Jaron said calmly, hoping that maybe he could settle this man down as well. "Perhaps you could help me find him."

"Help an Incendian?" The man let out a cruel, mocking laugh. "Like Scouts helped burn the trading docks years ago?"

His attention perked up at the mention of docks since there were none where he'd anchored. He'd had to row in on a dinghy.

"I am not a Scout," Jaron lied.

Incendian Scouts did the difficult jobs that no other member of the navy could do, the ones that were sometimes hard to stomach. But what they did, they did for the better of Incendia.

"I can smell fire from here," the man said. "You're an emberblood, aren't you? As if being a Scout wasn't wretched enough."

Jaron gripped the handle of his sword with both hands, wringing his fists, keeping the flames at bay. An emberblood without control was dangerous to everyone, including himself.

"I don't want to hurt you," Jaron said, his voice carrying over the whistle of the bitter wind. "I'm just looking for someone."

Two other men emerged from the shadows of the buildings on either side of Jaron with swords drawn. One of them had a face full of scars, the other a beard that reached halfway down his chest. Crooked smiles twisted their faces as they flanked the man in front of him. *Three against one?*

"You'll have to look somewhere else then," the man said.

Suddenly, he jumped forward with his blade pointed at Jaron's gut. Jaron leapt away and arced his sword down, their blades clanging when they met. He forced the tip of his opponent's sword down and kicked a cloud of snow into his face, making him stumble back.

The man's place was quickly taken by one of the others. Jaron had just enough time to block his attack, leaving a hole in his guard for Jaron to strike him in the nose. Blood poured down his lips and onto his chin.

Snow rustled as heavy footsteps ran toward Jaron from behind. He spun around, fire already flaming at his fingertips. His attacker gawked and he stumbled to a stop. Jaron let the flame explode from his palm and blaze through the air, hitting the man in the chest, quickly engulfing his long beard and coat in fire and smoke. His scream split through the harsh wind.

Jaron turned away from his thrashing body and faced his remaining two attackers.

"Monster!" the one with the scarred face yelled.

"I told you I didn't want to hurt you," Jaron told them. He winced at the searing pain in his hand that typically followed when he used the embers in his blood and burned his own skin. "You forced my hand."

This time the men attacked together. Jaron blocked a strike to his left and countered to his right. He took the offense and sliced long and wide across the middle, making both men bounce back. Their dance continued, clangs and grunts echoing over the crunch of snow and howling wind.

The man with the scarred face swung low, nicking Jaron's thigh. Hot blood poured out of the wound as Jaron limped back. His opponent smiled, satisfied with himself. Jaron dropped to his knee as the men stalked closer. They both lifted their swords above their heads.

Jaron raised his sword as they brought down their own. They clashed loudly, their steel weighing down on Jaron's. With his empty hand, he pushed against the dull side of his blade, holding them back from slicing him through. He didn't want to die. Not before he could find his lost brother. Not before he could claim the destiny that Magnus had promised him.

The sssword, Magnus whispered in his head.

He focused his energy on the obsidian blade, his palms burning again. Fire quickly covered his hands and spread across the blade until it too was in flames. The men gritted their teeth and pushed harder, bending Jaron's arms back, flames licking the air right in front of his face.

A sizzle hissed from the snow below. Then another and another, like the rhythm of raindrops at the beginning of a storm. The men's swords warped, morphing under the scorching magic, silver steel dripping in rivulets on either side of Jaron.

They dropped their ruined swords and stepped back. Jaron rose to his feet and kicked the blades out of his path. He held his sword firmly, ready for their next attack. The man with the scarred face reached for a pistol at his belt and Jaron flung his hand out, flames shooting toward the man before he could shoot him. The force of the blaze propelled the man backward onto the snow. He screamed and rolled, attempting to put out the fire.

Jaron took a step toward the last man standing, his sword raised at his side, but the man dropped to his knees, raising his hands in surrender. A wise decision.

"I'm looking for a man," Jaron told him once more, pointing his sword at him in case he had any ideas. "I'm told he made port here. No one comes here unless they don't want to be found. So, tell me, where is he?"

The man gulped. "House on the hill," he said.

Jaron nodded and sheathed his sword, stepping around the man.

"You're not going to kill me?" he asked.

Jaron stopped and turned over his shoulder. "Do you want me to?"

"No, I . . . I just thought you would."

"I know."

Jaron turned back around and left the man and his fallen comrades behind. Spots of blood trailed next to his footprints; the side of his pants were drenched. He was lucky the blade didn't slice deeper or he would've had to cauterize the wound. He just might have to anyway to avoid infection before he could see a healer.

Without the piling snow and the whip of the wind, the walk up the hill wouldn't have been as difficult. The higher he trudged, the fiercer the cold bit at his cheeks. Snow stuck to the ends of his dark hair and his lashes, making it hard to see exactly where he was going.

Up ahead a short squat house came into view. Crooked wooden slats made up the exterior, packed snow nearly caving in the roof. Smoke plumed from the chimney—a promise of warmth.

Jaron climbed the couple of steps to the front door and tried to peek into the windows, but they were covered with thick curtains. He debated knocking, then decided against it, grabbing the doorknob and giving it a turn. The hallway was dark and lit with candles. The walls were bare of any decor, dark spots of mold splattered across the wood. With each step he took, the floor creaked beneath him. If anyone was here, they'd surely have heard him by now.

Jaron grabbed a candle from the floor and held it in front of him as he walked down the darkened hall, leaving the blinding snow behind. Light bloomed from a room at the end. He stopped before the open doorway and pressed his back against the wall, afraid he might be walking into a trap.

"I know you're there," came a voice from inside the room. "Might as well show yourself."

Jaron took a deep breath and stepped out from behind the wall. Lit candles encompassed the floor of the room, wax spilling onto the floor. The place was an accident waiting to happen.

In the corner of the room, next to a roaring fireplace, was a man in a plush leather armchair. He wore a feathered hat and an ornamented overcoat. Shadows danced across his face.

"Ahh," the man mused. "You must be the emberblood he told me about."

"Who?" Jaron asked.

"The same one who's been whispering to you." The man smiled and leaned forward in his chair. "I've been waiting for you."

"Waiting for me?" Jaron's mind raced. He didn't know the man he sought already knew of him.

Why did he know of him, but Jaron didn't even know the man's name?

Do you not trussst me? the whisper asked him again.

Yes, he did. He had to.

"Who are you?" Jaron asked the man. "Why has he sent me to you?"

"They call me Turncoat," he said, playing with the end of his mustache. "You and I are going to be quite the team. You see, I fully support your cause. I also put my faith in Magnus."

Jaron watched him for a long moment. "You don't know anything about me aside from my emberblood. You don't know my cause."

"What would you say if I knew where to find the only living stormblood?" Turncoat's eye twinkled in the candlelight.

CHAPTER FIVE
CSILLA

Baltessa
Mid-Rainrise

The cliffs in Macaya would always be Csilla's favorite place in the entire world. It was where she and Rhoda had played when they were children, and it was the same place they returned to when visiting their mother between trainings. The day in Csilla's dream was just as beautiful as most others with the sun shining, birds singing, the waterfall pluming clouds of mist into the air. But just like every dream that Csilla had of Rhoda, the scene changed in an instant.

The grass at her feet stiffened and the leaves in the trees curled in, turning black. The waterfall darkened until it ran crimson with blood. Surrounding silence had never been so achingly loud. Then she'd glanced back at Rhoda, who was no longer smiling, her eyes replaced by gaping holes. Rhoda took a step toward her,

her jaw unhinging as a gurgling croak escaped her throat. Csilla took a step back, but when she blinked, Rhoda was right in front of her.

Rhoda grabbed her by the shoulders.

"You did this," she said. "I'm dead because of you."

"No," Csilla told the dream Rhoda. She shook her head. "No!"

"You did this," she repeated as teeth started falling from her mouth one by one. "You did this! *You did this!*" Rhoda's skin began to blister and bubble, withering away, decaying in a few moments until her dry bones fell into a pile at Csilla's feet.

Csilla bolted upright in her bed, her scream continuing from her dream. Sweat dripped from her temple and drenched the back of her shirt, damp hair sticking to her neck. She rolled her shoulders, trying to erase the feeling of Rhoda's fingernails digging into her skin as she melted away. Chest heaving, Csilla struggled to catch a breath that wouldn't come.

The dreams, she thought. *They're getting worse.*

Csilla remembered what the man from court had told her— the dreamwraith he swore he saw. Her skin pricked, a sudden chill sweeping over her at the thought. *What if . . . ?*

Her gaze traveled over her chambers, searching the shadows between the plush chairs, marbled tables, and wardrobes decorating the vast space. The room was the largest she'd ever called her own, yet the walls pushed in on her like she was stuffed in a crate below the deck of her ship. Moonlight streamed in through the open windows, the scarlet curtains ruffling in the sea breeze. Through the silence, her heartbeat clomped in her ears, her quick breaths splitting the quiet.

Unable to let the remnants of her dream swallow her any longer, she tossed the sheet from her legs and crawled out of bed.

The hem of her tunic tickled the bare skin of her thighs as she rounded the foot of the bed and pulled on the crimson overcoat draped over one of the chairs next to the unlit fireplace. She slipped on her boots without bothering to lace them and went to the door, opening it to the hallway beyond.

She had no inkling as to where she was heading in the middle of the night. Anywhere else was a welcome distraction though.

The halls and stairways were just as quiet as her quarters, but out here there were guards posted on corners, statuesque in their duty. Her flight led her through the royal wing and the guests' quarters, down the west staircase, past the courtyard, and into the rose garden. The stars scattered in the cloudless sky above her, the moon full and brilliant, illuminating the garden and sparkling against the pebbled path.

She stepped onto the grass and went to the nearest hedge of roses, her fingers reaching to touch one of the soft red petals. She reached into one of the hidden pockets of her overcoat and pulled out the small switch-knife the twins had crafted for her. When she placed the blade against the stem of the rose, a throat cleared from behind her.

"Breaking the palace rules, are we?"

Csilla spun on her heel, hiding her knife behind her. Flynn stood in the light of the moon like a different kind of dream. The collar of his shirt was crooked and one of the gold buttons on his vest was missing. His sand-colored hair was loose and his cheeks were flushed like he'd run to the gardens.

She hadn't been alone with him since he'd left with Kane those moons ago. He'd kissed her goodbye, but there were so many things left unsaid between them, leaving them in uncharted waters. Despite her doubts, her chest swelled when she saw him. Her feelings for him quickly bubbled to the surface—too quickly—so she turned away from him.

"What are you doing here?" Csilla asked, giving her attention to the hedge. She grabbed the nearest rose by its stem. "It's the middle of the night."

"I could ask you the same question," Flynn responded, his voice coming closer. "What are *you* doing roaming about the palace in the middle of the night?"

"It's my palace." She cut the rose free and tucked the knife back into the pocket of her overcoat. Then she turned back to face Flynn, holding the rose to her nose as she inhaled the scent of it.

"Ah-ha!" he said like he'd just solved a mystery, a wicked smile splitting his lips. "You must be the rose bandit I heard the kitchen staff whispering about earlier. Taking a rose from the royal garden is forbidden, yet once a week, a rose mysteriously goes missing."

"What were you doing in the kitchens?" Csilla turned the conversation back on him, keeping the rose over her mouth to hide her smirk, as small as it was. "Did you forget your way to the guests' quarters?"

"I just needed a snack." Flynn looked down at her. He was just like the sea that matched the color of his eyes—wild and unpredictable. "They have the best little tarts tucked away. Though I do hope they weren't planning to serve them tomorrow."

"None of that explains why you're here." Csilla brushed past him and went to the bench. She sat down, staring down at the red rose in her fingers.

"I came to investigate," Flynn said, crossing the space between them. "And look at the treasure I found."

Csilla scoffed even though her cheeks flushed. The forced poetry in his words should have made her cringe, yet instead she longed to hear more. "You truly are insufferable."

"Yet you're still here." Flynn sat down next to her on the bench. He leaned forward, his elbows resting on his knees. Craning his head back, he looked at her, then the rose in her hands. "I didn't know you liked roses."

Csilla didn't answer, swallowed in her thoughts. She rolled the stem of the rose back and forth between her fingers, watching the petals bleed together as they spun. The garden was quiet, waiting for Csilla to continue the conversation, but her tongue had turned to sand. Flynn moved to get up.

"I don't . . ." Csilla said, making him stop before he could leave the bench. He turned to look back at her again. ". . . like roses."

An unreadable expression fleeted across Flynn's face, and then it was gone as he looked back out at the hedges of roses. "Then why take one each week?"

"Rhoda liked them," Csilla managed to answer, finding it a little easier to breathe since she'd woken up. Talking about her sister in a positive light helped to mask the version from her darkest dreams. "She never told anyone that she did, but I always caught her collecting the wild ones by the falls back in Macaya. She'd say they were for our mother, thinking that I didn't see her smelling them during our trek back home."

After Csilla's coronation, she'd found herself a tearful mess in the garden, the roses reminding her of her sister—beautiful, yet thorned. She'd plucked one and kept it in her quarters, but just like all the roses that came after, it died.

"I'm sorry, Csilla," Flynn said.

"Don't be," she told him. Wiping the tear from her cheek before her sorrow could be witnessed. "Death comes, it takes, and it never gives back."

"Maybe one day it will."

A sad smile tugged at the corner of her mouth. "Always the optimist."

"One of us has to be, right?"

They watched each other for a moment, their silence filled with words unspoken. There were many things Csilla could have said, things she *should* have said, but the weight of her sister's death pulled her down too far into her sea of doubt and her lips remained sealed.

Flynn was the first to break away, glancing down at the rose in her hands with a sigh. He reached over and gently took the stem from her, his fingers lingering over hers, warmth spreading over her skin and into her heart. With his thumb, he snapped the thorns and brushed them away.

"Do you remember what I told you on Crossbones?" he asked, the humor in his voice vanishing as he watched the rose intently.

"You told me many things," Csilla answered coyly. She knew he was specifically talking about his confession made in the jungle deep, but she couldn't find the nerve to say it.

"Aye," he said, strands of his light-brown hair blowing away from his face with the wind. He turned to face her. "We haven't talked about it since then, but I want you to know that I meant it." Carefully, he tucked the rose behind her ear. "I meant every word."

Csilla's heart bloomed like petals reaching for the sun. Her lips parted, requited love resting on the tip of her tongue. She could tell him how she'd missed him during his quest at sea. She could tell him how he rarely left her mind or that seeing him again made her heart do wild things. She could tell him that she loved him too. But the memory of her sister's fading face stopped her words from leaving. A secret she'd rather keep bottled tight than unleash, because if she lost him too, there'd be too many broken pieces for her to put back together.

Flynn's fingers brushed her cheek as he pulled his hand back from the rose he'd placed behind her ear. The light in his expression dimmed and her stomach sank knowing that she was the reason why.

He cleared his throat. "I don't know what hurts more: being stabbed with a dagger or with rejection." He chuckled at himself, but it was a sad sound that she hated. "I should go."

He stood from the bench and Csilla fought the urge to reach out, grab his hand, and beg him to stay. She wasn't used to wanting someone, *needing* someone like she needed Flynn, and it scared her more than the dark abyss in the deepest parts of the sea. But what was even more terrifying was feeling alone.

She couldn't bear facing the shadows of her chambers by herself. So, she gathered the courage to be a different kind of brave, voicing what *she* wanted, what *she* needed.

"Wait," she told him, rising from the bench. He turned to face her, his face lighting with hope. "Will you . . . stay with me tonight?"

A smile split across Flynn's lips. "Wanting to make up for lost time?" He winked and she almost said yes.

"I just don't want to be alone," she replied, quickly glancing away from him and at the ground instead. "I haven't been sleeping well lately and I thought that maybe—"

"Say no more." Flynn held out his hand to her and she took it, his fingers curling around hers. "I'm yours."

She let him lead her back to the royal chambers even though she knew a much faster path. Silence between them rarely came, but as they wound through the hallways and staircases, hand in hand, the quiet was like the moonlight cutting through the open windows—soft and intimate.

When she curled into his side, their boots and coats discarded on the floor, silk sheets pulled up to their chests, she found peace in her sleep for the first time since he'd left.

But how long would it last?

CHAPTER SIX
KANE

Baltessa

Mid-Rainrise

Nothing good ever happened on birthdays.

Nineteen birthdays beforehand hadn't proved any different. Kane's mother had tried her best, always waking him bright and early with a locked treasure box and a hunt around the *Iron Jewel* for the key she'd hidden. As a child, he'd pretended he was training for the Trials should his day ever come, and those moments were some of the brightest in his memories. No matter how many brilliant moments he'd had with his mother, his father's cloud was there to darken the day, which was why he hoped for nothing when the day rolled around each year.

But this year could be different, he thought.

He stood in front of a full-length mirror, straightening the collar of his new black overcoat, an undeniable and unfamiliar feeling of hope taking root. It was his second birthday without his father and the first without his shadow looming over him. The golden threads on the embroidery of his overcoat laced around the hems of the black coat, sprawling intricately across his chest and up to his shoulders, forming the shape of a skull over his heart, glistened with the last bit of sunlight streaming into his room.

A black-and-gold mask rested on the small table next to the mirror. A masquerade—Flynn's idea, of course. A year ago, Kane wouldn't have been seen dead attending a ball like this, especially one arranged for his birthday, yet he'd had his wardrobe tailored specifically for tonight. *What am I becoming?*

When he reached for the mask, pain shot through his left shoulder, making his spine curl in on itself. His hand went to the spot where his chest met his shoulder. The pain was just as fresh as when he'd been stabbed by that half-soul nearly two moons ago. He'd ignored the wound for the most part—it was easy to since it rarely hurt—but now and then there were moments like this that had him stumbling into the mirror.

He leaned into the reflective glass with a grunt, propping himself up with his right forearm as he came face to face with reality. Chest heaving, he gripped the collar of his white shirt with his other hand and yanked, popping buttons and sending them rattling to the floor. A thick angry laceration was carved into the soft spot of his chest, its surface as black as the sails of his ship. The wound had turned this color a week after he'd received it, but now as the pain continued, black veins stretched out and away from it, pulsing, spreading.

"*Shit*," Kane hissed through his teeth.

There was a knock at the door and Kane pushed himself away from the mirror, straightening his collar. He kicked at the loose buttons on the floor, sending them rolling under the table as the visitor let themselves in.

"There's the birthday chum!"

Kane turned to see Flynn and Arius strolling into the room. Flynn wore a soft blue overcoat with gold buttons. His undershirt was visible half-tucked, but his hair was pulled back neatly from his face for once. He wore a cream mask that reminded Kane of a desert fox. Arius stood behind him, dressed in pearl white from head to toe, aside from his mask, which shimmered. A ridiculous white cocked hat sat on his head, black feathers lining the entire brim.

"I didn't know we were supposed to wear costumes," Kane said to Arius, stepping away from the mirror and walking toward them. He clenched his hand into a fist at his side, trying to bury the pain at his shoulder.

Flynn laughed, and Arius leaned on the back of a chair. "Hilarious, Blackwater," Arius said as Kane passed by him. "Do you think Lorelei will like my ensemble though?"

Kane stopped and turned to face Arius, his chest flaring with something other the subsiding pain.

"He was only joking," Flynn said, grabbing his best mate by both shoulders and giving him a light shake. "This fellow." A forced laugh. "Always with the digs." He elbowed Arius in the ribs and smiled sheepishly at Kane. "You meant Nara, right?"

Arius shrugged. "Meh, we fizzled out. A mutual parting."

"Mutual," Kane scoffed. "Keep telling yourself that, Pavel." Kane turned back toward the door, ignoring Arius as he tried to defend himself.

The hallway was like most others around the palace, oak doors lining the walls, small golden sculptures sitting on pedestals. The pain from his wound was nearly gone and he rolled his shoulder to be rid of the tightness that was left behind. It always came and went in flashes, which made it easy to ignore, but time was a fickle thing and there would come a point where Kane wouldn't be able to hide it from everyone. Until then, nothing changed.

"How's that stab wound doing?" Flynn asked from Kane's left. They walked in a trio down the hall, the echo of their boots muted by the scarlet carpet stretching across the middle of the marbled floor.

"Healing," he replied, unwavering.

Arius pretended to sniff the air. "I smell a lie," he sang.

"Are you trying to get decked in the face tonight?" Flynn asked. "Don't push Blackwater. My jaw still tenses from that last time when he—"

"When you cheated at Aces?" Kane interrupted.

"When will you let that go, mate? I didn't cheat."

"He doesn't cheat," Arius repeated.

"He definitely cheated," Kane said as they turned the corner. "I was dealt a perfect hand."

Someone else bustled around the corner at the same time, nearly running into them. The man stumbled back and mumbled an apology. He stepped aside to go around the group of them but Kane stopped him.

"Where are you running off to in such a hurry?" Kane asked, hitching an brow. He took note of the red mask the man wore, its outside edges curling up into points like the flame of a candle. A partygoer then. "The masquerade is down in the courtyard."

The man adjusted the mask that had gone crooked on his face. "Apologies," he muttered. "The palace is so large, it's easy to get lost in it."

"Aye," Flynn agreed. "I got lost a couple of times myself before I finally figured out the maze."

"I still get lost," Arius added in.

Kane looked closer at the stranger. They were the same height, and with his wide shoulders and the way his charcoal overcoat hugged his arms, Kane could tell the man had the physique of someone who'd been trained. Since Kane had been away at sea, there were probably many recruits that he wouldn't know, but that didn't stop him from checking.

"Do I know you?" Kane asked, investigating the stranger further. "I don't think I do."

"You don't," he replied. He glanced past the group of them like he had somewhere to get to, his body restless. "Sorry, but I've got to get going."

Quickly, the stranger brushed past them and hurried down the hall without another word, leaving the three of them behind.

Flynn turned around and yelled after him, "You're not even going to wish the birthday chum a merry evening?" But he received no reply.

Kane wondered about the masked stranger for a moment before Flynn and Arius whisked him away to the masquerade that he wasn't quite sure he was ready for.

—

The courtyard was full of partygoers by the time Kane and the two Sons of Anaphine arrived. Lanterns hung on ropes strung from pillar to pillar, candles flickered on tables strewn across the area, and guitars strummed to the tune of a familiar shanty. The sun had hit its lowest point, and stars began to peek between the few clouds in the sky. Soon the moon would cast everything in a hazy glow. Whoever oversaw the preparations for the party had done so with special attention to detail. He'd have to find out who the planner was and thank them after.

Flynn made a disappointed sound. "I don't see Csilla anywhere, do you?"

Trying to find someone familiar in a sea of masked faces proved more difficult than Kane had presumed. A few glances turned in their direction before returning to their pint of ale or the deck of cards in their hands. He recognized Borne, who was talking to a group of recruits. When Borne noticed Kane and the other two, he gave them a nod of acknowledgment, his beaded green mask shimmering in the light like an emerald.

Kane found Lockhart in a silver mask, and the Scarlet Twins, Serafina and Rosalina, in matching crimson ones. No Csilla. Nor Lorelei for that matter. Lorelei had told him she'd be there. He hoped this wouldn't be like all the other things she'd missed this week, like their nightly dinners with everyone else.

"Let's join a game of Aces while you wait," Arius told Flynn, slapping him on the back.

Flynn sighed. "Fine, I suppose so, but I'm not letting you win this time."

Arius laughed and hooked his arm over Flynn's shoulder, pulling him to the nearest table of card players. Kane figured he might as well join them to pass the time, but first, he needed a drink.

He made his way across the courtyard to an array of barrels where a man handed out ale. Kane motioned to the man, and he poured Kane a mug from the spout screwed into the side of the barrel. Foam spilled over the rim, dripping onto the courtyard's stone. Kane brought the mug to his lips, taking a long swig of the ale, letting it run down his throat and warm his belly.

"Well, will you look at what the tide washed in?" said a familiar silky voice from behind him.

Kane lowered his mug from his lips and slowly turned, recognizing the amber waves of hair that belonged to the voice. She wore a mauve dress that clung to her skin, scooping low in the front and woven with strands of silver, watching him behind her rounded silver mask.

"Clarissa," he said, giving her a nod. He hadn't seen her in nearly a year, since the night King Rathborne had died and the Blood Bell had rung through the city.

"I'd heard you were back," she said, taking a step closer. "I'll admit I was a bit disappointed that you didn't call on me."

"Those days are over, Clarissa," Kane said, his voice quiet.

A pout puckered her painted lips. "But they were such fun days."

Kane moved to step past her, but she stepped with him, in front of him, her nails tracing down his chest. "I'd rather not have this conversation again," he told her, lightly flicking her hand away from him. The relationship between them had been physical, nothing more, but it seemed she wasn't quite ready to let her flame die. His had flickered out a long time ago and had started to burn for someone new, different, brighter.

He hadn't even realized when it had happened until he asked himself the question. *When did I start to burn for Lorelei?* When she'd declared herself as his first mate. When she'd breathed life back into his drowned lungs. When she'd died and come back to life in his arms. All of those moments and more.

Clarissa sighed and leaned toward him. "You're so tense. You're sure you don't need someone to take your mind off things?"

The doors to the northern entrance of the courtyard opened, a stream of light from the hall pouring into the space. Everyone turned in the direction of whoever was entering, a hush falling over them; even the guitars faltered.

Kane first noticed Csilla, who led the group through the doors. Her black curls were pulled back from her face, woven through the golden curves of the Bone Crown on her head. Her eyes, one brown and one silver, assessed them from behind her gold mask. While most of the other women at the masquerade wore exquisitely tailored dresses, she wore a simple scarlet skirt that wrapped over the pants and boots she wore beneath.

Flynn appeared from nowhere at Kane's side. "Goddess help me, I'm a goner," he said with a sigh. "You've got to teach me how to be more stone-faced, like you. I mean, you're acting like you don't even see Lorelei. How do you do it, mate?"

"Lorelei?" Clarissa asked curiously.

Kane found her then, sliding out from behind Csilla. It wasn't the intricate patterns of lace on her dress or the golden headband she wore tucked into her soft curls that caught his breath. She was strikingly beautiful, but what really struck through his armor was the color she wore, matching the sails of the *Iron Jewel*, matching *him*. His palms went sweaty, his mouth dry. He gulped.

Clarissa was staring at him. "Oh," she said with realization. "I see."

As did he. Right then was the clearest he'd seen in many moons.

Partygoers cleared a path for Queen Csilla, nodding their heads in respect as she passed by them. At her side Nara wore a skirt similar to Csilla's, but it was the navy blue of the sea deep, and a matching mask sparkled with stars. Lorelei followed closely behind.

"Carry on," Csilla told them all with a wave of her hand. "Pretend I'm not here."

While everyone continued their dancing or games of cards, a flash of red darted past the wall, but when he glanced to his left, it was gone. The memory of the masked stranger he'd run into earlier flashed through his mind, and he tried to smother the feeling of dread that now crept up his spine.

Then Lorelei was in front of him, her fingers at his wrist, pulling his roaming attention from the courtyard walls and straight to her. Her lips parted to say something, then they closed shut, her cheeks rosing under the edges of her black lace mask. He glanced down at her hands, noticing the small parcel she carried in one of them. Curiosity sparked in him like the same little boy searching a ship for his mother's hidden treasures.

A throat cleared and Kane looked to see Flynn and the rest of them looking at him and Lorelei. Flynn smirked like he knew the thoughts racing through Kane's head. "How often are we all together like this?" Flynn asked, breaking the silence. "This calls for a round of Aces!"

"Oh," Lorelei said. "I've never actually played before."

"Sit with me," Kane told her. "I'll teach you."

CHAPTER SEVEN

LORELEI

Baltessa

Mid-Rainrise

Lorelei had seen the others play Aces enough to know the basic rules of the card game. Even then, Kane sat close, whispering in her ear about how much she should bet each round and which card she should play. Her hair tickled her neck every time he spoke, chills chasing each other down her spine. She let him think that he was helping her do so well, but she made her choices in her mind before he could say anything. At least it kept him close.

The longer they played, the more Kane seemed to be loosening up. He always stood so straight, calculative of everything and everyone. And smiles? They were like those short bursts of sunlight on cloudy days, warm then cold again. Tonight, however, there was something different about him, something hopeful, something that made her feel bold enough to scoot closer to him on the bench seat. Her heart fluttered when he didn't inch away, the side of his leg flush with hers as they were dealt hand after hand. When Flynn finally won, it felt like it had come too soon.

"Csilla," Flynn said, standing and throwing his cards in the air. "Would you like to dance with a winner?"

A small smile curved at Csilla's lips. She glanced out at the empty space near the band. "But there's no one dancing."

"Then let us be the first," he teased, grabbing both her hands and pulling her along.

"Fine," she said, but the happy tone in her voice didn't match her reluctance.

Lorelei stood and watched the two of them as they made their way to the open floor. Flynn wrapped his arms around Csilla's waist—hers were up around his neck. As they swayed to the slow strumming of the guitars, more masked dancers joined them, pairing and filling up the open space.

Kane stood right next to Lorelei, the quiet between them something that Lorelei felt the need to break even though her heart was in her throat.

"Do you . . ." she started, before she glanced down at the ground. "Do you want to dance?"

Kane sputtered the ale he was drinking. "Dance? Me? I don't dance."

Her stomach sank like a ruined ship. Her cheeks flushed, but she hoped her mask hid most of it.

"Excuse me, Miss Storm," said an unfamiliar voice. She glanced up from the ground to find a stranger in a brown mask that resembled an animal print. His smile was handsome as he asked, "I'd be honored if you'd spare a dance for me."

"Oh," Lorelei said, surprised. She wasn't quite sure how to answer as the one she truly wanted to dance with stood stoic next to her. "I suppose that—"

"We were just about to dance," Kane interrupted. She turned to look at him, noticing him assess the man through the holes of his mask.

"Perhaps another time." The stranger bowed slightly before running off to ask someone else.

Lorelei faced Kane and crossed her arms over her chest. She arched a brow at him. "I thought you said you didn't dance."

"It seems I've suddenly changed my mind," he said, holding out his elbow for her. "Would you like to dance with me, Miss Storm?"

She smiled at him then, and he smiled back just as fully. She wished that she could put this moment in a bottle—the first time she'd seen him smile like that. "I'd love to," she answered, slipping her arm through his. "It was my idea after all."

Kane chuckled and led her the few paces to the dance floor. He stopped at the edge and turned to face her, one hand finding hers, the other sliding to her lower back. She rested her other hand on his shoulder, warmth spreading into her from everywhere they touched. She swallowed, hoping to calm the beating of her heart, but it was pointless. As they began to slowly sway to the music, she looked up at him to find him already watching her, his rough exterior softening and melting away.

Then he stepped on her foot. She winced and gripped his hand and shoulder tighter.

Kane stood straighter, his hand wrapping farther around her back as he craned his head down toward her. "Is your foot okay?" he asked quietly, his mask hiding his expression. "I'm an oaf when it comes to dancing."

Lorelei nodded. "So, you weren't lying when you said you don't dance."

"I tried to warn you." One of the small scars by his lips dimpled with his smirk.

She shrugged her shoulders. "I just assumed you didn't want to dance with me." Her breath stalled, waiting for his response.

"If I'm going to be honest with you, Lorelei," he replied, lowering his voice like he was telling her a secret, "it's quite the opposite. I was only trying to protect your toes . . . and perhaps a bit of my pride."

"You haven't stepped on both feet yet, so I'd say you're doing okay."

He raised their joined hands above her head, her skirt fanning out as she spun. When she stopped and faced him again, both his hands went to her waist. Closer than they'd been before. The air was magnetic. The strums of the guitars slowed as her eyes caught his, their swaying falling to a standstill. He leaned down, she looked up, the space between them narrowing until he was all she could see, and if she stood on the tips of her toes, her lips would brush against his.

One of the guitars strummed a final chord and the party broke into applause. Lorelei and Kane stepped away from each other and clapped with the rest of them, but the warmth of him lingered on her. Sparks bloomed at her fingertips and she bit them back.

No, she thought to herself. *Not now. Not here.*

The guitars picked up again, their fingers strumming to a quicker tune. Someone hollered excitedly about the shanty choice, but their voice sounded so far away.

She felt Kane looking at her. "What's wrong?" he asked over the music.

Lorelei shook her head and forced a smile. The guitars were suddenly too loud, the lanterns too bright. She had to get out of there, but she didn't want to leave Kane behind. Then she remembered—the parcel, his gift.

"Come with me to the fountain?" Lorelei asked him, pulling on the sleeve of his coat. She couldn't quite read his expression under his mask, but he didn't argue with her so she dragged him away, stopping first to grab the parcel she'd left on the table.

The guitars faded away when they stepped through a curtained archway and onto a secluded terrace. Hedges lined the pillars, the clouds allowing in streams of moonlight. A three-layered fountain streamed in the center. She dropped Kane's arm from her grasp and walked toward it, the sound of its running water enough to quench the sea magic protesting in her veins, calling to her like a song. Just like the waves in Port Barlow used to do when she stood at the cliff. If she could, she'd spend the rest of the evening here, but that would only ruin Kane's night. It was his birthday after all and she'd done so much planning to make sure he liked the party.

"You're the one who planned the party?" Kane asked from behind her.

She hadn't meant to say the last part aloud. Her cheeks flamed, but she might as well own the slipup and run with it. Stepping back from the fountain, she spun on her heel to face him, finding him much closer than she'd anticipated. The moonlight reflected in his dark eyes, the black mask and his towering figure making him look more pirate than the man she'd gotten to know. Her courage flickered for a moment.

"Yes," she answered. "It's what I've been busy with the past couple of weeks. It's why I've been late for dinners with everyone."

Her words came out in a flood. "You said you didn't like birthdays, and with Flynn's idea of turning it into an entire masquerade, I thought I'd do what I could to at least make it enjoyable for you. It's okay if you don't like it. I completely understand."

Lorelei looked at the hedges, the ground, anywhere but at him. The parcel in her hands practically burned. If he announced his distaste for the party, there wouldn't be a shred of bravery left in her to give him the gift, so she had to give it to him now, before he could say anything.

"I also got you this," she said, shoving the parcel into his hands. She hadn't meant to do it so forcefully, but her nerves seeped into her bones. "I bought it in the Coin District the day you came back. I figured maybe if I gifted it on your birthday and you liked it, this wouldn't be such a hollow day for you, even if you didn't enjoy the party."

She cringed at her words and stared at the patterns in the marble instead of him. Paper crinkled as Kane tore into the parcel and then there was silence. Time passed. She wasn't sure how long, but it felt like the sun would rise before he said anything. Unable to stand it any longer, she raked her gaze to him.

In his palm he held the silver compass she'd bought him, its chain dangling down between his fingers. He'd pushed his mask up onto the crown of his head, the moon's light touching every curve, scar, and rugged angle of his face. His thumb pressed the button on its top and the lid popped open to reveal the face of the compass. Lorelei watched his lips as they parted and closed again.

"If you don't like it then I can—"

"I love it," Kane said, watching her with an intensity she didn't recognize from him.

"You do?" Relief trickled through her.

"Of course I do." He took a step closer. "The compass, the party, all of it. And you are . . ." Shoving the compass into his coat pocket, he reached for her hand, his callused fingers wrapping around her own. With the other, he lifted her mask away from her face. "You are beautiful. Tonight, and every other night."

Lorelei could've melted right there and become one with the water in the fountain, but instead she clenched her skirt with her empty hand and took a breath to steady herself. When she didn't respond, he crooked his finger under her chin and lifted, forcing her to look at him.

"Why did you wear a black dress?" he asked, as if it were a simple question with a simple answer.

She couldn't think. Not when he stood this close and he was touching her face. She remembered how delicate he'd been when he'd treated the burn on her arm back when they were just strangers to each other. That moment felt like so long ago, and now his touch was filled with a different kind of delicacy, something much more intimate.

"I don't know," she told him. Her voice only came out a whisper. His fingers held her chin so she couldn't look away.

"I think you do know," he argued.

"Perhaps I . . . wanted you to see me," she admitted. Her heart raced with her confession. "Not just as the stowaway, or as a stormblood, but as yours."

Kane stilled for a breath, then pulled her to him, his arms wrapping around her like he'd blow away in the wind if he didn't hold on tight enough. His nose brushed hers as he leaned down toward her.

"I don't deserve you," he murmured.

"What you deserve is to be happy." She traced the golden weavings on the collar of his coat.

She meant to say more. That he deserved to find happiness with or without her. That he should love with his whole being and forgive himself his past. But his lips met hers before she could say anything else. His kiss was a burst of warmth that spread over her cheeks and down her neck. Then he was gone, shying away from her as he searched her face.

"Is this okay with you?" he asked, his voice a rasp, nearly pleading. "Is this what you want?"

She answered by grabbing the collar of his coat with both hands and pulling him to her. He chuckled under her lips and kissed her back, his hands fitting back into place around her like it was where they were meant to be. She bowed into him as his hand traveled up her spine, his fingers twining into her hair.

She'd kissed a boy once back in Port Barlow, but not like this. Not with this type of hunger. She could kiss Kane under the stars until they faded into the bleeding light of sunrise and it still wouldn't be enough.

One moment they were holding each other, the next they were stumbling to a nearby pillar. Lorelei's back pressed against it as Kane leaned into her, kissing her again, deeper this time. Their rushed breaths filled the quiet space of the terrace.

His hands roamed over her ribs and onto her hips, clenching the black fabric of her dress. She lightly scratched the back of his neck and he sighed against her lips, the sound of it unraveling her.

Sparks started in her core, spreading up her chest, through her arms and into her fingers before she even realized what was happening. Her wild magic summoned itself so quickly, she didn't have time to bite it back. Like an uncorked bottle, magic poured from her.

The moment her sparks left her, Kane jolted. He convulsed under her touch, his entire body shaking like lightning swam through him. She let go of him, her heart in her throat as he crumpled to the ground. Though she no longer touched him, he still shook with tremors, his breaths more like ragged pants.

Lorelei moved to crouch down next to him, her trembling fingers reaching. But then she straightened back against the pillar, looking at her hands, afraid she'd lose control again. Attempting to make fear a stranger had only left it clawing at her door.

"What . . ." Kane said between breaths. He groaned as he rolled onto his side. "What was that?"

Her tongue turned to sand. Words were lost to her, swept away with the sea breeze.

"Lorelei?" He looked up at her from the ground, searching her with concern. "What happened? Were you harmed?"

Her heart throbbed. He worried over her even though he was the one shivering on the ground. She'd put him there. Her lack of control could've killed him. The more she thought of her grave mistake, the brighter the spark inside her grew.

She glanced down at her hands, her breath hitching. Her fingertips looked like they'd been dipped in gold. The terrace melted away and she was back in Limbo, her arms coated in the very same gold. In that realm, the power of her storm magic was unfathomable. Perhaps monsters weren't the only thing slipping through the cracks in Limbo. Lorelei rubbed her fingertips together, but the gold remained like paint smudged into her skin.

She couldn't stay there. No, she couldn't stay anywhere near the ones she cared about. It was foolish of her to think that she could find a sliver of peace, even for just one evening. A cloud of regret hung over her.

Kane grunted, drawing her attention back to him as he crawled onto his knees. He lifted his head back to look at her, blinking as if trying to see clearly. "What's wrong? Was it—was that *you*?"

His expression was unreadable. She'd never seen him look at her like that before. It was a mixture of shock and wonder, but did she detect disgust or was that her mind playing tricks on her?

"I'm sorry," she managed to say. Her voice didn't sound like her own, like she was speaking from behind a glass window. "I didn't mean to. I can't believe I—"

Kane rose to his feet, the movement wobbly and labored. "Shh, I'm fine." He reached out and cupped her cheek with his palm. "Are you?"

His thumb softly stroked her cheek and sparks pricked at her fingertips again. She stepped away and curled her fingers into fists as if her golden fingertips would cease to exist if she couldn't see them.

"I have to go." Lorelei's voice cracked. "I'm so sorry, but I have to go." She turned away from him, her face cold, her stomach churning, but she couldn't take the chance of hurting him again.

"Wait," he rasped, grabbing her wrist. His hand was warm. She wanted so much to hold on to it tightly. "Please. Stay."

The pools of his eyes and the scratch in his voice nearly pinned her where she stood. She'd stay with him. She'd let herself lie in his arms until the sun woke up. She'd kiss him and he'd kiss her like nothing else mattered, like they were the only two in the world. But she couldn't risk it.

She tore herself away from him before she caved in. "I have to go," she said, unable to hide the way her voice quivered. "Please. Let me go."

Kane dropped her wrist, his warmth leaving her skin much

too fast, the evening chill sweeping into her quickly. Tears welled as she half-ran away, spilling onto her cheeks as she stumbled through the empty side halls of the courtyard. Faded guitars and laughter drifted on the wind, deepening the cold in her heart.

What if the gold continued to spread up her arms, her power growing more uncontrollable? What was a future in a place where she put all of them in danger? Kane's smile flashed in her mind and she fell to a stop. If she left Cerulia, she'd never see it again.

She sighed and pulled the black mask from her head and held it in her hands, scanning the lace while she screamed on the inside. This night was supposed to be perfect, not for her, but for him, and she'd ruined it all.

Footsteps echoed behind her. Kane had followed her even after what she'd just done and it made her nearly banish thoughts of leaving. But when she turned to face him, it wasn't Kane who stood in the empty hall with her.

A man standing as tall as Kane, wearing a plain dark coat and pants, but with scuffed boots, stood behind her. In the shadows of the hall, she couldn't tell the shade of his hair, but his red mask stood out brightly.

"I'm a little offended that I didn't receive an invitation to such a grand party," the stranger said. He took a step closer and Lorelei took a step back.

"Who are you?" she asked. Sparks came to her fingertips without a thought. "If you didn't receive an invitation, then you shouldn't be here."

"Don't worry," he told her, hands splayed like he was trying to calm an animal. He took another step closer, then stopped when he noticed she retreated again. "You're scared."

"Not scared," she lied. "But of course I'm going to be wary of an intruder."

"I'm not your enemy. I'm here to save you."

Confusion made her sparks flicker, letting her guard down. "But I don't need to be saved."

"He said you'd said that," the stranger replied. "I didn't want to do this."

"Do what?" Her heart was in her throat. She could turn and run, but she wasn't outrunning anyone in heels.

The lanterns decorating the hallway snuffed out one by one, the flames inside dissolving to wisps of smoke. A scream lodged itself in her throat. She tried to summon her sparks, but they wouldn't come to her when she called. Damned magic with a mind of its own.

When the last lantern flickered out, everything went black.

CHAPTER EIGHT

JARON

Baltessa
Mid-Rainrise

Pirates had attacked Port Hullscar when Jaron was thirteen.

He still remembered the screams, the smoke, and how he'd searched for his little brother's tuft of charcoal hair in the chaos and never found him. He remembered how he'd abandoned his search when pirates started pillaging the street, and how when he'd finally found the courage to leave the crate he was hiding in, he returned to a home engulfed in flames. But what he remembered most of that day was his little sister staring unblinkingly at the sky, lifeless and empty as a broken bottle, her lungs filled with smoke from the fire. It was a shard in his memories, an ache that was present even in his dreams. Glenna had been so full of life, yet that life had been taken away so easily.

He'd vowed back then and there that he'd do whatever he could to avenge his sister and find his brother. He'd bury the pirates of

Cerulia at the bottom of their sacred seas. He'd burn their homes with a fire of his own, take away what they held dear, and when there was nothing left for them but hope, he'd snuff that flame out too.

He didn't know why carrying the stormblood through the shadows of the palace reminded him of that forsaken day. Perhaps it was her small frame and the way she fit in his arms the same way Glenna had. It was nothing but a fleeting feeling, something to be squashed. He focused on the tasks ahead, leaving no room for his mind to wander as he slipped through the last door and out into the night.

The moon painted the beach white, the wall surrounding the palace rising up like a tidal wave behind him while the true sea remained calm, lapping at the shore. His small ship was one of the several tied to the sleeping docks, waiting for him just as he'd left it. He breathed a sigh of relief that Crew hadn't run off with it like he thought he would. The man was as trustworthy as a pirate.

Had it really been as easy as Turncoat had promised? Using stolen white merchant sails had disguised his ship perfectly; the southern docks and servants' halls were unguarded, all just as he'd said. His boots echoed down the wooden path across the beach and to the docks. All he had to do was put the stormblood on his ship before she woke up, find Crew, and untie from the dock, and he'd be one step closer to fulfilling his duty.

An echo of footsteps that weren't his own. He stopped—one foot on the plank to his ship—and glanced over his shoulder. A silhouette stood where the path across the beach met the dock. He'd gotten all this way and of course, *now* someone found him. He sighed, frustrated that they'd been able to sneak up on him and annoyed that he'd probably have to use his embers. He turned back to his ship and crossed the plank, setting the stormblood down carefully on the deck before retreating back down to the dock.

The silhouette hadn't moved, but now Jaron could make out a feminine shape. Long, straight raven hair waved in the wind like a flag. There was something at her back and in her hands, but he didn't realize what it was until she nocked an arrow in her bow.

Jaron raised his hands in mock surrender. He was *this close* to getting out of Cerulia with their weapon. He couldn't let it slip through his fingers. Perhaps he could at least test the archer.

"Step away from the ship," the silhouette said. Her voice was as cold and smooth as a sheet of ice.

"I'm afraid I can't do that," he told her. "This cargo is too precious."

The silhouette didn't waver. "Then you should take your final glance at the moon because you won't be able to see it from the dungeons."

What an amusing threat. "Pity," Jaron said, lowering his marred hands. "I would've been inclined to hear more, but I'm on a bit of a tight schedule."

If she hadn't shot at him yet, then she either didn't have the aim from that distance or the nerve to do the job. Time was fickle and he didn't desire to waste it while standing around, trying to find out which one was her weakness. Turning on his heel, he took a step back up the plank to his ship.

A whir cut through the air. Then, *shuck*. An arrow sprouted from the wood where his foot would've taken its next step. Jaron whipped back to face the silhouette.

"You missed," he said.

"Did I?" the silhouette called, taking a step closer as she nocked another arrow in her bow. This woman wasn't what he'd thought. Perhaps he'd underestimated her. "That was just a warning shot."

She let go of the bowstring, her arrow splitting through the moonlight and finding its mark in his thigh. He cut off his own scream, holding it back with ragged breaths, the pain achingly sharp and dull at the same time.

"Missed," he grunted. "Again."

The silhouette stepped closer again, hand behind her head, ready to pull out another arrow. She wore a skirt over her pants, silver weavings on the sheer material shimmering as it fluttered with the sea breeze. He recognized her then as the quiet one who stood by the queen's side. The graceful one who didn't dance with the others when the guitars had started.

"If I wanted you dead," she said, her tone even frostier than before, "then you would be dead."

The muscles in his thigh tightened around the arrow, his knee nearly buckling with the pain. With one hand, he gripped the shaft of the arrow and held down his thigh with the other. He yanked the arrow from his leg, blood spurting from the wound. Then he summoned his embers, fire spreading over his hand as he closed it over the wound, cauterizing it so that he could still fight. He hissed and cursed and surprisingly wasn't struck with another arrow, but when he glanced to where the archer had been, she was gone.

The docks were suddenly so quiet, he could hear the tide washing. The sails above rustled and flapped with the wind. His heart thrummed in his ears, the pace of it numbing the stinging burn on his leg. He glanced down the dock, across the beach, but she was a ghost. *Where did she go?*

"So, you're an emberblood," came her voice from his ship.

He spun to face her, craning his head to look up at her from the bottom of the plank. The way she stood with another arrow nocked in her bow looked as if she'd done it a hundred times before. "How did you . . . ?" He cleared his throat and gripped his sword, unsheathing it slightly. "A bow is no match in close combat. Especially since you don't want to kill me."

"Don't flatter yourself," the archer seethed. From this angle, he could see her smoky black eyes through the mask she wore. "The only reason to keep you alive is for information about Incendia. We can twist, break, and peel every secret out of you—who you are, why you're here, how you got in and out unnoticed."

"*You* noticed though," he quipped. Maybe if he threw her off, she wouldn't realize that he was inching closer. "It appears I didn't do as well as I'd thought."

"It's my job to notice things. Are there more of you?"

"Don't you think they'd have attacked you by now?

A slight bit closer.

"What do you want with *her*?" She motioned to the resting stormblood on the deck behind her. "Was it the Incendian king who sent you or someone else?"

Jaron slowly slid his foot up the plank, another step forward. "I thought you were going to torture the answers from me. Why ask your questions now, archer?" He was close enough now that he could unsheathe his sword and attack.

"In case I have to kill you before I can ask them."

There was a pause, then she lunged forward, swinging her bow down. Its curved tip struck him across the cheek and he stumbled back down the plank, nearly falling flat onto his ass. He reset his feet and unsheathed his obsidian sword. She unsheathed her own blade, longer than his, but thinner, curved with a sharp pointed tip.

"Fine," he growled. "Have it your way."

They collided in the center of the plank, the clash of their steel echoing across the quiet beach. She had the advantage of the higher ground, her slender frame able to hold its own against the brute force of his. He slid his blade down and they clashed again, but this time he gained ground on her, pushing her back toward the ship. Again and again, their swords crossed until she was one step away from falling back onto the deck next to the stormblood. If she hadn't been so quick, his sword would've sliced through her by now, but she was swifter than most swordsmen he knew. Shame he'd have to take down someone as skilled as her.

He drew his sword back to strike again and swept it in a low-angling arc. The archer leapt away as his blade cut the ribbon on the tail of her skirt. He stepped down onto the deck and she jumped back, tearing at the ties on her skirt until she was able to toss it away onto the wood. There was a rip on the lower leg of the pants she wore beneath. Blood shimmered in the moonlight. It seemed he'd cut more than just the ribbon on her skirt. If it hurt, she didn't show it, her expression just as much of a mask as the one she wore over her face.

He took the opening to slice the rope tying his ship to the dock and cut the one holding the sails closed. Once free, the sails billowed with the wind, the ship sailing forward, leaving the dock behind.

"What are you doing?" the woman said, craning her neck as if she could somehow escape with the stormblood before the ship was too far from the dock. But they were already being carried out with the waves. Her only option now would be to kill him and commandeer the ship. She couldn't though, *could she*? Crew had told him it took at least two people to man the ship and he still wasn't anywhere to be seen.

"You're brave," Jaron said as he made his way to the helm of the ship, only a few paces away, never turning his back to her. "But you don't have to die." It would be such a waste.

Jussst kill her and be done with it, came the whisper. *Leavesss more room on your tiny ship.* The whisper chuckled, a dark scratch in Jaron's mind.

"Death would be better than whatever grim fate you have planned for us." She didn't lower her peculiar sword like he'd thought she would. "Take us back to the docks at once."

This nearly made Jaron chuckle. Were all Cerulians this demanding or just her?

When he gripped the wheel and straightened the mast instead of turning back in the direction of Baltessa, she tossed her sword to the deck and reached behind her back to grab her bow.

Jaron jolted around the wheel and raced toward her before she could grab an arrow and nock it. He grabbed both her wrists and when he went to pin them behind her back, she clocked him with an elbow to his gut. If he let her get away, he'd be dead in mere seconds from an arrow in the head. He stumbled after her and grabbed for her again, his other hand reaching into a pocket at his belt and pulling out his cuffs. In one swift movement, he slid his hand down to her wrist and slapped the silver band on it.

The moment the metal slid into place over her wrist, he snatched her other arm, forcing it into the band. She kicked back, the heel of her boot hitting below his belt and everything went black for a moment, pain exploding through him like he'd just been shot with a pistol. A scream that didn't sound like his own ripped into the air. He curled in on himself, clutching himself in the precious spot where she'd hit him.

"What is this silver contraption?" He heard the archer's panicked voice over the raging thrum of his blood in his ears.

Blinking away the tears that had forced their way out, he looked up at her from the deck. He hadn't even known he'd fallen; the pain had been that immense and overwhelming—his soul, *what was left of it*, had nearly left his body. He squinted up at her, watching her squirm as the silver band tightened on her wrists.

"What kind of evil contraption have you placed on me?" she hissed at him. The silver clicked the more she moved, constricting her wrists even tighter.

"Those," he said between breaths. "Those are cuffs, designed—" He coughed and rolled up onto his knees. "Designed specifically for pirates like you. The more you squirm, the tighter they get. Keep squirming and you'll lose your hands." He glanced at the pack of arrows on her back. "How would your shot with a bow be then?"

Jaron expected her to scream at him or at least react in some way, but her face remained a stone carving beneath her mask. He wished she had ripped it off already so he could read her properly, yet for some reason he didn't think it would've aided him.

A defeated sound escaped from the archer's lips. If he wasn't listening carefully enough, he would've mistaken it for a wave washing against the ship.

"Are you going to kill us then?" she asked, her knuckles white, her expression calculative.

"If I wanted you dead," he told her, repeating the same words she'd told him earlier, "then you would be dead."

"You won't get away with it." She glanced past him at the

fading capital island behind him. "The Queen of Bones and the pirate fleet will hunt you to the edge of the seas."

Jaron rose to his feet with a groan. "Then it's a wondrous thing that where we're heading, there is no sea."

PART TWO

CHASING THE STORM

CHAPTER NINE

CSILLA

Baltessa
Mid-Rainrise

"Don't tell a soul," Csilla whispered to the guard who'd brought her the news. "Especially not Blackwater."

When Kane had come back to the courtyard searching for Lorelei and she wasn't anywhere to be seen, Csilla had sent a couple of guards to the rose garden and the guests' quarters. She'd sent her best and most trusted sword down the servant wing and through the dimmest lit hallways. The fact that Nara hadn't yet returned set off alarm bells in Csilla's head.

"We have a maid who thinks she might've seen something," a guard, Tio, muttered quietly. They stood in an alcove on the edge of the courtyard, away from the rest of the partygoers, who were all unaware that the Storm—as well as Csilla's dearest friend and first mate—had gone missing. How could she have spent her time dancing and twirling with Flynn and let something like this happen in *her home*?

"Take me to her," Csilla said, pulling the gold mask from her face. She had no use for it anymore. She turned to follow the guard, but then Flynn was there in her path, his crooked smile pulling at his lips.

"Don't tell me you're leaving." Flynn twined his fingers into hers. "Put aside your queenly duties just for one night."

She had, and now her friends could be missing. She slid her hands away from Flynn. "Duty never rests. I'm sorry, but I must go."

"I understand," he told her, his usual sparkle losing a bit of its glimmer. "Try not to think of me too much while you're gone."

A small smile was all she could spare him as she turned away and followed Tio, winding through the halls to the servants' wing. The roast she'd eaten earlier started to churn in her stomach, threatening to come back up, dread leaving a sour taste in her mouth.

The guard stopped at a door to one of the large storage rooms and opened it, ushering Csilla inside. The space was dimly lit by a hanging lantern, while shelves stocked with sheets, quilts, and other bedding lined the walls. A woman in the center of the room turned to face them when they entered. Her hands were wrapped around her arms as if she was chilled, her nervous eyes flicking from Csilla to the floor.

"Your Majesty," the maid said, bowing her head. A strand of honey hair escaped from the cap on her head. She didn't look a year older than Csilla.

"What did you see?" Csilla asked her, sweeping past all formalities. "Please tell me everything."

"Yes, ma'am," she said with a quiver in her voice. "I wasn't too sure of what I saw at first because of the party and the dark hallways and I wrote it off as people roaming because people roam when they have too much ale and rum you know?" She spoke much too quickly, her words falling from her mouth like loose marbles. "By the time I realized that what I saw could've been foul it was probably too late to have made a difference but I still went to find someone on patrol in the inner halls of the palace."

"You're nervous," Csilla said, softening her tone even though her heart raced the longer she stood there. "It's all right. Just take a deep breath and tell me exactly what you saw. I promise you, every detail will help, even if you think it's too late."

The maid nodded and took a breath before continuing. "There hadn't been much of anyone in the halls after we served dinner. Everyone either went to the masquerade or home to their families since we were finished early tonight, but I still had shelves to stock. I was alone and when I heard bootsteps, I was curious to see if maybe some lovebirds were trying to find a quiet place to be . . . alone, you know?"

She wrung her apron in her fingers as she continued. "So, I took a peek through the door, and sure enough a man came walking down the hall, carrying a girl in his arms. I thought perhaps she'd had too much to drink and he was helping her." Her voice lowered then. "I didn't notice it then, but after he'd left, I started thinking about how the hallway seemed darker when he passed, like the lantern flames were flickering out. Then I talked myself down because what were the odds of an emberblood being in the palace?"

The maid glanced at Csilla as if she'd tell her different, that the very thought was ridiculous, but Csilla couldn't provide her with any solace. If they had been infiltrated by an emberblood, then he was a skilled enough Incendian Scout to not leave any clues behind. "What else do you remember about him?"

"He wore a red mask," she answered with a shrug. "But that's it. Not too long went by before I heard another set of footsteps. I barely heard these, but they were much faster, like someone was running on the tips of their toes. By the time I got to the door to peek and see who it was, they were gone. Whoever it was, they were fast."

Nara. She must've been on his tail.

"How far apart were the two sets of footsteps?" Csilla asked.

"I'd had enough time to fold the four bedsheets on the bottom row of that shelf." The maid hooked her thumb to the right. "I folded five more shelves before I fetched a guard."

"Five more shelves' worth?" Csilla hadn't meant to yell, but too much time had gone by. If Nara and Lorelei were in danger, then she might be too late. "It took you that long to realize foul play?"

Tears welled up in the maid's eyes and her chin wobbled. "I'm sorry, Your Majesty! I was afraid. The halls were dark and I was alone. I lacked the courage to report what I'd seen sooner. Please! Don't punish me!"

Csilla stiffened. "Punish you?" She placed her hand on the maid's shoulder. "I could never. Tio, be sure this maid receives the remainder of the week's end off with full coin. She's to be compensated for the information she has given."

"What?" the maid asked through her tears. "I've never had the week's end off."

"Spend your time however you choose," Csilla told her. She opened the closet's door and stepped into the hall, with Tio following close behind.

"Where are we heading?" he asked, trying to keep up. Her stride was quick, despite her limp.

"If you were planning to make a swift and unseen escape from the palace," she asked him, "where would you go?"

They raced to the southern docks, tucked away on a stretch of beach behind the palace. It was known only to the most trusted merchants who brought shipments directly to the palace, but if that information had slipped into the wrong hands, it was exactly where the emberblood would've run.

The docks were empty aside from the ships that swayed with the tide. Everything seemed mostly untouched under the moonlight, the beach as calm and serene as any other. Just as Csilla was about to tell Tio to rally a group to search the districts of Baltessa, something caught her sight. The stretch of dock in front of her seemed off. There was no ship in the spot, but a rope was tied to the post.

Csilla hurried forward and grabbed the rope, pulling until the other end came up from the sea. Frayed. Cut by someone. With the rope still in her hand, Csilla glanced around the stretch of dock finding nothing but crates and discarded netting, until she saw the discarded plank. When she stepped out of the way and let the moonlight hit it directly, there were splatters of blood across it, still fresh enough to be red. She kicked at the plank of wood, revealing an arrow hidden beneath. Its tip was coated in blood, the striped fletching on the nock familiar.

Nara's arrow, but no Nara.

Csilla spun to look out at the sea, hoping for a glimpse of the ship the rope had once been attached to, but there were only waves in the darkness.

She threw the rope back into the sea. "Damn!" she yelled, her heart flaring in her chest. "He got away!"

Csilla half debated commandeering one of the docked ships

and chasing the sea, hoping to find them, but she knew that the journey would be fruitless. She'd be nothing without a crew and she had no idea which direction they'd have sailed once they left the capital's waters.

"What are your orders?" Tio asked. She'd forgotten he was there, his voice making her jump.

"Gather my crew," Csilla said, grinding the toe of her boot into the dock. "We meet in the War Room."

—

Everyone gathered quickly, circling around the table in the center, poring over the map covering its top. Flynn and Arius squabbled to Csilla's right about the possibility of more than one intruder while the twins, Rosalina and Serafina, silently tweaked the new midrange wrist weapon they'd been working on as Borne watched them curiously. Lockhart mumbled in the corner of the room with a handful of upper-ranking court officials. Even though she'd sent a guard to find Kane, he was still missing. She couldn't help but think of Rhoda. If her sister had been the one in charge, they would've started figuring out their plan with or without Kane.

"Where is Blackwater?" Arius asked, cutting off Flynn's last argument. "Shouldn't he be here, considering his lady is the one who died?"

Flynn backhanded Arius in the chest, making him cough. "She isn't dead. Didn't you pay attention?"

"There was blood on the dock and she's missing," Arius continued. He rubbed at his chest where Flynn had swatted him. "Death *is* a possibility."

Flynn rubbed his temple like he was dealing with a child.

"He's right," Csilla said, her finger tracing the map. "Lorelei and Nara could both be dead." The word tasted strange. The thought of both of them . . . she stopped herself, unable to let her mind wander there. She pointed to the Gold Sea on the map, the water between Baltessa and the earth-worshiping kingdom, Terran. "With all the harbors between here and—"

The doors to the War Room burst open, bouncing off the walls with an echoing bang. Kane stumbled into the light, stopping, then straightening his collar. "Apologies," he said, his voice slurring slightly. "The door was in my way."

"Aye!" Arius called. His sun-kissed curls were a mess on his head from the ridiculous hat he'd worn earlier. "Where have you been, mate?"

"Testing the ale," Kane said. He walked toward the table without fault, but Csilla couldn't tell if it was because he was perfectly fine or if walking a straight line was trained into him so hard that he could drink a tavern's worth and still function. "Don't worry," he continued. "The ale is fine."

"Blackwater"—Flynn's nose scrunched as he assessed Kane—"are you drunk?"

"Don't think I've ever seen Blackwater drunk," Arius chimed in.

Flynn nodded. "We tried to find you earlier, but you were gone."

Kane sighed deeply, the sound of it filling the whole room. "Have you ever wanted something that kept slipping from your grasp?" His stared hazily forward at nothing in particular, almost like he was picturing something or someone else in front of him instead. "There. Right in front of you, but if you become too eager, move toward it too quickly, you'll lose it?"

The air in the room felt heavy. Csilla knew what everyone was thinking. They all knew his tipsy mind was talking about Lorelei, but he didn't yet know how much he'd lost her tonight and from the look on everyone's faces, no one wanted to be the one to tell him.

"Well, that was romantic," Arius mused. "Poetic even, considering that Lorelei is either missing or dead."

Quiet swept over them all. The crackle of the fireplace was the only thing Csilla could hear aside from her own breathing. Leave it to Arius to blow out the only candle in a dark room.

Kane stood eerily still, his fist gripping the table, his shoulders rising and falling. He hadn't attempted to throw a chair yet, so Csilla broke the silence before he could.

"We don't know everything yet," she told him, her voice even calmer than she'd hoped for. "But I don't believe she is dead."

Kane glanced up at her then from under his brow, his eyes black and bottomless. "Where is she?"

Csilla proceeded to tell Kane what she believed to have happened—that the intruder took Lorelei and Nara confronted him, wounding him on the docks, but ultimately was taken as well. She could be wrong, but if his plan had been to kill them, then why not leave their bodies to be found? Incendia was up to something.

"There's more," Csilla said. She hadn't told the rest of them about what she and Tio had found out. "The maid wasn't sure if she was imagining it, but she said the flames in the lanterns flickered out when he walked by. It's possible the intruder was an emberblood."

"Truly?" Lockhart asked from the corner of the room. She'd forgotten he was over there with the court officials. "You think they'd send a Scout? Explains why they've been so quiet the past moon."

Arius craned his head into the conversation. "A Scout? I thought Csilla said an emberblood."

"All emberbloods are Scouts," Flynn reminded him. "Scouts are a rank in their navy, remember?"

"Aye, but just to make sure I follow, all emberbloods are Scouts, but not all Scouts are emberbloods?"

Everyone's voices kept growing louder, merging together until they were the same wave whipping against a cliff. Rhoda would've stopped this. She wouldn't have let this carry on. Csilla clenched and unclenched her hand.

Kane rubbed his hand down his face. "This is my fault. I should've been with her. After she touched me with lightning, I thought it was best to give her room. She seemed so scared and I left her alone."

"Wait," Flynn said. "Touched you with lightning?"

Arius snorted. "How much ale did you drink exactly?"

Kane slammed his fist on the table. "Not too much to know that you're *still an imbecile.*"

"Do you men *ever* stop prattling?" Rosalina said from the chair she slouched in. Her braided ringlets fell over her shoulder as she looked up from the weapon she was working on. The twins didn't pipe up much, often listening and observing, so when Rosalina's quiet soprano voice joined in, everyone turned to look at her. She blinked at them. "What? You're like ships without sails trying to find your way through conversations."

She smiled sweetly, her tone remaining soft while her words sliced sharply. "The pieces are there if you just look close enough. The Incendians sent one man because they knew how difficult it would be to send an entire troop unnoticed. Must be one of their best, if they sent him alone. We should be making a plan, yet the only thing you all can contribute is a change of topic."

"Well," Arius scoffed, fists on his hips. "At least I'm contributing *something*. Have you finished playing with your toys?"

Too much. Csilla's thoughts were fragments in her mind. *It's all too much.*

Serafina stood up next to Rosalina, holding the weapon she'd crafted in front of her. "These are not toys," she told him, her voice rougher than her twin's. "These cuffs can shoot a poison dart with a click of a switch. Quick as an arrow, needle sharp enough for whatever potion we can buy off a witchblood. What do the Sons have again?"

Arius laughed. "We have pistols, dove. It's all we need."

"Enough," Csilla said, the ringing in her ears muffling her voice. No one quieted. She withdrew one of the blades from her belt and stabbed it into the war table, pieces clattering over onto their sides. "Enough!"

A hush fell across the room.

"If I could," she continued in a hushed voice, "I'd have everyone board this instant and we'd chase down the ember-blood with no direction. But we don't know what we're truly up against here." She glanced down at the war table's map again, looking over the jagged scar of islands, and stopping on a splotch marked with ruin. Its stark familiarity rooted her boots to the floor.

The Lost Isle.

"Borne," she said. "I think we should pay your mother a visit. See what the trees have whispered to the Ruin Witch."

"She hates having visitors," the former witchblood replied,

"but these are strange times. I can send her a gull, let her know we are coming."

"Send one tonight. We'll leave dock at first light. Flynn, Kane, gather your most dependable men and I'll recruit my Maidens. Serafina, Rosalina, visit the armory and place an order for *everything*. Give them all the gold they need to get it done."

"Hold on a minute," Lockhart said, emerging from his corner of the room. "You plan on going with them? What about Cerulia? You have a duty to fulfill here." The few court officials behind him murmured in agreement. "You can't just sail off into the sunset on a journey to find your friends."

Csilla's hand curled into a fist on the face of the table. "Yes, I will be going. You and the court officials will keep things running smoothly in my absence, I presume?" She didn't give him a moment to answer though he grumbled something under his breath. "And someone be sure Blackwater sleeps off the ale."

The room burst into motion, everyone scuttling like crabs to where Csilla had sent them, but one person came toward her instead. Lockhart held his hands behind his back as he surveyed her. Salt-and-pepper hair was tucked behind his pierced ears, the handle of his whip protruding from his belt.

"You have a responsibility here that you can't sail away from," Lockhart told her.

"Lorelei Storm and my first mate are missing, General," Csilla replied, straightening her spine. "I'm not sure what you're suggesting I should be doing otherwise."

"Send a team, yes, but you don't need to go." Lockhart quieted his voice. "That's for *them* to do, not for *us*."

"Excuse me?" Csilla looked him square in the face. "I know you were never a captain, so you wouldn't understand. If the ship sinks, we go down with our crew. Nara and Lorelei are a part of my crew. Yes, they are *my friends*, but I cannot stay behind when they could be out there, waiting."

Lockhart's face turned to stone, distaste etched in his frown. "If you can't put your duty first, then maybe you're not cut out for the island throne. Perhaps the Storm was wrong about you. Perhaps your grandmother was too."

Csilla took a step closer and lowered her tone to a menacing level. "Choose your next words carefully, General. I can easily find someone else to fill your position. There are many eager, young minds that you're so terrified of who are waiting to step into a position of such status. Tell me, can you fulfill *your* duty as your queen asks?" Using her title in such a way felt wrong, but she couldn't allow disarray in her court. She had to prove she was strong in ways they believed she wasn't.

"The court officials and I will run the kingdom like you never left," Lockhart said with a smile that didn't quite reach his eyes. He bowed his head and turned to leave, but Csilla cleared her throat, stopping him.

"And one more thing, General," she said. "This isn't a kingdom anymore. It's a queendom."

CHAPTER TEN
KANE

Baltessa

Mid-Rainrise

Kane's temples pounded as he headed to the docks with the dawn.

The only reason he'd been able to sleep when he returned to his chambers was because of the ale he'd had earlier. He'd lost count of how many precisely. He was half-tempted to drink another just to chase off the headache, but he'd rather suffer through it and have a clear mind when setting sail. Everything had to go right after it had gone so wrong.

The docks were still quiet, the capital only beginning to wake up as the sky began to lighten. His heart, however, remained dark.

He blamed himself for what had happened to Lorelei. He probably would until the day he found her. It was still difficult for him to grasp that not even a day ago she was kissing him under the moonlight, their feelings laid bare, and now she was gone. He truly was cursed with the rotten luck of his father. *Black spot of a Blackwater.* He faltered to a stop where the path met the dock. Grief hung on him, weighing him down like an anchor, but then anger rose again in him, lifting him back up.

He tightened the strap on his shoulder and turned back toward the waiting sea, nearly running into Csilla. Her curls were pulled back from her face, determination curving her brow, lighting a fire behind her gaze. He noticed the blouse and pants she wore were simple, like those she used to wear when she was only a captain. A queen with a ship instead of a crown.

"You're coming after all?" Kane asked her, watching her reaction closely.

"I don't take orders from Lockhart," she responded. She paused. "He should remember his place."

"He did make a valid point, you know." Kane knew she didn't want to hear the truth, but she still needed to. "Cerulia doesn't need to lose its queen as well."

"I'm surprised you remember what he even said." Csilla laughed, the sound small, clipped. "You were pretty sloshed last night."

"And I'm still feeling it this morning," Kane said, rubbing at his temple.

"But if anyone is going to be out there looking for Nara and Lorelei, I'm going to be with them."

"Then we will find them," Kane said, holding out his hand to her like he was offering her a deal. She grasped his hand and they shook on it.

"Together," she said.

Many ships rested at the docks, waiting to be taken on another voyage. Men carried crates and rolled barrels up the plank of one ship in particular, its gray sails tucked away.

As they walked toward the dock, Kane glanced down to where the tide met the ship, eyeing the line of silver peeking out of the water. A steel bow ran from the keel, across the bottom, to the back end. It was magicked by a witch during the Old War, allowing it to cut through waves and even bergs. Pity such a beautiful ship belonged to someone who couldn't value its worth.

"We're taking the *Wavecutter*?" Kane asked as Csilla turned to walk up the plank of the ship. "Does Tomas know about this?"

"Not yet," Csilla responded. He jogged up the plank to catch up to her. "But what he doesn't know, and won't remember, won't hurt him. This ship is the fastest in the fleet and we'll hoist merchant sails to disguise ourselves, but if anyone recognizes the steel, the *Wavecutter* also has a reputation of being manned by drunks. Fast and inconspicuous is exactly what we need."

—

It was a four days' sail to the Lost Isle, thanks to the *Wavecutter*. Kane had never visited the ruins of the ancient city of Alannis, but he'd sailed past it a time or two. To get to the Ruin Witch's home, Csilla told them they would need to row in on the narrow river that cut into the middle of the island. Flynn had insisted on sharing a boat with Csilla since he was the best shot and needed to protect the queen, even though they all knew the truth, while Kane sat in a dinghy with Borne and Arius, who wouldn't keep quiet. All Kane wanted was a moment to think and he clearly wasn't going to get that.

The vegetation on the island was wilder than on Crossbones, trees filling every space, winding around each other and through withered stone ruins along the riverbank. The farther inland they rowed, the narrower the river became. The canopy of the jungle grew closer, vines hanging down like ropes, brushing over their shoulders as they rowed on.

Kane was finally getting a moment of quiet when Arius yelped and let go of the oar to point out into the jungle. Borne quickly grabbed the handle before it could fall into the water, leaving them stuck with just one.

"Did you *see that*?" Arius yelled. "That lizard was as big as a dog! Do you think it was a dragon?" He looked at Kane, then to Borne who sat on the middle bench between them. "Borne, was it a baby dragon? I've always wanted to see a baby dragon. Do you think they came through the crack in Limbo as well?" His voice dropped to a whisper then, his head turned back and forth between each riverbank. "What if its mother is here *right now*?"

Borne glanced over his shoulder to where Arius had pointed. "I don't see anything," he replied, then looked forward again. "I've seen lizards bigger than a horse while growing up here, so odds are it was only a lizard. However, you shouldn't sound excited about the possibility of the return of dragons."

Arius chuckled. "You wouldn't want to see one? A real fire-breathing dragon? I'd bet all my gold that they're damn magnificent."

"And destructive," Kane said from the other end of the dinghy where he sat, elbows on his knees. "They're too difficult to tame and were put in Limbo for a reason."

"Whoa." Arius feigned surprise. "Hold the sails! Is there some knowledge tucked away in that head of yours, Blackwater?"

"Don't think I won't kick your ass on this dinghy," Kane growled. "Just keep rowing."

"Now, *that* would be a sight to see, mate."

"Kane is right, Arius," Borne interrupted, moving to block Kane from staring a hole through Arius. "Dragons burn with no mercy. If Incendia were to somehow be able to train or control them, then I'm afraid the Kingdoms of Four would fall to just one."

Arius scoffed. "Then what about the ice dragons in Ventys? Why didn't they get locked away in Limbo?"

"Have you ever seen an ice dragon, Arius?" Kane asked.

"No."

"Have you ever heard stories about them turning villages to blocks of ice?"

Arius hesitated a moment like he was cycling through his memories. "Hmm, no."

"There is your answer."

"Are you getting lippy again, Blackwater?"

Borne cleared his throat, interrupting them once more. "The ice dragons are docile and are used for Ventys's transportation and keeping the Frozen Gap surrounding their kingdom frozen."

"Huh . . ." Arius curled his lip like he was lost in thought for a moment. "You really are a little bundle of history, aren't you?"

Borne shrugged his shoulders. "My mother taught me everything I know."

"It's been great having you with us," Arius went on. "Useful to have that brain of yours on board."

"For once," Kane said, hating that he had to say the words, "I actually agree with Arius. Your knowledge is valuable."

"Agree with me?" Arius laughed. "We really are in strange times."

They rowed on a bit more, Arius exclaiming a few more times—once about a white snake that had to be as long as the width of the deck of the *Iron Jewel* and another time about a turtle with what looked like jewels sprouting from its shell. Kane was ready to kiss the dock by the time they got there. The three of them climbed out quickly and joined Csilla and Flynn on the riverbank.

"Where to now?" Kane asked, wanting to be in and out of the Lost Isle as soon as possible. The quicker they found out what they could, the quicker they could find Lorelei and Nara.

"We go to the Ruin Witch or she'll find us," Csilla said. "Whichever comes first."

This made Kane cock his head. "You've been here before?"

"I've made many deals with the Ruin Witch." She motioned them forward. Borne joined her at the front of their group while they began their trek through the jungle.

"What kind of deals?" Arius asked as they followed Csilla and Borne through the jungle thicket. Arius swiped at a vine that hung down. "Did you ask for gold or . . . wait, did you ask to become captain of the *Scarlet Maiden* over your sister?"

"Arius!" Flynn snapped, shoving him in the shoulder. "We talked about this. Some things we don't ask. Some things we don't say."

Arius brushed off his shoulder like Flynn had left a mark. "I'm just curious, mate."

Csilla stopped walking, the tall grass she was marching through covering her boots. She didn't turn to look at them as she said, "I made deals to keep my mother alive for as long as I could. It wasn't enough in the end."

Kane remembered the crate of fruit he'd had sent to the Abado sisters when he'd found out about their mother's passing. He hadn't known what Csilla had done to keep Soleil Abado alive though.

"Oh," Arius said, his voice dropping. "I'm sorry. Truly I am." He leaned closer to Flynn and asked so quietly, Kane almost didn't hear him, "Can I ask what she gave up to trade?"

A new voice entered the thicket. Rich, warm, and as unfamiliar as the jungle ruins. "She gave me some childhood dolls, a favorite sword, and even an eye."

Csilla looked back at them then. One eye of silver. One of brown. "She found us," Csilla said.

Kane turned in the direction of the voice, watching as the Ruin Witch slid from the jungle, a part of it in every way. She moved with the graceful danger of a snake, every step making the group shrink back slightly. Her curly red-gold hair was twisted in a knot on her head, wisps blowing as she walked, a scarf tied across her hairline. Golden eyes flitted to each of them, her expression unreadable. Then she smiled.

"My son," she said, opening her arms.

Borne stepped forward, embracing her. "Mother."

She pulled back from him, her hands at his cheeks as she looked up at him. "You're just like the trees here. You never stop growing." She hugged him again. "I'm so very glad you've came to visit me, my son. The trees told me that you'd arrived, but did you have to bring along *pirates*?" She bit out the word like it was a curse.

Arius cleared his throat, all heads turning to him. "Excuse me, Miss Ruin Witch?"

Kane let out a frustrated sigh and Csilla silently shook her head, mouthing the word *don't*. Flynn pulled at Arius's sleeve. "Some questions don't need to be asked," he repeated through the side of his mouth.

"Do the trees *really* speak to you?" Arius asked, taking a step away from Flynn. "Or is it in a metaphorical sense? You seem a little cryptic like your son, and I just want to be sure."

"Are you mocking me?" the Ruin Witch asked, the gold in her eyes swimming.

"No," Arius said quickly, his words stumbling from his mouth. "No, no, I'm only curious. I think it would be brilliant if you could really hear the trees." He beamed from ear to ear, dimples cutting his light-brown cheeks.

The Ruin Witch studied him for a moment, the tension so thick it could be cut with a blade. If Arius's uncaged mouth thwarted this mission to get information, Kane would personally see to it that he was left to rot on the nearest wild island. It didn't matter how close he was with Flynn or if he was a good shot. Lines had to be drawn in the sand at some point.

"She magically sealed Rhoda's lips the last time we were here," Csilla said quietly to Arius. "You should apologize and—"

"I like this one," the Ruin Witch said, the corners of her lips turning up the slightest bit. She turned to Borne then. "He can come visit us in Terran anytime."

Kane's mouth popped open. He could practically feel the pride swelling in Arius at the witch's comment. Relief washed over him for the moment after the shock.

Borne whipped his head to his mother. "Terran? What are you talking about, Mother?"

"Come," she said, waving at them to follow. "We have much to discuss."

—

The Ruin Witch's cabin wasn't too much farther, but Kane would've preferred standing in the jungle with how cramped it was inside. Various jars filled with different herbs and dead insects that made Kane's skin crawl were scattered on shelves and tables. The Ruin Witch walked around the space lighting candles, and a sweet aroma reached him, almost like the smell of bayberries during peak sunspur. The unease he'd been feeling slowly started to slip away along with his suspicions that the cause was something magic in the candles.

"So," the witch said, snuffing out the rolled-up paper she'd used to the light the candles. "You've lost the Storm."

"We didn't lose her," Csilla explained. "Or Nara." She leaned against the wall next to the window, her arms crossed as she looked out at something in front of the cabin. "Someone took them from us."

"And you came to me to figure out where to find them." The Ruin Witch clicked her tongue. "You pirates always want something."

"Mother," Borne intervened. "You know the realms are restless right now. I don't believe we'd have come here if there were any other choice. We don't want your help, we *need* it."

The witch reached for her son, fingers twitching, then quickly dropped her hand back down by her side. "I see. With your magic gone, have they now turned you against me in your time away?"

Borne sighed, the sound of it filling the space. "You know much, but you are wrong about that. I'm no longer a witchblood, and I thought you'd come to terms with that before Rove took me from here. We knew where my path led."

Listening to the exchange between Borne and his mother was a twist in Kane's heart. He remembered the time his own mother had asked him to stay and play cards with her instead of going and training with his father that day. He'd left her and ran off to train, leaving her alone in the captain's cabin, his expression drooping with sadness. If only Kane could go back, he would've stayed with her every day. He wouldn't have let another moment slip through his fingers. Perhaps Borne should stay with his mother too.

The tense expression on the Ruin Witch's face remained unchanged. "When you come back with me to Terran, we can find a way to fix your magic." Her expression darkened then, worry creasing her brow. "You'll need your magic in the days to come."

"What's coming?" Csilla asked, finally pulling her focus from the window. Kane briefly wondered if she'd been thinking about her own mother too.

The Ruin Witch cut her gaze to Csilla, her golden eyes flickering in the candlelight. "I think you know very well what's coming."

Kane thought back to Death's Cove. The ravaging hunger of the comoras, the reek of the half-souls on the abandoned deck of a *Bonedog*. His shoulder throbbed in response. He imagined the blackness of his wound stretching farther, rotting the blood in his veins, spreading across his skin like a disease.

"The crack in Limbo is real then?" Csilla asked. Kane anchored himself back in the conversation, suppressing the urge to grip his shoulder. The pain would fade soon. If he'd just distract himself, it would be over even quicker.

Flynn cocked his head at Csilla. "Did you not believe my story about those man-eating birds? I didn't make it up just to woo you. It's fine if it worked though." He mumbled the last bit, getting a snicker out of Arius.

"No, it's not that," Csilla explained. "I just want to hear it from *her*."

"Yes, Queen Csilla," the Ruin Witch said, putting emphasis on her title. "It is true." The words would've shocked Kane had it not been for what he'd seen on that day.

"You should know it," the witch continued, pointing at Csilla. "From the dreamwraith that haunts you."

"Dreamwraith?" Flynn rounded on Csilla. "What is she talking about?"

"They're just nightmares," Csilla assured him.

"The bags under your eyes are from more than just nightmares. Tell me, do the dreams come every night or just on the nights your anguish eats away at you?"

Csilla scowled and turned her head back toward the window, her jaw working. Flynn moved closer to her, placing his hand softly on her shoulder. She shrugged him away but his hand remained and she didn't move away from him again. Kane thought the two of them were like the tide, push and pull. This time it seemed she let him win their little game of back-and-forth.

Seeing the way Flynn looked at Csilla made Kane think of blue eyes and the way they'd gleamed at him in the moonlight. It was hard to believe that night hadn't even been a week ago, though it felt like an entire season had flown by, his thoughts always returning to her one way or another.

"What does one do about a dreamwraith?" Flynn asked, cupping his chin with his fingers as if in profound thought.

The Ruin Witch glanced between Flynn and Csilla, interest lighting her expression. She continued to move like a snake even out of the jungle, her walk slow with a deliberate sway in her hips. She reached a pelt-covered chair and turned to face them. "Like one ends most things." She slid into the chair, her pointed fingernails tapping its wooden arms. "By killing it."

"And how do I kill something that I've never seen?" Csilla asked, her voice raising slightly. "I've never seen this supposed dreamwraith."

The Ruin Witch took a deep breath and sighed like she was about to tell a long story. "You wouldn't have seen it because you're asleep when it comes. Dreamwraiths are difficult creatures as they tether their essence to the dream realm while their physical form remains in our mortal realm, feeding from the terror they create in our dreams. It must be killed in *both* realms."

"How can I kill it in this realm if it only comes while I'm asleep?" Csilla asked, taking a step forward, her voice suggesting both hope and desperation. "If I kill it in my dream, will I wake up and have time to slay it?"

The Ruin Witch tilted her head, one of her stray amber curls swaying. "Doing it alone would be difficult, but not impossible. It would be better done with a group present. After you kill the wraith in your dreams, it must quickly be struck down in its physical form."

"That part will be easy," Arius said from the floor. He sat on a rug near the Ruin Witch's chair like a child listening to a story.

"Don't be naive, golden one," she said to Arius, patting his sun-kissed curls. Kane rolled his eyes. She'd only just met Pavel and he'd already earned a nickname from her. "It won't be that simple. If you kill the wraith's physical form before Csilla is able to kill it in her dream, then its essence could keep her trapped in the dream realm. Once a wraith loses its essence, its physical form grows stronger—that's when you'll know to deliver a fatal strike . . . if you're able to land one."

"You underestimate my shot," Flynn said, his hand resting at his pistol.

"Let's hope that remains true when it matters most then." The Ruin Witch looked at Flynn for a long moment, like she was studying him or knew something none of them knew, which was likely, considering all the things the trees told her.

If she knew so many things, then she had to know where Lorelei and Nara were. Kane had sat back, patiently listening to the rest of them, letting his mind wander to places, while the two of them were out there, waiting for them to help.

Kane cleared his throat, drawing their attention like someone had shouted about a fire. "I don't mean to be the black spot in this conversation and steer it off course, but do you also know where to find our friends?"

The Ruin Witch smiled full-tooth at Kane. It looked almost unnatural with her gold eyes. "There you are, Blackwater. I was wondering when you were going to speak up. Your voice is just as dark as I thought it would be."

"I've been listening." Kane pushed himself from the wall he'd been resting against and took a step forward. "You seem to know everything. Surely you must know who took Lorelei and Nara and where we can find them."

"Straight to business then." The Ruin Witch chuckled. "I can only assume it is the emberblood that the hollow trees in West Incendia saw. He went to the wasteland alone and dug up a magicked sword that had belonged to Magnus when his war had raged across this realm. If he knew where to find this sword, then he knew where to find Lorelei. I suspect he has a connection to Magnus, just as the flame god did with Rove and Rhoda."

Magnus. He'd see a world of flames and ashes. Molten men with their dripping lava and obsidian armor fighting alongside the flame-worshiping Incendians to conquer the other Kingdoms of Four. But the question still lingered: what was stopping him?

"Why hasn't he slipped through the crack in Limbo?" Kane asked. "Plenty of other creatures seem to be slipping through."

"Ah." The Ruin Witch raised one sharp-nailed finger into the air. "That's the correct question, isn't it? Mortals can navigate between realms. We do it in our dreams, we do it in death, we can even project our spirit into another realm if we will it enough and if there is a path to take. But a god cannot walk our realm in their form. They must have a willing vessel."

"A mortal body for him to possess?"

Csilla bristled from the window, straightening her stance once more. "Then we have even more reason to hunt down the ember-blood. If he has Magnus's sword, then perhaps he is the vessel Magnus is seeking."

"Why a vessel now though?" Kane asked, trying to piece it all together. "There was no mention of this when he nearly escaped the last time."

"The curse to hold him in Limbo was broken," the Ruin Witch explained, "and though it was partially resealed, a curse cannot be broken a second time. The spill of Storm blood was supposed to release him to the realm of the gods, where he could still wreak his havoc, but now Magnus seeks a different path, one that leads directly to our realm."

"Well, isn't that just peachy?" Arius threw his head back and laughed. "We thought we saved the world, but we only screwed it up further."

Kane's head was swimming as he tried to figure out the ember-blood and Magnus's motives. "Why take her then?" The question was barely a whisper, something he hadn't even meant to ask out loud.

"They must have other plans for her," the Ruin Witch replied. "Though I cannot say for sure what their reasoning may be, she is the only stormblood who walks this earth. Perhaps they have a use for her."

"I'll be damned if I let that happen," Kane growled, white-knuckled.

"How can we find them?" Csilla asked. "We have no idea where exactly they're sailing to."

The Ruin Witch shook her head. "They're still at sea, so the trees have told me nothing. I cannot track them if the trees cannot as well."

"What about a loophole?" Flynn tested. "There's always a loophole."

"Well, I might not be able to track them, but I do know of someone who can track anyone . . . for a price." The witch tapped the arm of the chair and smirked.

"Another witchblood?" For the first time since they'd left Baltessa, Kane felt a kindling of hope. "Where do we find them?"

"I'll tell you," the Ruin Witch said with a calculative gleam in her eye, "but only if Borne comes with me back to Terran."

"Mother!" Borne turned on her. "You can't just—"

"Deal," Kane said without hesitation. Borne would thank him one day when he had his magic back and more time with his mother.

"Now hold on," Arius interrupted. "This kid knows everything there is to know about everything. He answers all of my questions. Who will answer them now?"

"The tracker is a witchblood," Kane told him. "Ask your questions to them."

"Terran isn't my home, Mother," Borne pleaded. "I've only just gotten decent with a sword."

"This is about more than what you want," the witch told him. "If Magnus gets his vessel, it won't just be Cerulia in danger. After all this time, he won't stop there and you will need your magic back, so you *will come*."

Borne hesitated, eyes shining for a moment before he blinked them clear. "I understand," he said quietly.

"The Serpent can be found in Smuggler's Harbor. I can't promise he'll help you though." She gazed out the window, squinting. "The sun is already setting. I'd hurry there if you want to reach him before someone else has made an offer."

"Then we should go," Csilla said, straightening from where she was leaning by the window.

The group mumbled their goodbyes to the Ruin Witch and wished Borne well as they headed out the door of her cabin, Kane following after them. Before he could step through the doorway, the Ruin Witch's voice stopped him.

"Blackwater," she called. He slowly turned to face her. "Don't think I didn't smell the death on you. What do you plan to do about that wound of yours?"

"It was a dead man's sword," Borne said in his mother's ear. "He hasn't spoken about it with anyone."

"Denial will not make your wound any less fatal," the Ruin Witch told Kane, her gold eyes pinning him where he stood. He'd already told himself the words, but hearing them from someone else laced them with a finality that darkened his mood. He didn't look back as he walked through the door of the witch's home and back out into the wild jungle.

CHAPTER ELEVEN

LORELEI

Silver Sea

Mid-Rainrise

Thunderstorms used to frighten Lorelei when she was still small enough to curl into her mother's lap. The raging winds that blew in from the sea always hit the coast hard, and high up on the hill above Port Barlow, near the cliffs, they struck even harder.

Storms might be unpredictable, but one thing was certain: they always brought darkness with them. Every time dark clouds rolled in, they draped over the windows, reaching into their home and into her heart. During one rainrise, a storm with clouds nearly the color of charcoal hit their harbor town with wind and thunder that shook the walls of their cabin. Her mother had always told her that fire brought destruction, but Lorelei had seen the chaos that storms left behind. The storm that had hit that night many years ago had left the docks and rooftops in such a mess, they'd needed to be rebuilt.

Lorelei didn't know when she'd fallen asleep, but her dreams were filled with lightning and thunder. Rain and tears. A biting wind.

A different breeze blew across her cheeks, almost warm. Cerulian winds.

The storms in her dreams ripped away, the copper spires of Baltessa emerging from the clouds. Her vision flew between the spires like a bird in flight, narrowing in on the palace. The sun stretched in an arc across the sky, racing like someone had sped up time, the moon chasing daylight until stars splattered across the black and she was standing on the terrace with Kane's callused hands in hers.

A moment later he crumpled to the ground, his body twitching as lightning swam through him, but unlike the last time, the sparks didn't die.

"Please," Kane rasped. "Stop."

"I . . . I can't!" Lorelei looked down at her open palms, watching in horror as the gold on her fingertips bled up her arms, up to her shoulders. She coughed, struggling to breath as it reached her neck, squeezing.

"Why?" Kane shouted between shocks. "Why are you . . . doing this?"

"I can't control it!" she screamed, her voice breaking as the gold continued to crawl up her neck. Coldness crept over her jaw, along her cheeks as she clawed at it, her fingernails scraping against the hardened gold.

Is this what her magic would do? Devour her whole?

She glanced down at the ground, trying to see if Kane was still hurting, but Kane wasn't there. The molten gold sealed her lips closed; a scream caught in her throat. Someone else stood in front of her, a red mask like flames hiding his face. Two empty holes sat where his eyes should be. A too-wide smile peeled across his lips as fire flickered to life behind him, burning across everything like the gold trailing up her face. Smoke filled the last breath she took.

Lorelei woke up, blinking once, twice from the blinding sun. Everything was so bright, she couldn't see anything yet, but she could smell the brine of the sea and hear the whip of sails.

Where am I?

Lorelei bolted upright, her hair sticking to the side of her face. She shielded her eyes and cracked them open, glancing down at the black dress she still wore from the masquerade. She sat in the middle of a small deck that was no wider than the small cabin she'd grown up in.

The first thing to pop into her mind was the man in the mask. Him standing in the hall with her was the last thing she remembered. The flames in the lanterns had blinked out, then it all went black. She thought she remembered a glimpse of the night sky and someone with a bow—was it Nara?—but it all seemed hazy, like it was another scene in the nightmare she'd just woken from.

She stood up much too fast, the world tilting. The sea stretched in all directions, endless as the sky. She whipped around, her heart in her throat, spotting Nara, who rested against the railing of the deck. Lorelei ran the few steps toward her, dropping to her knees.

"Nara," she said quietly, afraid to talk too loud in case the man with the mask was somewhere on the ship. "Nara, wake up." She shook Nara's shoulders.

Nara's head lifted, her eyes groggy as they opened and closed at Lorelei. Then, as if she suddenly realized where she was, she tensed, her shoulders moving but her arms remaining pinned behind her back.

"Damn," she said under her breath. "He still has these cuffs on me."

"He?" Lorelei asked, peeking behind Nara's back as she leaned forward, trying to pull her wrists from the contraption that held them. Lorelei had never seen anything like the silver coils that restricted Nara. It seemed the more she moved, the tighter they became.

"The man who took us," Nara whispered through her teeth. "He was trying to make off with you and I tried to stop him on my own." Her head dropped, her ebony hair falling like a curtain around her face. "I wasn't enough."

Lorelei looked closer at the cuffs, searching for a button or some switch to release the coils' hold. If she could free Nara, then the two of them together could overtake him. Lorelei might not be a fighter, but if she could make her lightning cooperate with her, then perhaps conjuring it as a weapon could be an option. But the cuffs had a smooth surface and Lorelei couldn't even tell where they connected.

"You'll be needing a key to get those off," came a familiar voice from behind her. She recognized it from the hallway at the palace, before everything had gone dark. She whirled around to face him, her hair whipping her face.

Gone was the coat he'd worn the night before, his white shirt and charcoal pants more casual and sea-ready. His mask was gone, revealing the sharp features on his olive-toned face, his dark hair cropped close to his head. She expected a cruel smile to twist his lips, but his expression remained hidden.

"I was wondering when you'd both wake up," he said, rolling up his shirtsleeve. Scars marred his hands, reaching past his wrists and up his forearms. Lorelei watched as he rolled up his other sleeve, revealing the matching scars on the other side. He pulled out two gloves from his back pocket and slipped them over his hands.

"Are you going to continue staring?" he asked, making Lorelei's breath catch.

She glanced up, fear holding her still with an icy grip. Hands that were scarred to that extent only meant one thing. "You're an emberblood."

His gaze narrowed on her as if contemplating what direction he should take the conversation. "And you're a stormblood. The only one in existence actually. There's a pretty high price on your head, you know."

Lorelei felt unsteady, like one strong gust of wind would knock her sideways.

"The last I heard," he continued, "even bandits in Terran are interested in the girl with the power of the storm brought back from the dead."

"Don't let him mess with your head," Nara said. "He sinks into your mind and that's when he attacks."

Lorelei glanced over her shoulder at the Maiden, whose shoulders were hunched as she sat leaned back against the ship's railing. Nara had done her best to protect Lorelei when she could do nothing for herself; now it was Lorelei's time to return the favor. She curled her fingers into fists, thinking of her sparks, hoping they'd race to her hands.

The emberblood looked down at her fists. "I'd rather not fight you too." He took a step forward and she noticed the limp in his movement. Perhaps Nara had wounded him during their confrontation. His wince curled into a wicked smile that didn't reach his eyes. "But I don't think you know how to fight, do you?"

"Can't fight, can't fight!" A squawk from the other end of the small ship broke the silence. She glanced back to see a stout man leaning against the mast of the ship, a parrot on his shoulder, both of them watching the scene unfold on the deck. Two against two then, plus the bird. Unless there were more hiding on the small ship.

Lorelei ground her teeth. She knew nothing about the man in front of her aside from his affinity for flames and his seeming hatred for Cerulia, but he somehow knew plenty about her. If Incendia, or Magnus, or whoever he reported to had intentions of killing her, why take her away from the capital instead of finishing the job right there?

"You're not going to do anything," Lorelei said, surprised by how even her tone was. Calling his bluff was a risk, but it was the only leverage she had. "Or else you wouldn't have wasted the effort of stealing me from my home."

"Your home?" The emberblood laughed then, a cold and mocking sound. "Don't act like you're a Cerulian when you were raised in Incendia."

"How do you—" Lorelei stammered over her words, her lips unable to keep up with her thoughts. "Why are you doing this?"

"Well." His voice trailed off as he stared off into the rising sun. "I'm not allowed to say too much, but I can promise you that you're not in imminent danger, if that's what you're worried about."

"Thank you for the reassurance." She didn't hide the sarcasm in her voice. "If you mean us no harm, then can you uncuff my friend?" Lorelei motioned to Nara behind her, but didn't take her sight off the emberblood.

"That's something I cannot do." He turned away from them and walked the few steps to the wheel of the small ship.

Lorelei spun to face him. "And why not? You say we're not in danger, yet you keep her in shackles."

He looked as if he was ignoring her, focusing instead on the sails as he turned the wheel a few notches.

"Are you a liar then?"

That got his attention. His gaze flicked back to her with lightning speed.

"I am a lot of things, stormblood," he said. "But I'm no liar."

"Then prove it," she said, lowering her voice, hoping she sounded like she'd unleash hell on him if he didn't do what she said. "Uncuff her."

"And die?" The emberblood laughed, gazing past Lorelei to Nara. "I'd prefer not to."

Lorelei glanced back at Nara, who watched the emberblood like a hawk watching its prey. If a glare could kill, he would be dead on the deck.

"See?" He laughed. "I've already got one boot in the grave with that one."

Nara's heated stare burned into him as she remained quiet.

"How else was she to react?" Lorelei turned back on him. "Was she supposed to surrender to you? I assume you'd defend your men."

"What men?" He looked around his empty ship. "In case you haven't noticed, this is a two-man ship. It's just me and Crew."

Confirming that it was just them, him, and a bloke with a parrot on the ship brought an odd comfort. Perhaps they did stand a chance if the two of them caught him off guard. For now, she'd play along in hopes of buying them more time before something changed, and he decided that she and Nara were both disposable.

"You must be very trusted to be sent alone to Baltessa," she mused. "One of the Incendian king's top Scouts, I assume."

The emberblood chuckled. "Valiant attempt, but you're not getting any information from me."

Worth a shot.

"Where are you taking us then?" Lorelei pushed even though Nara grumbled behind her. "What are your plans for us when we get there?"

"And what good would that knowledge do you?" he said, his glare shooting in her direction. "What solace would it provide you?"

A gust of wind blew Lorelei's hair across her face. "You're right," she replied, ignoring the strands. "Knowing won't bring me any peace. Only being back home will."

The emberblood stared straight ahead, his jaw working as he locked the wheel into place. It seemed getting any answers from him would be as difficult as her trying to fight her way out of this. Lorelei sighed and turned back to Nara, lowering herself onto the deck next to her. She rested her hand on Nara's shoulder and Nara finally tore her murderous gaze away from the emberblood.

"I don't understand what his plan for us is," Nara said only loud enough for Lorelei and the wind to hear. "The last we knew, the Incendians wanted you dead to raise Magnus. So, what has changed?"

Everything, Lorelei wanted to say. With the cracks in Limbo, the unknown had become a new foe. Lorelei's dress suddenly felt too tight, the bodice squeezing her ribs, constricting her lungs. She tried to take a deep breath to calm herself, but it couldn't get past her throat. Again she tried, but it wasn't enough.

"Clever idea," Nara said, a bite in her tone, not realizing that Lorelei wasn't faking. "We'll lure him over here and when I attack, you go for the key. It's around his neck. I saw him tuck it in there last night."

Lorelei looked up at the sky, trying to open her throat to allow a deep breath to get through, but instead of finding comfort in that breath, her hands started to tremble. She'd felt anxiety like this before, back when she was in the cellar of the cabin in Port Barlow, waiting for the storms to strike. She wanted to tell Nara that she couldn't breathe right, but her throat had closed in on itself.

"Aye!" Nara yelled at the emberblood. Even though she yelled from right next to her, her voice sounded so far away. "Help her! Can't you see something is wrong?"

Boot steps clomped toward her. "What's wrong with her? She was just fine."

"She obviously can't breathe!" Nara yelled at him.

The emberblood growled something back at Nara and they continued to bicker, the sound of them blurring together with the wind in Lorelei's ears. She focused on the sails above and the rhythm they played in the wind, trying to distract her racing nerves before they did something dangerous.

At the thought, her fingertips pricked. Dread seeped into her bones. Her magic seemed to only show itself when it wasn't wanted and never when it was needed.

The emberblood stepped into her line of vision, cutting off her view of the sails. He looked at her panicked face for only a moment before grabbing her shoulders and pulling her forward to expose her back. "The corset of this dress is a part of the problem," he said. She felt his fingers pulling at the threads on the back of her dress, trying to loosen the seams so she could breathe, but black spots started to fill her vision.

Suddenly, Nara rammed her shoulder into the emberblood, knocking him back onto the deck. "Now, Lorelei!" she yelled. "Get the key! Lorelei?"

Her head swam as Nara and the emberblood's shouts became muffled, like she was underwater and they were yelling on the deck of the ship. Her body felt tingly, her limbs weak and limp as hands grabbed her and ripped at the bodice of her dress.

Just when she was on the brink of passing out, the pressure on her ribs was lifted, the tear of fabric snapping her back into place. Her vision focused back into place like she was turning the barrels of a telescope and her breaths came in quick pants. Her arms and legs still trembled like they were sailing through the Frozen Gap.

"Lorelei," Nara said, inching toward her on her knees. "Are you all right? My judgment was clouded and I should've realized—"

"Don't worry though," the emberblood said, cutting Nara off. "My knife was able to save you. No thanks are needed."

"If we weren't here in the first place," Nara argued, "then she wouldn't need to be saved."

"And you can't seem to protect your friends very well."

"At least I have friends," Nara scoffed. "It seems you do not."

The emberblood tucked his knife into his belt and smirked. "Will you tell me your name yet, archer? Perhaps *we* could be friends after this is all over."

"Never in your wildest dreams would I—"

"It's okay," Lorelei said, stopping their argument. "I'm all right. I just got a little overwhelmed is all."

Nara's mouth was agape, her expression reminding Lorelei of the way her mother used to look at her when she'd get hurt while playing, hoping that she was unscathed. "I'm sorry I didn't see it. Do you have attacks like this often?"

Lorelei took another deep breath, her trembles beginning to calm slightly. "When I was a child, yes, but I thought I'd outgrown it."

"Or recent events made it resurface," Nara said. "You can't wear that dress out here." She turned her attention to the emberblood, her face changing from soft to sharp in the blink of an eye. "Surely you have some clothes she can wear that are better fitting for a voyage, even though you've taken us prisoner. Or are all Incendians truly so coldhearted?"

The emberblood quickly glanced away from them, then stood up. "Coldhearted," he scoffed. "Do you even know what happened to Port—you know what? There are extra clothes in the downstairs cabin, but they will probably be much too big for her."

"I'll make it work," Lorelei said, using the ship's railing to pull herself up onto her feet. She'd done it before when she'd donned Kane's clothes to enter the Trials as his first mate. The thought of him and what he was doing right then was nearly enough to send her back into a breathing fit. Did he loathe her for what she'd done to him? Did he notice she was missing?

"Are you coming?" the emberblood asked.

Lorelei nodded and followed, trying to clear her mind, but the fog refused to release her.

CHAPTER TWELVE
JARON

Silver Sea
Mid-Rainrise

Smoke and ashes: two things that were always promised at Ember Keep.

When Jaron had first arrived there, the smoke and ashes were a constant reminder to him of all he'd lost in Port Hullscar. After the pirate attack, many of the survivors enlisted in the navy, prepared to endure the hellish training at the Ember Keep. Jaron was the smallest and youngest, but he was more determined than anyone else.

He wanted to learn to sail. He wanted to fight. But what he wanted more than anything was to be an emberblood. If he'd been able to wield fire that day, maybe he would've been able to save Glenna and Alrik; maybe now he could save others from the same fate.

Emberbloods were not born with their powers like other

magicked-bloods. Stormbloods and frostbloods had been blessed by their gods during ancient times, their power passed down through their familial lines. Witchbloods made a sacrifice to their god in exchange for their unique magics. Emberbloods, however, were chosen, their magic earned and bestowed upon them by the fire god Vulcan, brother to Magnus.

That was the whole purpose of the Ember Keep—to train navy recruits to near death and let their god find those who were worthy of the flame. Even with nothing left but an empty stomach and a broken body, the strongest of desires could still ring above all else. During Jaron's time at the Ember Keep, he'd seen only one man become an emberblood, and he'd fought tooth and nail to get there. He'd watched the sacred flame burn long after the ritual had been completed.

Jaron had arrived in the sunspur season and wasn't allowed to start dueling until the first frost. Being the youngest and the smallest didn't spare him any beatings, nor did it earn him any extra servings of food or any pity. He should have died by the end of frostfall, but his will to live was too strong, his thirst for vengeance coming before all else.

Moon after moon, duel after duel, Vulcan's flame remained unlit. Many had given up the chase, choosing to join the ranks of the navy instead, but not Jaron. Faces and names came and left, but he remained. It was nearly a year after he had arrived at the Ember Keep that the sacred flame ignited once more.

On that day, the Commandants had grown weary of the recruits, pushing them beyond their limits with training drills and duels that left the losers unable to walk away on their own. Jaron was chosen to duel against Corvin, a recruit older than him by four years and nearly double his size. Since Corvin's arrival a couple of moons earlier, the Commandants had only praised his strength and quickness to learn. In hopes of appeasing Vulcan, perhaps they'd thought to choose an opponent who would be a swift and easy win for Corvin. They'd underestimated Jaron's tenacity.

Jaron knew that Corvin would be the one leading the dance, so when the Commandants signaled the start of their duel, he was sure to be the first one to attack. His blade was dull, but his strikes were quick and relentless. Corvin blocked his attempts again and again, then countered Jaron with a strike of his own, sending him stumbling into a water trough for the horses. Jaron had promised himself he would silence their laughter.

He faced Corvin again, soaking and slipping through the mud. Jaron didn't wait for his opponent's attack and ran forward, striking Corvin in the upper arm. If they had been real blades, the wound would've been deep, but Corvin only groaned and switched his stance. He attacked then, a flurry of slashes and jabs that Jaron couldn't keep up with.

One strike hit Jaron's temple, dropping him to the ground as stars filled his vision. The whole side of his head hurt and something was wrong with his leg, but he still crawled up onto his knees. Corvin's footsteps neared, then a kick to Jaron's face sent him flying onto his back in the mud. Jaron rolled and curled in on himself, unable to see out of his right eye as it closed up, as the surrounding men laughed again.

Keep fighting, he told himself. *If you want the flame, you have to take it for yourself.*

Jaron put his hands in the mud and slowly lifted himself from the ground, despite his body begging him to stay down. He reached for his sword as he stood, and once he was on his feet he pointed it at Corvin.

"What are you doing?" Corvin asked with a hard-set brow. "You've lost."

Corvin attacked, striking both of Jaron's arms and his side. Jaron fell to his knees and wobbled as he stood back up, sword still in his hand. Again and again, Jaron found himself on the ground and each time he got back up, unwilling to give in. The men's laughter hushed.

"Just stay down!" Corvin yelled. He dropped his sword and grabbed Jaron by his shirt.

"No," Jaron said, looking up at him as blood streamed out of his nose. "I will keep fighting for my destiny. I will take the flame for myself."

Corvin raised his fist to strike Jaron, but gasps of the recruits and Commandants around them stopped him. Their gazes turned to the adorned fire pit, the altar in which Vulcan's flame lit nearly a year ago. The flame that danced in the obsidian altar was brighter than the one Jaron had seen that day, the tendrils blue instead of orange as they licked the air.

The Commandants muttered among themselves as Jaron was released from Corvin's grip. He had looked to the altar each preceding day, wondering when and if it would ever light again, and that day it burned brighter than ever.

"Come." A Commandant suddenly stepped in front of Jaron, blocking his view. Jaron wasn't sure which one of them he was speaking to, but when he looked up, the Commandant was in front of him instead of Corvin. "You've been chosen."

The breath whooshed out of Jaron as relief flooded through him. He followed the Commandant up the stone steps to the altar. It was as if he was in a dream, the moment unreal, the scenery around him slipping away until there was nothing but him and the blue flame. He knew what was to come next and the pain that would follow, yet when the Commandant told him to put his hands into the flames, Jaron did not hesitate. He would take the flame for himself.

His scream ripped through the air as the fire consumed his hands. His flesh melted away, the searing pain reaching inside his hands and up his arms until it was as if the fire was inside his entire body. After what felt like a lifetime, the Commandant pulled him back as the blue flame began to die. Jaron could barely see through his swollen eyes as he looked at his palms, thinking he'd see nothing except bones, but his skin was healed with thick scars that covered his hands like gloves. One moment he had been looking at his hands; the next, flames exploded out of him. They spread across the wooden awnings and surrounding structures in the fort, devouring everything in sight. Men scrambled about, the few emberblood Commandants doing their best to control the wildfire.

Someone shook his shoulders. "Jaron!" the Commandant yelled, though his voice sounded muffled to him. "You must control it."

Jaron took a deep breath and thought of pulling the fire to him, but the flames only continued to rage. "How?" he asked frantically. "I don't know what to do."

"You have to become a stable vessel for your magic," the man explained, sweat dripping down his brow. "Your magic comes from the realm of the gods, so you must find what it is in *this* realm that grounds you. You have been here longer than any recruit I have ever seen. What is it that keeps you fighting?" Jaron closed his eyes. "Find that spark. Hold on to it."

Glenna's hazel eyes that sparkled when Jaron chased her

around the fields behind their uncle's cabin. Alrik's laugh as he tried to keep up with him. He would do anything to see them both again, to return to those simple days, but there would be more. He could learn to wield his newfound flame as a weapon. He could make sure that other Incendians would keep living their own simple days. When he opened his eyes, the flames were gone, white smoke rising from where they had reached.

Once Jaron found that spark, he kindled the flame, never letting it die.

—

The farther north Jaron sailed with his two captives, the colder the wind blew.

Having one stolen female on his ship was not something Jaron was thrilled about, but having two of them on board was a cruel punishment, especially when one was an Incendian led astray and the other was as cold as she was dangerous.

The archer's frosty glare usually rested on wherever the storm-blood was, protecting her with her watchful gaze since she could do nothing else. Today, however, Jaron noticed the archer's sight was keen on the horizon, her brow knit with concentration as if she was trying to figure out where they were sailing to. Strands of her long black hair blew across her face, her cuffed hands unable to sweep them away. Not that she would sweep them away if she could. Even Crew's noisy parrot hadn't gotten under her skin in the days they'd been at sea. That was a feat even he couldn't conquer.

Lorelei, however, brewed like a looming storm in the distance, her demeanor turning darker and more frantic each day. The clouds followed suit, barely allowed a sliver of sun to shine through during the day. But at night, when she slept, the clouds dissipated just enough to see the moonlight and the shimmering of stars beyond.

Today, the clouds were nearly as deep a color as the endless sea. The wind whipped at the sails, the sound of it so loud that Jaron didn't hear Crew amble up next to him.

"Looks like a storm's rolling in," Crew mused, as he surveyed the obvious. "Boat this small won't fare very well."

"I am well aware of the circumstance," Jaron said, gripping the wheel tighter. Crew was right. A proper sea storm would pick apart their small ship and leave it as nothing but driftwood. This storm, however, didn't seem like any storm created by nature.

It'sss her, his god whispered. Jaron noticed his whisper sounded less like the hiss of a dying flame, almost as if he'd somehow grown stronger. *Her magic bleedsss.*

"Take over for me." Jaron stepped away from the wheel and around Crew, heading across the deck toward the true storm.

The stormblood noticed him coming right away and stood as stiff as the ship's railing behind her, brushing her hair from her face. She quickly tucked her fingers away in the sleeves of the too-big charcoal overcoat he'd given her to wear. Jaron caught the glimmer of gold shimmering up past her knuckles before she could fully hide her hands from him.

"Are you causing this?" he asked her blankly, his finger pointed toward the sky. "I don't know what your plan is, but a storm like this will only kill us all."

Nara appeared at her side, stepping slightly in front of the stormblood like a shield. This was the third time she'd silently snuck up on him. She truly would be deadly to him if he released her from those cuffs.

"And you condone this?" Jaron asked, throwing his hands up. "If she sinks this vessel, are you going to swim to the nearest island?"

The archer glanced over her shoulder at the stormblood, whose focus was drawn to her trembling fingers. Then she turned back to Jaron with a frost-filled glare.

"And if she did unleash a storm?" the archer asked. "You've stolen her from her home for means unknown to her. You are nefarious. Do not pretend to be anything otherwise."

Jaron curled his hands into fists as his sides. "Spent some days at sea with me and you believe yourself to understand my motives then?"

"It doesn't take much to read an open book," the archer replied, lifting her chin at him. "Relic of a sword and hands marred with scars? You're an emberblood with something to prove to your meddling god. What did he promise you? Power?"

Each word was so precise, yet spoken with the calm of unrippled water. This made the heat in his chest flare even more. The whisper in his mind hissed.

"You know nothing," Jaron told her. "Have I not fed you? Provided you with clothing suitable for seafaring? I even recuffed your wrists in the front at the stormblood's request."

"Yet I'm still cuffed." The archer perked one brow.

"You and I both know that those cuffs are the only thing keeping you from attempting to kill me."

The stormblood's head was tilted back toward the sky, rain openly falling on her face. He glanced down at her hands, watching as the gold slowly crawled up her skin toward and past her wrist. The wind picked up, roaring in his ears.

Watching her, Jaron expected to see some sort of triumph

written across her expression—a look that meant that this storm was a successful part of her and the archer's plan. But as he searched her face, he noticed her chin trembling.

Her magic bleeds.

It suddenly made sense to him. She couldn't contain her magic and it was pouring out of her like wine from an uncorked bottle. Letting himself drown out in the middle of the Silver Sea without avenging his sister, without finding his brother, would be an unfair fate. Death was not an option when he still had to finish what he'd started.

"You have to try to control it!" he yelled at her over the raging wind of the storm. He had to say something that could reach her. "Forget about me. If your storm sinks this ship, the archer—your friend—dies too."

The archer scowled at him and then glanced back at the storm-blood. "He's right," she told her. "Can you try to pull it back in?"

The stormblood shook her head, wet hair clinging to her face. "I can't!" she cried. "I don't know what to do!"

Jaron scoured his brain for some way to help her see that she could. He remembered what the emberblood had told him that day at Ember Keep.

"You have to find your spark!" Jaron yelled over the crashing of waves into the side of the ship, hoping he could be heard.

The archer scoffed. "How is that supposed to help?"

Jaron thought of a way to get through to them both in a way they might understand. "Our magic is not from this realm! Whatever it is that anchors you to this realm, you have to find it or your storm will consume you and anything or anyone close to you." His eyes connected with the archer's for a moment, something strange passing between the two of them. Almost as if she

140

understood what it was that he was trying to say.

The stormblood, however, did not hear his words.

The wind and rain whipped at his cheeks, the sails flapping violently. If they took too much more of this, they'd be finished. If the Storm couldn't control her chaos, then they had to at least try to outlive it until she was completely drained.

"Archer!" he yelled. She turned her attention back to him, hair sticking to her face, an unfamiliar look of uncertainty and worry fleeting before she blinked it away. "We have to try to furl the sails."

The archer glanced down at her wrists, then pushed them toward him. "Then uncuff me."

Jaron hesitated for just a moment, wondering if perhaps the archer truly would take the opportunity to end his life. But from the desperation hiding behind her frosty glare, he could tell that he would be safe for at least this moment. He would worry about what came after when the time came. He groaned and reached into the pocket of his pants, pulling out the ring of keys he'd stowed away. The archer shoved her fists into his hands. He fumbled with the lock as he tried to remain steady on the deck. When the metal clicked and opened, the archer yanked her arms back and rubbed at her wrists. His attention lingered on the red marks on her skin, and he quickly smothered the pang of guilt that rose in him before it could spread.

Jaron rushed to the mast with the archer behind him. He grabbed the halyard for the throat sails and handed her the one for the peak sails. He nodded at her and they both started to pull the ropes together, the sails protesting the force of the wind as they rose.

He looked to check on the stormblood, noticing that she'd

moved to the center of the deck. Her eyes glowed blue like lightning, sparking with gold like a hammer against hot iron. She stood motionless as her hair danced wildly in the wind. The golden shimmer on her fingertips began to spread up her skin.

Crew left his place at the wheel and ran past them, toward the stormblood. He grabbed her shoulders and shook her, but she remained untethered to the moment.

"Crew!" Jaron yelled over the storm. "Stay back!"

A flash blinded Jaron, followed quickly by a boom. The sound of something heavier than rain dropped onto the deck as Jaron's vision cleared. Several feet away from the Storm, Crew's body lay motionless, steam rising as rain sizzled against his charred skin. Shock kept Jaron frozen at the mast, hands still gripping the rope.

The archer, however, left his side and rushed to the stormblood. Jaron looked from the rope in his hands, up to the sails, which needed to be tied off, and back down to the two of them.

"Damn it," Jaron said as he hooked the halyards. He headed toward the middle of the deck, slipping in the sea-slick and nearly falling. "Wait!" he yelled to the archer. "You could get struck too!"

Jaron grabbed her arm to try to keep her back, afraid of the reaction the stormblood might have if she killed her friend the same way she'd killed Crew. The archer spun around on him and quickly flicked his hand away. She raised her fists, ready to fight him. He raised his hands to show he meant her no harm. "I'm only trying to protect you."

"I don't need you to," she said, lowering her fists and turning back to the stormblood. "Now back up."

Jaron took a couple of steps backward.

The archer stood in front of the stormblood, but she didn't grip her shoulders like Crew had done—like the Commandant had done to Jaron all those years ago. Instead, the archer grabbed her hands, holding them in her own as she spoke to her.

"Come back, Lorelei," she said, her voice calm even though a storm raged around them. "You are Lorelei Storm, and you wield a storm's power, but you are not chaos and destruction. Remember how you got here and where you come from. Think of your mother's stories and the simple but happy days you lived with her. Think of everyone waiting for you back in Baltessa, even Arius and the ridiculous things he says. Think of Kane. I know he must be searching for you."

The lightning in the stormblood's eyes began to fade, the golden sparks dying completely. The wind calmed to a breeze and the rain to a mist. The sky remained blanketed with dark clouds, but the storm had ceased its rage for the moment.

The stormblood blinked and hugged the archer, who stood with her arms still at her side for a moment, like the affection was not something she was used to. Neither was Jaron. He watched with interest as the archer finally lifted her arms and embraced her back. When she pulled away, her face twisted into a fear-filled sob, as she noticed Crew's charred body on the deck.

"Don't look," the archer said, stepping in front of the stormblood.

"Did I . . . ?" She took a deep breath. "Did I do that to him?"

"It was an accident," the archer assured her. "It was the storm, not you."

"It was me," the stormblood cried, grasping the archer for support. "Oh, Goddess, I killed him." A sob escaped from her then, her knees buckling as she fell into the archer. "I'm going to be sick."

The archer helped the stormblood get to the side of the ship before she could vomit. Jaron remembered the day his magic had exploded out of him. If he'd hurt or killed someone that day, would his reaction have been the same? Would he have cared the way this girl did?

The stormblood leaned over the railing and emptied her stomach into the sea. The archer rubbed her back and glanced back at Jaron, their eyes meeting. Her expression remained unchanged, frosty and closed off, but something was different. Something had shifted.

"I won't cuff you again," he said. When her icy demeanor wavered, he couldn't deny that his chest swelled in the slightest. "We will need to stop at the nearest harbor to make quick repairs. Just try not to kill me."

"Your life is safe," she replied. She glanced out at the calming sea, then back at him again. "For now, emberblood."

For now, he'd enjoy the peace.

CHAPTER THIRTEEN
CSILLA

Silver Sea
Mid-Rainrise

Csilla sat in the crow's nest of the *Wavecutter*, her feet dangling down over the edge while she craned her head back to watch the sky. She'd hoped that tonight there would be stars to distract her from sleep, but there were only clouds to greet her.

Sleep wasn't something she allowed to come anymore. It would creep up on her every night, dragging her eyelids down, her dreams trying to take her captive, and every night she'd find herself in a different part of the ship, awake with her mind wandering.

Catching sleep in spots during the day was something she resorted to, but even then, she'd started to feel the dreamwraith's presence lurking under the sun with her, looming over her like a shadow that no one else could see. She'd tried to tell herself differently, that it was just her guilt eating away at her, but she knew the truth. The dreamwraith would continue haunting her until it had its fill of her torment. Would anything be left of her then?

There was a flash of blue in the distance. Odd. The cloud cover had been increasing the past couple of days, but they hadn't seemed dark enough to promise a storm.

"Storms out there," suddenly came a voice from below.

Csilla glanced behind her to see Flynn's sand-colored mop emerging through the hole in the middle of the crow's nest. She turned back to the railing she straddled. "Looks like it."

A bit of knocking and scooting around and Flynn sat down next to her, letting his own legs hang down by hers. "That storm in the distance isn't the only thing on that mind of yours though, is it?" One of his wry smiles threatened to unlock her secrets.

"You always seem to know when I'm swimming in my thoughts," she said, tucking back a curl that had blown loose from her scarf.

"You disappear every night," Flynn said, leaning back onto his hands and looking up at the sky. "It wouldn't take a brilliant mind to figure that out." A smile lifted his tone. "Unless you think I have a brilliant mind?"

Csilla chuckled. The first genuine one since the masquerade party.

"Do your dreams plague you in the day?" Flynn asked. "It's fine if you don't want to talk about it, but I am curious."

"You always are," Csilla said. In the past, this would be the part where Csilla would push him away and mock the idea of vulnerability, but up in the nest it was just the two of them, two birds flying high above the sea. As she gazed ahead into the night without the comfort of the stars to guide them, the unknown should've rattled her. Yet next to Flynn she felt safe. With him she could spread her wings; with him she could be free.

"The wraith only visits me at night," she said. She glanced down at her legs, focusing on the scuffs at the knees of her pants, trying to somehow anchor herself to the conversation. "I've stopped sleeping at night because . . ." She paused. Csilla could wear an intimidating mask and say the words that needed to be said to gain the upper hand against those who challenged her. She always promised herself that she wouldn't let others see the holes in her armor, but the holes had only grown larger.

"

. . . I'm scared that if I fall asleep, I won't wake up again."

Flynn grabbed her hand and she didn't pull away this time.

"So that's why I found you sleeping in the cargo the other day," he said. "You were even snoring."

A small smile escaped from Csilla. "It seems to feed on my dreams only at night," she said. "But lately I've been feeling its presence during the day too. Maybe it's getting stronger."

"You must be feeding it well." Flynn turned his head to look at her, his cheek resting against the wooden post in front of him. "I didn't know you were such a good chef, Csilla."

Csilla threw her head back and laughed, earning a chuckle from Flynn. They smiled at each other and for a moment it was just the two of them, alone in the world.

"What do you dream of?" he asked, his tone soft and gentle. "Are they always nightmares?"

"It always starts off pleasant," Csilla said, remembering the beauty of Rhoda's smiles in the dream. "Rhoda and I—we're together—and we're happy. The air is warm, the jungle alive. I never know I'm dreaming and I just want to stay there, you know? It's a dream I could easily get lost in." She sighed and rested her own cheek against the railing in front of her, looking into the sea of Flynn's eyes as she continued. "But each time, the dream twists and I'm fighting Rhoda once more."

"You duel Rhoda every time?" Flynn asked, concern knitting his brow.

"And every time she dies," Csilla said. She closed her eyes, trying to erase the image from her mind. "Over and over again. Everything around me dies."

Flynn squeezed her hand. "Aye." His voice was so quiet she could barely hear it over the wind. "It wasn't your fault, you know."

"It was my sword," Csilla said. "Of course it was my fault."

"You can't blame yourself. Magnus tainted Rhoda's mind. You didn't ask for any of that to happen."

"Yet it still did." Csilla sighed. "If I'd tried harder to fix our relationship, maybe even if I'd just let her be captain, things would have been different." Would Rhoda have listened to Magnus's whispers if she'd already had what she wanted?

"But you can't change any of it." Flynn pulled away from the post and turned to her, sitting with his legs folded and crossed. "You can only move forward. You *have* to move forward. I see it in your eyes sometimes, you know. The guilt. I can't watch this dreamwraith eat away at you."

"I won't let it," Csilla said. She let go of the post and swung her legs around until she mirrored him. She leaned in and lightly kissed his lips, then the scar on his cheek that he'd gotten when fighting on Crossbones. The look of surprise on his face was one that she wished she could capture and revisit again. "I will defeat it. I promise."

Smuggler's Harbor was a small, isolated island at the northern-most point of Cerulia.

It was one of the first trading ports established by the island nation, its location a convenient middle point between Baltessa, Incendia, and Ventys's old port, Icehaven. But since the fall of Icehaven years ago, Smuggler's Harbor had turned into more of a black market, a place where people went to do crooked things.

When Csilla had heard the Ruin Witch say they'd find the Serpent in this place, her feelings about it teetered. On the one hand, it made sense. Witchbloods and their dealmaking ways would find the most work on a busy island like this. However, this was Smuggler's Harbor and the handful of times she had docked for resources, something had always gone missing.

"Keep your guard up," Csilla told everyone as they stepped onto the dock. "This may be a Cerulian island, but some folk will do anything for coin." She glanced at her crew, noticing how Kane's attention flicked nervously around the area.

The harbor was alive with men unloading barrels and crates from a ship docked next to the *Wavecutter*. A small dog barked at one man and nipped at his ankles while his comrades laughed. Gulls circled the area, ships groaned as they rocked against the tide, and the sky remained gray, almost as if the dark cloud was following them. Or perhaps they were the ones chasing it.

"How long will you be docked?" A burly man stepped in front of Csilla. He wore a hat made of straw and his pants had been cut so that his legs were bare from the knees down.

"We should be gone by nightfall," Csilla answered.

The docker hitched his brow. "Not even planning a night's rest?" His assessing gaze traveled the white merchant sails they had hoisted from the masts. "Name and trade?"

Csilla hesitated, wondering, trying to quickly produce a name that was not her own. Something that would not draw attention in case spies from Incendia lurked about.

The docker shifted his weight, growing impatient. "I can't let you dock if you do not—"

"The name is Jack Rattler," Flynn said, taking a step forward. "Though you may have heard of my other alias, Handsome Jack?"

The docker stared forward at Flynn, expression unchanging.

"The greatest tea trader this side of the Silver Sea? Also known as the Silver Tea?"

Arius snorted as he tried to hold in his laugh. Csilla squashed his toe with the heel of her boot.

"Are you here with a shipment of tea?" The docker scribbled something in the book he carried.

"No, no tea today." Flynn laughed casually. "I only have some quick business to address, a messenger gull or two to send. As my lovely partner stated, we will be out of your docks and sailing away from your harbor before day's end."

The docker nodded and snapped his book shut. "Very well, then. Three hundred gold pieces."

"Three hundred?" Csilla asked. "That's more than asking price."

"You bring no goods to our harbor, yet you take up two docking stations with your massive ship." He crossed his arms. "Three hundred gold pieces."

Csilla looked at Flynn, then to where Kane had been standing before. Suddenly, Kane was in front of the docker, his hands clenching the man's shirt. He shoved him into a stack of crates, knocking over a barrel of fish next to them. The gulls that had been circling above swooped in, collecting a free lunch and drawing more attention to the scuffle.

"It will be one hundred gold pieces," Kane said in the man's face, still fisting his shirt.

Csilla and Flynn both navigated through the gulls to get to them.

"But the asking price is two hundred," the docker whimpered.

"You're lucky if I give you any gold, you—"

Csilla's hand at Kane's shoulder made him freeze. He quickly let go of the docker and yanked his hands back like they had been burned. When he turned around, his face was pale and his eyes were troubled. He gripped his chest and winced.

"Are you okay?" Csilla asked quietly, but he wouldn't look at her.

"I'm fine," he grumbled, shrugging her off. "I apologize. I . . . I'm not thinking straight." He walked past her, not waiting for her to respond to his apology for his outburst. She watched him with concern as he blended back in with the crew. Something was going on with him and that wound of his whether he wanted to admit it to them or not.

"Mate's been out at sea too long," Flynn said as he brushed off the man's shirt. "Do hope you'll understand. You were saying that the cost would be asking price, yes?"

"Aye," the man groaned, rubbing the back of his head.

Flynn clapped the docker on the shoulder. "You have a merry day, sir."

Csilla motioned for the crew to follow and they left the dock behind, making their way into the market streets of Smuggler's Harbor. The short, slanted buildings that lined the dirt road were stacked so close together, the spaces between them were only wide enough to allow a person to walk through. Mud had made its own path down the center of the roads, coating their boots as they continued on, searching for signs of where they could find the Serpent.

"Spread out and listen in on conversations," Csilla said to her crew. "There must be word of him somewhere."

Csilla took to the left side of the road, browsing through the stalls of rare jewels and suspicious jarred substances. She kept her sight wandering over the items for sale, shaking her head subtly at merchants as they tried to make deals with her. She would not be tempted by any of their haggling. She only wanted to hear what the folk had to say.

"My husband swears he saw it," said a merchant who stood in a stall filled with intricately woven tapestries. The merchant turned to a woman who stood gawking next to her with dark hair twisted up in a pile on her head. She quieted her voice. "A seagrim."

"A what?" the woman said, confusion twisting her brow. "What is that?"

"It's a dark creature of the sea. Old tales say that once a seagrim marks you, you'll drown within the next moon."

The woman looked suspiciously at the merchant. "I don't believe you. Creatures like that don't exist any longer."

"Listen," the merchant said, quieting her voice even further. Csilla had to take a step closer, standing behind one of the long tapestries that hung nearby. "My husband sails with a trading crew from here to Terran, and he's heard rumors."

"Rumors?" the woman asked. "What kind of rumors?"

"Well, you know about the Storm heir, right? My husband heard that something happened on Crossbones they're not letting the island nation know. Something about that girl and Limbo. What if . . . she's the one bringing these creatures in?"

Csilla fought the urge to expose herself right then and there and demand that the women stop their wild rumors. Crown officials had decided that it would be best to not cause panic among Cerulians regarding Magnus almost rising, but what worried Csilla was how many others had heard this rumor and how many believed it. If only these women knew that Lorelei fighting the fire god in Limbo was the only reason he wasn't creating havoc and destruction right then. Csilla quickly left the stall and went back toward the center of the road where the crew had gathered.

"Anything?" Kane asked as she joined them.

"Nothing of substance," she said. "You?"

The rest of the crew shook their heads as Arius strutted in. He wore a new hat that he hadn't been wearing before and carried two long skewers of stacked meat chunks and vegetables.

"I thought we were supposed to be searching for information," Flynn said, snatching one of Arius's skewers for himself.

"I was hungry," Arius admitted. "However, the man who sold me this hat said we can find the Serpent at the tavern at the end of the road."

"How did you . . ." Csilla's voice trailed off, confused and amazed at the same time.

"Oh." Arius laughed. He shrugged and took a bite of one of the meat chunks. "I just asked him."

There was no point in pondering Arius's ways any longer and the crew continued down the muddied road. Merchants yelled for them to buy their wares, to come try their trusted elixir, but they paid them no mind—except for Arius—and made a direct line for a shabby-looking tavern.

The inside didn't look any better than the outside, and slanted planks had been nailed to the wall in an attempt to cover up holes. A bartender looked up from the bar top he was wiping down. When no one asked for a drink, he continued back to his chore as if they weren't even there. The tavern was oddly quiet; folk were scattered around the clustered tables, some alone and others in pairs or small groups, all chugging down their drinks.

Csilla's gaze traveled over them all, trying to find the one of them who would be the Serpent. It wasn't until she looked into the far corner that she saw him. He sat alone, his hands shuffling cards. His brown skin was as unblemished as the Ruin Witch's, his silver locs bundled and tied at his neck. There was an aura about him that exuded the magic in his veins. Csilla could have assumed his identity based on that alone, but what truly gave him away were his golden eyes looking back at her.

CHAPTER FOURTEEN
KANE

Smuggler's Harbor
Mid-Rainrise

Smuggler's Harbor was the last place Kane wanted to dock. The small island wasn't even on the map of the Kingdoms of Four, either purposely left off or forgotten like Kane wished it would be. He hadn't returned here since the days he'd dealt with Rove and he'd much rather the memories of those days stay buried at the bottom of the Silver Sea. Damned fate, however, seemed to have other plans for him.

In the year since, the island and its inhabitants hadn't changed much. A couple of lanterns were scattered across the tavern, some hanging, some knocked over on tables, dimly lighting the space. The building, like all others in Smuggler's Harbor, seemed to be barely holding itself together with rusty nails and those inside were most likely still drunk from the day before. No one paid Kane and his crew any attention, their gazes on the drinks in their hands or on the crooked tables.

Except for one with eyes of shimmering gold. He was already watching Kane when Csilla pointed him out sitting at a table in the corner.

A witchblood.

Kane made a bullet's path to him, unwavering and nudging aside stray chairs that stood in his way. The crew followed close behind, but Kane noticed that the witchblood did not let his attention wander and remained transfixed on Kane. This made his fingers curl into fists as he wondered why.

Even with the horrid lighting, Kane could see the gnarled scar that sliced down the side of the Serpent's face, the rest of his skin unblemished and as youthful as Kane's own even though his bundled locs were silver. Kane stopped at the table, spying the deck of cards that the Serpent shuffled with his long skinny fingers even though he sat at the table alone. Perhaps the witchblood was waiting for someone and if so, they needed to request his skills before then, but the words couldn't leave Kane's mouth.

The Serpent glanced up from his cards, his golden eyes falling back on Kane. "The tide brings in the Blackwater, I see." His voice was deep and warm and filled with the promise of many stories of adventures. He tapped the deck of cards once with his pointer finger and cocked his head to the side, assessing Kane. "But what is curious is why he would come to this place. To this very tavern."

Kane's blood pumped faster as he wondered what exactly this man already knew. All witchbloods seemed to know more than they should. Kane blamed the damned trees.

"We came here looking for you," Kane said, gripping the compass in his pocket to help calm his nerves. Lorelei's face flashed in his mind as he rubbed his thumb over the smooth surface. "I've heard from a reliable source that you're the best at finding what is lost."

A small smile hooked at the corner of the Serpent's lips. "Your source tells no lie." He shuffled the cards once more. "But I do hope she also told you that I do not offer my services freely."

Kane hadn't told the Serpent that the Ruin Witch had sent them, yet he seemed to already know. Unease crept up Kane's spine as his mind drifted to what else the witchblood knew, how many secrets he kept tucked away in his odd purple overcoat.

"I am a captain of the pirate fleet," Kane told him. "I can acquire however many gold pieces you may desire."

The Serpent shook his head. "I don't want your gold, Blackwater."

"I need your help," Kane said, not having spoken the words often, ". . . please."

"Did Blackwater just say please?" he heard Flynn whisper behind him.

Kane's brow furrowed. "What is it that you want, Serpent?"

"Fancy a game of Aces?" he asked, his smirk deepening. "Let's make a little deal, shall we? If you can beat me at Aces, then I will seek whatever it is you have lost."

"Aye!" Arius said excitedly. "Blackwater is a master at Aces. The bloke always wins."

Flynn piped up from next to him. "Not necessarily. Remember that time in Sarva, when I won?"

Kane turned his glare on Flynn. "For the last time, you cheated."

Flynn tried to argue but was quickly shushed by Csilla.

"I'll play," Kane said. "But what's the catch?"

"Catch?" The Serpent feigned confusion, his eyes shimmering gold. "There is no catch."

"If I win, you help us, but what if you win?"

"Then I get to stay right here and enjoy my ale." The Serpent smiled widely before picking up his mug and taking a long drink from it.

Kane slid into the chair across from the Serpent, watching as he dealt out the cards, seven each. Then he set the remainder of the deck down and flipped over the top card, revealing a four of spades, making the trump suit for the game spades. Kane stopped fidgeting with the compass in his hand and set it on the table. As he picked up the cards and splayed them in his hand, he glanced at the suits in his hand, spying three decently high cards but only one spade. The odds were not in his favor, but he didn't let his expression show this.

"You know," the Serpent mused, "I'm truthfully surprised that you came back to Smuggler's Harbor."

Kane slowly looked up from the cards in his hand. "What's your bet?" Kane asked, attempting to bring focus back to the game.

The Serpent tapped his chin. "Hmm, I believe I will win four tricks." He looked at Kane then. "And your bet?"

"Four," Kane said without hesitation.

The Serpent chuckled. "We only have seven cards, Blackwater. Only one of us will win four tricks."

Kane leaned forward, resting his elbows on the table. He was already tired of whatever games the Serpent was trying to play. "And it will be me."

The Serpent laughed and slammed his fist on the table, rattling his mug of ale. "Is he always this serious?" he asked.

"It's truly dreadful sometimes," Arius replied.

"I don't even remember the last time I saw Blackwater smile," Flynn added.

Kane turned and glared at them both, making their mouths snap shut. "Play your first card," Kane said with a low voice.

"Very well," the Serpent said. He pulled a card from his seven and laid it down between the two of them.

A king of hearts.

Kane had to play the same suit as the Serpent if he had it. He could only lay down his trump card if he didn't have any matching suit of the card played. While he focused on the two hearts in his hand—an eight and a queen—the Serpent continued pressing him.

"You know," the Serpent said. "Whatever it is you've lost, it must be a big deal for you to come back to Smuggler's Harbor. I mean . . . after all the things you've done here."

Kane could feel the eyes of his crewmates on the back of his head. He was sure everyone knew of his dealings with Rove, but not the dirty details. He'd rather those things remain unknown so that he could remain unjudged.

He plucked the eight of hearts from his hand and tossed it to the middle with the Serpent's card. "All of us have done things that we regret," Kane said.

The Serpent smirked as he took both cards and slid them to his side of the table, having won the trick since his card was higher than Kane's. "Some of us more than others," he said with a chuckle.

The Serpent tossed another card out, this time the nine of diamonds. Kane glanced through the cards in his hand, his hopes rising when he spied his ten of diamonds.

"Though you are right," the Serpent said. "I'm sure the man whose market stall you trashed regrets not repaying Rove on time."

The small bit of hope Kane had was squashed by his heavy heart as the Serpent reminded him of one of the many cruel things he'd done when working to repay Rove of his own debts. He tossed his ten of diamonds to the middle of the table and took the two cards he'd won without a word.

"It seems I have struck a nerve with you, Blackwater." The Serpent watched him closely. His gold eyes eerily seemed to glow against the light of a nearby lantern. "It's your play now."

Growing tired of the Serpent's taunts, he quickly flicked a jack of clubs to the space between them. The witchblood scanned the cards in his hand. "Well, that's no good," the Serpent said, fingering one of the cards. He tossed it onto the table, revealing a six of clubs.

Another trick won. Kane breathed a sigh of relief and pulled the cards to him.

"Although . . ." The Serpent's voice trailed off as if he were lost in thought. "I would say I'm doing better than the man you crippled in this very tavern."

Kane remembered that evening vividly. The man had owed Rove gold and when Kane had tried to collect, the man had pulled a blade on him. During their scuffle, Kane hadn't meant for the man to fall from the second floor of the tavern, but he'd heard the fall had left the man bedridden.

He wondered what terrible thoughts his crewmates behind him were thinking, and even worse, what Lorelei would think if she found out. Would she still look at him the way she did when he returned to Baltessa?

Kane tossed a five of diamonds and the Serpent quickly beat him with a king of diamonds. "I wonder if anyone in this tavern recognizes you," the Serpent said, tossing a jack of hearts onto the table after collecting his trick. "I'm sure there are quite a few people on this island who miss the men who vanished each time you docked here."

His crewmates had gone so silent behind him, it was as if they weren't even there. Camaraderie was something that was still fresh and new to him and the feeling that he might lose it due to his past was an anchor that made him sink farther into his chair.

His wound began to ache again, pulsing with each angered, heavy breath he took. He gritted his teeth as he tossed out the queen of hearts he'd kept back earlier. A small flicker of triumph in raising the score was enough to help him calm down enough to finish the match. One more trick was all he needed to win, but his next card was swiftly defeated by the Serpent.

After all the back-and-forth, and all the jabs from the Serpent, the score was even. The next trick would win the game.

"And what about you?" Kane asked, finally speaking up after the Serpent had his digs at him. "Let us not pretend that witch-bloods are innocent people. You lot have to sacrifice something great to be blessed by your earthen god. I've even heard of witch-bloods sacrificing their own family to be granted magic."

This made the glimmer in the Serpent's eyes die, his back going rigidly straight. "What do you know of sacrifice, Blackwater?" He laid his final card on the table.

An ace of clubs, the highest playable card.

Kane leaned forward, despite the pain radiating from his wound and across his chest, speaking low enough that only those close to him could hear. "I know that I will do whatever it takes to get back what I have lost."

The Serpent raised his scarred brow. "Would you sacrifice your own life to ensure the safety of the stormblood?" The surprise must have been readable on his face because a sly smile split the Serpent's lips. "You would, wouldn't you? Tell me, Blackwater. Do you love her?"

Kane looked away from the Serpent and laid his final card on top of the witchblood's. A two of spades typically wasn't worth much in this game, but since spades was the trump suit, it didn't matter.

"Aces," Kane said, not hiding the triumph in his voice.

"You held that card until the very end," the Serpent said. "I must say I'm impressed with your restraint."

"Enough with the pleasantries," Kane bit out, tired of the Serpent's mind games. "How do we find Lorelei?"

Saying her name aloud made his heart drop and he wondered where they'd end up finding her. If she was scared, if she was hurt, if she missed him just as much as he longed for her. He wasn't familiar with love, but this feeling of not being whole without her . . . was this what love felt like?

"There are a couple of things I'll need," the Serpent said, pulling Kane away from his thoughts. "But what I've come to learn is that sometimes what we seek isn't too far away after all."

CHAPTER FIFTEEN

LORELEI

Smuggler's Harbor

Mid-Rainrise

Lorelei had only seen Kane look lost once before.

It was the night they had snuck into Rove's camp on Crossbones and stolen a key piece. The sky had already been dark when they'd left for Rove's camp, but the group decided to try to get what rest they could while the stars remained in the sky above. But while everyone else got rest during the brief time they had before the sun rose, Kane sat with his back against the trunk of a tree, watching the dying fire. His brow was furrowed as usual, but his eyes held an untold story behind them.

"How are you feeling?" Lorelei asked softly from where she lay next to him in the grass. Her voice sounded like a shout in the quiet. She glanced to Csilla and the rest of them sleeping nearby to make sure she hadn't woken anyone.

"I still feel like I got my ass kicked," Kane grunted, staring into the dimming fire. The dull orange glow cast shadows across his face.

She remembered the panic she'd felt when she'd seen him lifeless by the mermaid lagoon, when she'd tried to help him breathe again and had nearly failed. It wasn't as if the two of them were truly dear to each other, yet she couldn't deny the ache in her chest when she'd thought he was dead. He hadn't let her in enough for her to know about his past, but from what she'd seen from him, he was a man of honor.

He could've killed her when he realized who she was. He could've left Borne to drown in the mermaid lagoon. So why did regret hang on him like wet as he looked into the fire?

"It was brave what you did," she told him. "Saving Borne from the mermaid. In a place like this, I don't believe many men would have done the same. It's a true strength of yours."

"Strength," Kane scoffed, his gaze refusing to meet hers. "Yet you had to come to my rescue in the end, didn't you?"

"We all need a little saving sometimes." Lorelei rolled onto her back and stared up at the canopy of the jungle. "I'm sorry we couldn't save your father's compass."

"Don't be sorry," Kane muttered. "It's better off lost."

"Then why are you the one who looks lost?" Lorelei held her breath, hoping that what she said wouldn't push him away.

"Why do you always ask the most soul-prodding questions?" Kane sighed. She felt the heat of him watching her, but she kept focused on the leaves tangled together in the dark.

"It is fine. You don't have to—"

"Ever since I can remember," Kane said at the same time. "That compass was in my father's hand. Whether it was on the ship or on an uninhabited island we were exploring, he had it with him, looking to it when we weren't even navigating." Kane paused for a moment before continuing, almost as if he was trying to make sense of it himself.

"My mother must've given it to him because when she died, it was the only thing about him that remained unchanged. He drank more heavily, trained me harder, shoved me aside even more, but the one thing that always brought him back was that *damned compass.*"

"You sound like you hated it though," Lorelei said, turning her head to look at him.

He was already looking at her. "I did. That compass meant more to him than I ever did."

"Yet you carried it with you."

Kane watched her carefully like he was trying to figure out a puzzle. "Why?" His brow knit. "Why did I do that?"

"Your mother's dresses still hang in the wardrobe of your cabin," Lorelei told him. "Perhaps keeping these things is your way of holding on to the treasures of your heart." She smirked then. "I mean, you are a pirate, after all. Aren't treasures your heart's calling?"

Kane's face held an unreadable expression and she thought she'd gone too far, had pushed him too much. She noticed the small blush in his cheeks before he looked away.

"You should get some rest," he told her, looking back to the fire.

Lorelei nodded and rolled over onto her side, facing away from him so that he couldn't see her own cheeks reddening. She'd noticed how handsome he was the moment she'd first seen him and the way his muscles moved under his shirt, but this vulnerability was something new, something that she longed for more of. As she drifted to sleep, she wondered, if she'd been just a girl from the harbor, and if he'd been just a boy who liked to sail, what could have been between the two of them? What could be then if they survived the cruelty of the world? It wasn't that long ago, but the Kane from that night was so different from the Kane she saw now in the tavern below.

She'd been in the market of Smuggler's Harbor when Jaron quickly pulled her and Nara into an alley. They'd followed him up onto the rooftop and to the wall of a tavern that was falling apart. He had promised to show them something they'd find interesting. She nearly yelled out when she saw Kane, Csilla, and the others enter the tavern, but Jaron quickly shushed her.

"I saw them enter while you two were stuffing your faces," Jaron told her, glancing past her to Nara. "Let's listen in. After this, I'll let you decide what you want to do."

"What?" Lorelei asked, shocked. "Why even wait? Of course, I want to go with my crew."

"I don't know what kind of game you're playing at," Nara said menacingly. "But I see no point in waiting when our comrades have come for us."

Jaron sighed. "They didn't come here for you. They're here for him." Jaron motioned to the man with golden eyes sitting at the table Kane just sat down at.

"A witchblood?" Lorelei asked.

"Yes," Jaron answered.

He said something else, but his words didn't reach Lorelei as she was too wrapped up in watching Kane. Dark circles lined his eyes, his complexion missing the warmth of the sun she'd come to know. It reminded her of that night he'd stared into the fire, but now he looked more lost than ever. Something silver rested in his hand.

Her compass.

Her heart bloomed at the sight of him holding it as dear as he'd held the one before. Knowing that he kept the compass close made a small and content smile play at Lorelei's lips.

The feeling, however, didn't last long. Something was wrong with him.

He set her compass on the table and picked up a deck of cards the witchblood had dealt him and Lorelei listened intently as the conversation continued, hoping to figure out why Kane didn't seem like himself.

But the longer the Serpent spoke, the less she wanted to hear.

"*I'm sure the man whose market stall you trashed regrets not repaying Rove on time.*"

"*I would say I'm doing better than the man you crippled in this very tavern.*"

"*There are quite a few people on this island who miss the men who vanished each time you docked here.*"

With each sentence, the light in Lorelei's heart dimmed. Magnus had warned her about Kane's past and now she understood why he'd kept his actions a secret. But he'd shown her such kindness; he'd done such heroic things. How could he be capable of both?

Her enemy had been right.

She didn't truly know the Blackwater.

"Pirates," Jaron muttered. He turned his attention to Lorelei. "They aren't truly your friends. They just want your storm, but I can teach you how to control it if you choose to leave here with me."

Lorelei hesitated.

"Lorelei," Nara said. "Don't listen to him. He is the enemy."

"I extend the same to you," Jaron said to Nara. "I can help you return to Ventys. Neither of you belong with them."

"I've chosen my family," Nara responded, "and I will continue to choose them."

Her words lodged themselves in Lorelei's heart. "As have I," she said.

"You will lose control of your storm again," Jaron said. "And when you do, which one of them will you hurt next?"

Nara's gaze turned glacial. "You are cruel and—"

"And telling her the truth she needs to hear."

Nara's mouth snapped shut.

Lorelei let his words sink in before she said anything. She glanced back at Kane, who was standing from the table, motioning to the witchblood to follow them. The last time she'd touched him, she'd nearly killed him. The image of Crew's scorched body flickered in her mind. She could never live with herself if she let the same happen to Kane.

"I don't trust him, Lorelei," Nara said. "And you shouldn't either."

Lorelei took one last long glance at Kane, then Csilla, Flynn, and Arius, before moving away from the hole in the wall. "Neither do I, but I also don't trust myself anymore." She looked down at her golden hands. "I need to learn to control this before it consumes me and everyone else."

"Are you certain about this?" Nara prodded once more. "This is our chance to escape. We still don't know what the emberblood's plans are for us."

Lorelei nodded. "I am certain."

"Then I will go with you," Nara said.

The sudden sound of scuffling and shouting drew their attention back to the hole. A group of men surrounded Kane and the rest of them, swords drawn.

"What's happening?" Lorelei asked frantically. "Who are they?"

"Incendian soldiers," Jaron said, surprise in his tone. "They were here the whole time, dressed as common Cerulians. Now is our chance to leave without them seeing us."

"We can't just leave them," Lorelei said, as Jaron pulled on her wrist.

"We must help them," Nara argued.

"If they're captains of the fleet, then I'm sure they will be fine," Jaron said. "I only spotted one Scout among them. We must make our leave if you wish to come with me instead. Otherwise, it will be difficult for you to cut ties. Don't you agree?"

Lorelei looked down into the tavern one last time to see the crew making their way successfully to the doorway as a group, fending off their attackers as they moved forward. She forced herself to pull away and turn back toward the way they'd come across the rooftop.

She quickly balanced herself on the crooked shingles, following behind Jaron and Nara as the sound of fighting faded. A ladder waited at the end and then they would sneak back to Jaron's ship. A couple more steps and shouts from men and women in the street below made her stop.

The group had escaped the tavern and now were fighting a couple of the disguised Incendians in the street. The crowd backed away as Flynn punched one in the face so hard that he fell backward into a stall. She found Kane and saw him grip the spot where his shoulder met his chest. He grimaced and glanced around the market street. As if he was drawn to her, his eyes scaled the building and locked onto her.

He mouthed her name.

"Shit," Jaron said. "We've got to go *now*."

Lorelei took one last glance at Kane before following after Jaron across the rooftop. Kane called her name from the street below and as much as it clawed at her heart, she kept her gaze forward and moved ahead.

"Lorelei!" he called again. He turned to the rest of his crew. "Go on without me!"

Lorelei, Jaron, and Nara got to the ladder at the end, but when Jaron made the move to climb down, Kane appeared at the bottom. His fists gripped both sides of the ladder as he looked up at the group of them.

"Lorelei," he said breathlessly. "What are you doing?"

"Come on!" Jaron yelled before jumping to the next rooftop. The gap was narrow since the buildings were stacked so close together, but the thought of missing the jump made Lorelei's heart leap into her throat.

Nara jumped next with ease and turned to Lorelei. "If this is what you want, then you have to jump before he makes it up that ladder."

Lorelei looked down at Kane, who was now climbing, and back at Jaron and Nara, who waited for her on the other rooftop. She took a deep breath, whispered an apology, and braced herself to jump.

She took a step and leapt forward, her toes finding the edge of the roof as Jaron and Nara both grabbed her and pulled her to the other side. Then they all took off in a run across the slanted rooftops.

Lorelei struggled to keep up, her gaze flicking between Nara, who ran in front of her, and where she should put her feet next. Behind her, she heard Kane chasing after them while shouting to her to wait. But if she waited, if she let herself talk to him, she wasn't so sure she'd be able to walk away.

A shingle dislodged itself under Lorelei's foot and she slipped, nearly falling before picking herself back up again. As she ran, she pictured Kane—the way he'd asked for her forgiveness on Crossbones, the way he'd held her in his arms when she'd returned from Limbo, the way he'd looked at her when they'd danced together on his birthday. Then, just like every other time she thought of Kane recently, the memories were followed by him on the ground after she'd hurt him with her lightning.

She could never let that happen again. She'd make friends with her enemy before she'd let herself hurt Kane once more. She blinked away the tears that sprang up as they neared the end of the rooftops.

Jaron stopped at the edge and looked down for a moment before turning back to Nara and Lorelei as they both stumbled to a stop. The docks and their ship waited just beyond.

"That pile of hay could do for a safe landing," Jaron said. "I'll leap first and then you two follow me. Make a break for the ship as quickly as you can and I'll meet you there."

Lorelei didn't respond. She nervously looked from the hay to the ship.

"You're still deciding what to do," Jaron said quickly. "But you have to make that choice now. Come with me and learn how to use your magic, or go back and risk his life. The choice is yours, Storm."

Lorelei knew that she was being manipulated. Jaron didn't care about whether or not she hurt Kane, but he was very much aware that she cared. Her leaving with Jaron by choice was exactly what he wanted, and as much as she wanted to refuse and run toward Kane, she couldn't. Jaron was right: she would face whatever plans he had for her if she could just control her storm.

"I'll go," she said.

Jaron nodded and jumped from the edge of the roof. Lorelei leaned to peer over, watching as he plopped safely into the hay. Nara leapt down as soon as Jaron had cleared the way. As she scrambled out of the hay, Lorelei readied herself to jump.

"Lorelei!" Kane yelled. His footsteps slowed to a stop behind her. "Wait!"

She stopped the tip of her toes, frozen except for her hair, which blew in the wind. *Jump*, she told herself. *Let go.*

But she couldn't. The desperation in his tone from that one single word had her hesitating when she had just made up her mind a moment before.

"Please," Kane begged, his voice even closer. "Why are you running from me?" His fingertips brushed against her wrist.

She quickly spun around and pulled her arm from him. "Stay back," she told him, the ache in her heart making her words tremble. "I don't want to hurt you."

"You won't hurt me, Lorelei," he said, gaze swimming. "You'd never hurt me or anyone else."

Kane could say those words over and over, but they would never be the truth. She had hurt two people now and had killed one of them. Crew's charred remains haunted her—a memory that returned no matter how many times she tried to bury it.

"You don't understand," Lorelei said. She swallowed back the tears that threatened to form. She held up her hands, her fingers trembling as she showed him the gold that had spread from her fingertips to her forearms. "Look at me, Kane. Look at what's happening to me."

His gaze was wide-eyed for a moment, taking in the spreading gold. "It's okay," he said. His breathing picked up speed. "We can figure this out. We can fix you."

"Fix me?" Lorelei shook her head. "You think I'm a monster, don't you?" Perhaps he was right. Perhaps she was a monster.

"What?" Kane rubbed his hand down his face. "I didn't say that, I—"

"I'm not going to be a monster." The wind blew Lorelei's hair in front of her face. "I'm going to learn to control it. Don't follow me, Kane. Let me go."

Kane's jaw worked. "Don't say that," he said, his voice low. "You can run, and I will follow, but don't tell me to let you go because I will not. I refuse to accept that fate. I can't."

His words nearly made Lorelei change her mind and throw herself into his arms, but the shimmer of the setting sun on her golden hands reminded her of her unsettled magic. She took one last look at him—his dark restless eyes and the small scars scattered across his face. At least she'd gotten to see him one last time. She bit her lip and took a deep breath.

"Goodbye, Kane," she whispered.

Then she turned and leapt from the rooftop, landing in the soft hay below. She quickly climbed out and ran toward Nara and Jaron, who stood waiting by the docks. As her foot hit the wooden planks, she snuck a glance back to see if Kane had jumped after her, but he remained on the rooftop, watching her go. He gripped his shoulder as if in pain. Was she the cause? Her lightning must have hurt him deeper than she'd thought.

"Are you okay?" Nara asked as they climbed onto Jaron's ship.

"I will be," Lorelei said, closing her eyes.

The words tasted like a lie.

PART THREE

ASHES

CHAPTER SIXTEEN

KANE

Silver Sea

Mid-Rainrise

The skies were clear for the first time since they had set sail on the *Wavecutter*. The stars above were a sea of their own and the moon shone bright, reflecting on the silver of Kane's compass. He traced the smooth surface with his thumb as he stared out at the calm dark waters, thinking of the one who'd given it to him.

He wondered where she was now and if she was okay. She had seemed different, scared almost. No matter how much he had tried to tell her that he wasn't afraid of her, that she wouldn't hurt him, she still wouldn't accept it. He tried and tried, but he couldn't think of why she would willingly go with the emberblood. Unless she felt like she didn't have choice. Perhaps she had heard the Serpent's taunts during their card game and realized all the terrible things that Kane had done. Now she might want nothing more to do with him.

Damn it all.

Kane gripped the compass hard and reared back his arm, ready to throw the compass out into the sea. He stopped himself as he swung his arm forward, catching himself and holding the compass tight against his chest. His heart sank further into its abyss. He wasn't sure what hurt more, his wound or watching her run away. Even now, as he stood alone at the railing of the *Wavecutter*, the pain was just as fresh as when he had stood on that rooftop. What would it take to get her back? He'd pay whatever price if it just meant that she was safe, whether it be in his arms or not.

He couldn't wait any longer.

Kane left the railing, tucking the compass away as he crossed the deck to where the Serpent lounged on a stack of netting. Arius leaned against a mast as he told him the story about the comoras in Death's Cove. The Serpent, his gold eyes shimmering, slid his gaze to Kane the moment he stopped in front of him.

"Beautiful night," the Serpent said with a smile. He looked up at the stars above. "Don't you think, Blackwater?"

Kane gritted his teeth, still unhappy with the way the Serpent had laid Kane's crimes bare in front of his crew, his friends. But however he felt, he had to suppress it and ask for the witchblood's help. They were sailing in the same direction that Lorelei had gone, but it was easy to get lost on the seas.

"Can you track her?" Kane asked, ignoring the Serpent's question.

The Serpent's smile spread even farther, his eyes twinkling at Kane. "I thought you'd never ask."

The witchblood burst into action and moved to a crate nearby, sitting on his knees in front of it. He brushed off the wooden top and pulled a folded parchment out of his pocket. Kane followed him, watching as he unfolded the parchment and laid it down on the crate's top, a map of the Kingdoms of Four now covering the surface.

"I can't wait to see this," Arius said excitedly as he sat across from the Serpent on the other side of the crate.

Kane remained silent as he searched over the worn map, wondering how the Serpent would use it to locate Lorelei.

"In order to find the lost, I will need something that they have touched." The Serpent looked to Kane to provide an item.

"Something she's touched?" Kane asked, slight panic rising in his tone. "She hasn't set foot on this ship. There is nothing here that she has touched."

"Can we use Blackwater?" Arius asked with a grin. "I'm sure he's let her touch him more than once."

"If you don't shut your—" Kane stopped, suddenly realizing that he *did* have something she'd touched. His pocket felt heavier as he remembered. "What about this?" Kane reached into his pocket and pulled out the compass. "This would work, right?"

The Serpent took the compass and turned it over in his hands, assessing it. "It should, as long as she's touched it."

"She's the one who gave it to me." Kane would remember that night until he took his last breath. It was the only gift he'd ever received aside from his mother's.

"Very well." The Serpent rested the compass in the bottom right corner of the map, where a narrow strip of sea divided Eastern Incendia and the southern continent of Terran. Then he closed his eyes and started to recite an incantation.

The words were ones Kane didn't know, but they were similar to the ones Borne had used to bring Lorelei back from Limbo. After several moments, the Serpent fell silent, but nothing happened aside from the groan of the ship as it swayed on the waves.

"Well?" Kane pressed. He crossed his arms over his chest. "Anything?"

"Be patient, Blackwater," Arius said, his voice calm. "Hush and let the man do his magic."

"That's absolutely rich coming from you," Kane huffed.

Just as Kane was about to say more, something on the map caught his attention. It was the tiniest of glimmers at first, but as he stood there, holding his breath, it grew. Gold shone like a light in the dark, a small blip in the Silver Sea, about where their ship would be right then. The gold started to snake north, creating a sparkling path and stopping a hands-length away.

"It looks like they're heading toward Icehaven," Kane said. "Why would they go there? That place is a ghost island."

"Your guess is as good as mine," the Serpent replied. "I only track the lost, not their reasoning."

At least they had an eye on her. At least they knew where to find her.

"You're very different from the Ruin Witch," Kane said, finally finding enough relief in himself to sit down. "When we visited her, it felt like she knew everything."

"She does." The Serpent laughed. "Her relationship with the trees is much stronger than mine."

"Why is that?" Arius asked. "Why don't you sprout trees from the ground or grow instant flowers?"

"Really, Pavel?" Kane sighed deeply.

"What? I'm just curious," Arius said. "The other magics are very elemental-based while the witchbloods' are not."

"It's because our god, Crysso, lets us choose our talents," the

Serpent replied. "While your friend the Ruin Witch chose to mirror our gods with dealmaking magic, I chose to be an excellent tracker. I will find anyone who is lost if they're still in this realm."

"And what did you give up for that power?" Kane asked. Arius's curiosity must have been rubbing off on him.

The Serpent's golden gaze was on Kane for a long moment before answering. "Love," he replied simply.

"Love?" Arius's face twisted in disbelief. "I thought it would be a bigger deal, like sacrificing your most prized pig or something."

The Serpent ignored Arius and continued. "My wife was stolen by a group of bandits, witchbloods who had gone rogue. When I begged Crysso for the power to track her, I gave up the only thing I had that was of any worth—the strength of my love for her."

"Did you find her?" Kane asked. The Serpent's gaze held pain that reminded him of his own.

"I did," the Serpent replied, his voice unchanging even though he wove a story of despair. "But one of the witchbloods had erased her memory to keep their identities and their plans secret. This included all her memories of me."

"That's a tragic story," Arius said. "To go through all of that for her to not even remember you?"

"I don't know what's worse," the Serpent said with a sigh. "Her forgetting me or me not having any feelings about it. My ability to love was truly lost, and I will die alone." He took a deep breath as if centering himself once more. "But at least she is safe, even if she is happy again with another."

Sometimes Kane wished that he could be rid of his feelings. If he didn't care so much for Lorelei, he wouldn't be so reckless. His heart wouldn't be heavy and weighing him down with rejection. But then he remembered the way Lorelei's eyes sparkled when she smiled, the way her cheeks rosed when he stood close to her. The warmth inside him when he thought about her was not something he would be willing to give up easily, but he understood the Serpent's choice. If he could guarantee Lorelei's safety, he would do the same.

Shouts and hurried footsteps pulled Kane out of his thoughts. He turned toward the sound, seeing Flynn, who raced across the deck toward them. His hair was a wild mess, his face pale like he'd seen a ghost.

"Aye," Arius said as they all rose to their feet. "What's got your sails in a knot?"

"It's Csilla," Flynn said breathlessly, already turning back the way he came. "Hurry!"

Kane chased after him across the deck and into the Captain's Quarters, anxious about what kind of horror they would find based on Flynn's panicked demeanor. Inside the cabin, Csilla lay on the plush bed, her eyes closed in sleep. Kane's breath left him as he took in what filled the space over her.

A figure hovered above her, levitating in the air. Its tattered black cloak fluttered softly as if being held there by the wind. The room smelled like a musty wardrobe, which it hadn't the last time Kane had set foot in it. The longer he stared at the creature, the colder he felt, his skin prickling, his insides chilling.

"The dreamwraith," Kane whispered.

"Aye!" Arius squealed. "What should we do? Set it on fire?"

"No," Flynn said quickly. Usually, he'd find humor in the ridiculous things Arius said, but right then his face held nothing but fear. "Remember what the Ruin Witch said. We can't kill it unless Csilla defeats it in the dream realm first."

Csilla's body jerked on the bed, but she remained asleep. He wondered what she was seeing, if she was fighting. He hoped to Goddess she fought like hell. They needed her. Lorelei needed her. After all that Csilla had been through, it would be a travesty to lose her fight to a creature such as this. When she woke up, they would be here to kill the thing.

But until then, she was on her own.

CHAPTER SEVENTEEN

CSILLA

The Dream Realm

The jungle of Macaya felt as much like a home as the small cottage Csilla had grown up in. In her dream, the cacao flowers were in full bloom. No, not a dream. She could smell the jungle flora and feel the humidity clinging to her skin. That wasn't possible in dreams.

She was crouched behind the trunk of a tree with gnarled roots sprouting from the ground, peeking around the side to see if Rhoda was coming. Then she heard the song Rhoda always sang when they played hide-and-seek in the jungle.

". . . *the snake slithers by,*

"*The owl flies at night.*"

Csilla leaned farther around the trunk, her hand over her mouth to keep from giggling. She still couldn't see Rhoda, but her voice seemed closer than before.

"*And when you least expect it . . .*"

Suddenly, Csilla was grabbed from behind.

"The fox will strike!"

Csilla squealed and spun around, coming face to face with her elder sister. Rhoda wore a smile so big it lit up her eyes, something that Csilla didn't see very often. Her skin held a glow that made Csilla feel warm.

"Rhoda," Csilla said with a laugh. "You're in such high spirits today."

"Well," Rhoda said, her hands falling to Csilla's and gripping them excitedly. "It is my twelfth birthday today."

The smile fell from Csilla's face. "It is today?" Guilt crept into her heart. "How could I forget? I'm so sorry, sister, I—"

"Little Cub," Rhoda said softly. "Birthdays come every year. How about you just surprise me next year?"

Csilla smiled. "Aye aye, sister!"

"Csilla!" came the call of a familiar voice. "Rhoda!"

The smile Csilla wore slowly dropped. Tears sprang up and she didn't know why. That voice. It was one she longed for desperately, one that she held dear to her heart. She'd seen her just that morning, but somewhere deep inside her was an ache that felt deeper, like she hadn't seen her in ages.

Something wasn't right.

"Come home for dinner!" yelled the voice again.

"Mother!" Csilla yelled back through the jungle, even though there was nothing but tangled trees. She was surprised by the desperation in her tone.

"Let's go home," Rhoda said, pulling Csilla forward as she stepped back farther into the jungle. "Mother's waiting on us."

Csilla shook her head clear and donned a smile, hoping the unease would slip away. "What do you think she cooked for us?"

Rhoda grinned at her, but there was a strange gleam in her eye. "I suppose we will just have to see." She turned away, still holding Csilla's hand, and started trudging through the jungle, pulling Csilla along.

As they walked, the jungle grew quieter. When she looked up at the tree canopy, it seemed as if the leaves had bundled closer together, blocking out any sunlight that tried to stream in. Just moments before, they had been surrounded by vibrant life, yet the farther they trekked, the darker the jungle grew.

"Rhoda," Csilla said, her voice sounding small. "I'm scared." She'd never felt more like a child.

Rhoda squeezed her hand tighter. Too tight. Their pace picked up speed. The jungle grew darker, the shadows becoming sinister.

"Rhoda?" Csilla asked, her voice a whimper.

Rhoda dropped Csilla's hand and spun around. She suddenly wasn't twelve anymore and stood tall over Csilla, staring down her nose at her. Gone were her still-full cheeks, replaced by sharp cheekbones and an even sharper gaze.

"Why do you always have to ruin everything?" Rhoda sneered at her.

Csilla's chin wobbled. "What's happened to you?"

"*You*," Rhoda replied through her teeth. "If you would've just stayed quiet for a little longer, we would be home by now." She fiddled with the sword at her waist that hadn't been there before. "If you would've let me be captain of the *Scarlet Maiden*, then I would've been queen. If you wouldn't have dueled me in that cave, then I would still be alive. Perhaps I should've just left you to hang in Port Barlow."

With each accusation, a memory flashed through Csilla's mind. Climbing cliffs and playing hide-and-seek with Rhoda, arguing with Rhoda over captainship, Csilla's sword piercing Rhoda's stomach. Rhoda was dead. Csilla had killed her own sister. The realization was a punch to the gut that almost had Csilla falling to the lush jungle floor.

"That's right, Little Cub." Rhoda slowly unsheathed her sword. "You can wake up to what you've done, but I won't let you awaken from this dream."

Csilla jumped back from her and reached for her waist on instinct, surprised to find a sword waiting. Once her hand touched the hilt, her mind suddenly felt clearer. None of this was real. She remembered going to sleep on board the *Wavecutter* with promises that Flynn would keep watch over her.

"You're not Rhoda," Csilla said, no longer her child self.

The dream Rhoda smiled, her lips stretching too far, her cheekbones jutting out. "You've been sleeping for too long, Little Cub."

"I know what you are now," Csilla said, unsheathing her own sword. "And you will not drown me in your dreams any longer."

Rhoda growled, the sound inhuman and echoing in the jungle, and attacked Csilla with her sword high. Their steel clashed. Csilla pushed Rhoda's sword away with her own and raised it again to block the next attack. Left then right. High then low. Block after block Csilla executed, their dance ever familiar.

"*Fight me!*" Rhoda yelled, her voice vicious.

"I don't want to fight you!" Csilla yelled back as she stumbled over a root. She quickly caught herself before Rhoda could swing at Csilla's side. "I've never wanted to fight you!"

A cruel laugh came from Rhoda. "We were made for this. We were born to compete against each other. This was always our fate." Rhoda sliced at Csilla with each sentence, barely missing.

"That's a lie," Csilla grunted, pushing her sister's sword back once more. "Our mother wanted us to be close. That's why she always had us come back home between trainings. She didn't want this for us."

"Our mother was weak." Rhoda's face twisted even further into a demon's—one that Csilla couldn't even recognize. "Just like you."

The dream Rhoda's attacks were relentless, making Csilla retreat farther and farther until they stood at the cliff by the waterfall. The same one where they used to play when they'd been small and innocent.

"Do you truly think someone as weak as you can lead a nation of pirates?" Rhoda laughed. "Lockhart doesn't respect you and neither do the council officials. No one truly does."

"More lies!" Csilla yelled as she blocked one more attack, but this one was so strong it nearly had her stumbling backward over the edge of the cliff.

"You should be back in Baltessa, leading them all, instead of chasing after the stormblood."

Rhoda's sword came too close, slicing her upper arm. Csilla dodged Rhoda's next attack and ran around her, putting Rhoda between herself and the cliff now.

"You chose her over me," Rhoda hissed. "You chose her over your own blood."

"It's not my fault!" Csilla finally yelled. "I am so sorry that it happened, but it is not my fault. You made this happen. You left no room in your heart for love, only hatred."

Rhoda's eyes gleamed. Csilla realized her anger was only feeding the dreamwraith.

"I loved you, Rhoda," Csilla said calmly, letting her sword

relax in her hands. "You let Magnus's whispers taint your mind, but I still love you. I forgive you."

Her sister's face froze for a moment before her expression dropped to one of fear. The dream jungle around Csilla quivered, and splotches of the cabin where Csilla slept appeared through the leaves and bark before becoming whole again.

"I forgive myself too," Csilla said.

Rhoda's face became stone, unreadable and cold, as she stumbled backward like Csilla had stabbed her. Her foot lost bearing as she came too close to the edge of the cliff and she fell back, her scream echoing as she dropped out of sight.

Csilla called out her sister's name on instinct, reaching out for her like she could save her. Then she remembered that this was a dream and she wondered why she wasn't waking up yet if she'd defeated the wraith.

A hand appeared at the edge of the cliff, grabbing at the ground. Csilla watched as they pulled themselves up. Long silky black hair covered her face as she rose to her feet and adjusted the arrows at her back. Her hair parted to reveal Nara's smiling face.

Csilla's heart tugged. She had missed her dearest friend. It was so nice to have her visiting them in Macaya. She knew her mother would have treasured Nara as her own daughter if given the chance.

Csilla shook her head.

Wait.

Nara didn't smile.

Not Nara.

"I won't let you win!" Csilla yelled at the dreamwraith. "This is my dream. You're just a part of it."

The dream Nara laughed, then her smile fell into a flat line, her expression dead of emotion. "We will see about that, Csilla Abado." She inhaled, as if gathering a scent. "Your guilt and regret is divine. I've never had a meal this tasty before."

Csilla readied her sword as Nara unsheathed her own. The attack was quick and precise, just like Nara's true self. The dreamwraith must have studied Csilla's loved ones so that they could be authentic in her dream. It nearly had her fooled, especially when it said things that Csilla only worried about to herself, keeping it buried deep so no one could see.

"I always liked your sister better," Nara said. She spun gracefully on her toes and lunged, her sword nearly missing the side of Csilla's rib cage. "I only watched out for you because I felt sorry for you."

Csilla reminded herself that Nara's words weren't true, that the dreamwraith was only feeding on her emotions. She couldn't let herself succumb. If she did, the Ruin Witch said she'd be stuck in the dream realm forever. She looked to the trees, hoping to see the cabin walls fading back through the pretend jungle, but only leaves greeted her. Csilla swung her sword as Nara swung hers, the collision sending Nara's sword into the jungle.

Nara stood, defenseless, her hands splayed in surrender. "How could you abandon me in Smuggler's Harbor?"

Csilla blinked and the dreamwraith had changed its appearance. Blue eyes stared back at Csilla now.

"How could you abandon *us*?" asked Lorelei. Her eyes flickered with gold sparks like the day she'd woken up from Limbo on that cave floor. "After all that we've been through."

The hairs on Csilla's arm raised, the air changing as Lorelei's fingers curled. Csilla jumped back just in time as lightning left

Lorelei's hand and struck the spot where Csilla had stood just a moment before.

"I was there the entire time and not one of you could save me?" Lorelei's voice amplified like thunder in a storm. "I'm just a girl from the fish-reeking Port Barlow, right? Perhaps Incendia *is* where I truly belong."

A fierce wind whipped at Csilla and she braced her feet on the ground. She took a step forward, the force of the wind pushing her back. Csilla's heart raced faster and faster. Was this the power of Lorelei's magic that she'd been so afraid of that night on the balcony at the palace? If she was still unraveling, Csilla had to find her *now*. She couldn't let her friend down when she'd begged her for help.

The dream world flickered again, like a candlewick threatening to snuff out.

"Your mind games won't work any longer!" Csilla yelled over the roar of the wind. "I won't let you win!"

The dreamwraith smiled at her with Lorelei's face, her hair unmoving even though the wind circled wildly around them. Lorelei flicked one finger and a burst of wind hit Csilla like a cannon, throwing her into the jungle. Her head knocked against the trunk of a tree and the dream world went black for a moment.

When Csilla cracked open her eyes, the jungle of Macaya was gone. She lay in the sand on a beach that stretched for miles, not a single dock or person in sight. The sea lapped gently at the shore. In the distance, gulls squawked and waves crashed over each other. The sky was a blue as endless as the sea. Just a moment earlier she'd been visiting her mother in Macaya and now she was . . . she didn't know *where* she was.

"There you are," came a familiar honeyed voice.

Csilla glanced in the direction the voice had come from and saw Flynn walking toward her, holding his boots by their straps. He stopped at her toes, which were buried in the sand.

"I've been looking all over for you," Flynn said, a smile hooking at his lips. His sea-colored eyes glimmered in the light of the sun as the breeze blew at the sand-colored hair. "And here you are, right back at the sea. I should have known." He winked, the scar on his cheek dimpling.

Her heart warmed from the sight, but it didn't cease the confusion swimming in her head. "Flynn, where are we?"

"Are you all right?" Flynn crouched down in front of her, searching her face. "Did something happen?"

Csilla shook her head. "No, I'm fine. I had the strangest dream is all. But I"—she looked down the unfamiliar shore once more—"I don't recognize this beach."

Flynn squinted at her. He reached toward her and brushed her curls away from her face, then rested his palm against her cheek, his thumb tracing once under her silver eye. "Are you sure you're fine? How could you forget our home?"

"Our home?" Csilla's voice broke off. She turned her head away from his hand and to the left, finding a planked path that led to a quaint cabin on a hill. It sat alone, overlooking the shore. Nothing more than a whisper left her lips when she looked back at Flynn. "Our home . . ."

Flynn's smile was uncertain. "Yes, our home. Do you truly not remember, love?"

Csilla watched him for a moment, remembering all the times he'd looked at her with such confidence, even when she'd been adamant in her feigned distaste for him on Crossbones. This uncertain expression of his was something she wasn't sure she'd seen from him before.

Something wasn't right.

"Where is everyone else?" Csilla asked. It was odd being in a place so quiet, not surrounded by the chaos of her friends.

"It's just us," Flynn said. "We came here together after Crossbones, a little island to call our own."

Csilla cocked her head. "I don't understand."

Flynn sighed and looked out at the sea. "You didn't understand then either, but everyone thought it was in your best interest to take a break from everything after what had happened with Rhoda."

"Oh." Csilla's voice trailed off. "Sounds like something they would do."

"Is your lack of remembrance just a facade?" Although his question was an accusation, his voice held pain.

"Flynn, no, I—"

"You don't truly want to be here with me, do you?" Flynn rose from his crouch and dragged his hand down his face.

She reached for his other hand, gripping it tightly and trying to shake some sense into him. "What? Why would you say such a thing?"

"Do you even love me, Csilla?" Flynn turned back on her then, the sea swimming in his eyes. "After everything, after all this time, you still haven't said it. Just let me off easy before I sink any further into you."

"Flynn." Csilla's voice was soft. Much softer than she ever allowed herself to be. "It's not that simple."

"How is it not?" Flynn said, desperation seeping through him. He dropped to his knees in the sand. "Stay here with me. We can forget about the rest of the world."

If he only knew how tempting that offer truly was. To forget about the troubles of the world and the crooked ways of pirates would be a freedom unlike any she'd ever experienced, but having Flynn there with her would be like a dream.

But she couldn't forget about her friends. Her found family. Not after everything they'd done for her.

"I can't," she told him. The words tasted horrid on her tongue, but they were necessary. "I will never step away from my responsibilities. It's a part of what makes me who I am."

Flynn's eyes shone with tears for a moment before he blinked them away and looked down at the sand between them. "What can I do to make you stay? Have I always fought a losing battle?"

"Oh, Flynn . . ." She put her hand over his that rested on his thigh. "Perhaps we can stay a little while longer."

Flynn looked back up at her then, a smile stretching across his face. Something was off about it again, but this time it seemed a little more wicked. The sinister nature behind it seemed familiar though.

She suddenly remembered Rhoda smiling at her like that, and Nara, and Lorelei. It all suddenly linked together in her head like a chain. Returning to Baltessa. Her coronation. Flynn and her together in the rose garden. The dreamwraith invading her dreams.

Her breath stilled for a moment.

"Csilla?" Flynn asked, standing and holding out his hand to her. "Ready to go home?"

Csilla soaked him in, capturing the moment and etching it into her mind. Of all the masks the wraith wore, this one was nearly perfect. She'd almost let herself fall into the dream peacefully with just a promise of having him by her side for as long as she needed.

She knew what she had to do.

She placed her hand in his and let him pull her up onto her feet. Looking into his eyes, she took a deep breath and let it out while she let her words settle on her tongue.

"I love you, Flynn Gunnison," she said. "Across the seas and back." She placed her hands on either side of his face and closed the distance between them.

The moment her lips touched his, the dream faded to black.

The first thing she heard was Flynn's voice, only this time it wasn't a dream.

"Csilla!" he yelled, relief pouring out of him. "You're awake!"

There were yells and shuffling as Csilla blinked, trying to see through the black, but as her gaze focused, she realized she wasn't in the black of the dream anymore and instead was face to face with the dreamwraith.

It hovered over her, cloaked in black, a bottomless abyss for a face underneath its hood. Csilla was frozen in shock for a moment, then she remembered what the Ruin Witch had told them. She'd defeated it in the dreamworld; now she would finish it herself.

She reached under her pillow and pulled out the dagger she kept hidden away and stabbed the black hole where its face should be. The wraith shrieked and wailed in the air above her. The air hissed as smoke rose from its body, which dissolved in the air like ashes. The weight that had pressed her down into the bed lifted, and the shadow that loomed over her each day on the deck faded away until she was the lightest she'd felt in moons.

"You've done it," Flynn said from next to her.

Csilla let her arm drop to the bed and let go of the dagger. She turned her head to look at Flynn and smiled widely at him.

Surprise lit his expression and then he smiled back at her.

"Flynn," she started. She felt anxious, but the time had come. If anything, the dreamwraith had helped her realize that she didn't need to keep her feelings bottled up anymore. "I want to tell you something."

"What is it, love?" His voice was tender, sweet.

"Holy hell!" Arius said with a clap of his hands. "That was actually kind of scary. Were you all scared? I'm not going to lie, I was shaking in my boots a bit."

Csilla's gaze flitted around the room, taking in the audience she hadn't realized was there. "Another time," she told Flynn. "I promise."

CHAPTER EIGHTEEN
JARON

Northern Silver Sea

Mid-Rainrise

Jaron pulled his overcoat tighter around him, wishing he'd brought a scarf for their journey up north. Although the bitterness of the frostfall season had faded, a chill still lingered in the air, getting colder the farther north they sailed.

They'd almost made it. Finally.

You have done well, my champion, came his god's whisper. *You are one ssstep closer to achieving your full potential.*

Jaron looked out at the early morning mist creeping across the waves. He'd trained harder than most; he'd obtained the obsidian sword; he'd gathered the stormblood. So, he found himself wondering what more he needed to do to reach his full potential and what exactly it was.

Don't worry your mortal mind over such trivial thingsss, Magnus whispered. *Your reward is coming sssoon.*

Yes, his reward. Magnus would help Jaron find his brother, Alrik. Jaron didn't question how; the thought of seeing his big round charcoal eyes again was enough for him to do whatever Magnus asked of him.

"Are we nearly there?" the archer asked suddenly from beside him.

Jaron jumped, nearly dropping the spyglass he'd been peering through a moment before. He would never get used to how easy it was for the archer to sneak up on him. He was surprised it hadn't gotten him killed yet. Perhaps she didn't wish death upon him after all.

"Nearly where?" Jaron asked, watching the mist.

"Our destination," the archer replied. "Your demeanor has changed. You're slightly on edge. This must mean we're close to whatever fate you have in store for us."

"You still do not believe that I mean you and the stormblood no harm?" Jaron returned his hands to the knobs on the wheel.

"Your mouth says one thing, but your actions say another."

"Do enlighten me as to what actions I have taken to make you believe that."

"Coming into our home and kidnapping Lorelei is the foundation on which you stand, emberblood." Jaron didn't need to look at her to know she was scowling at him.

"You say emberblood like it's a curse."

"Because you are one," she said coldly.

Jaron looked at her then. She was already watching him, frostier than usual. As much as he tried, he couldn't wrap his head around why she hated him so much. Perhaps she did want to kill him after all. The thought hit him with an unexpected pang.

"I didn't force you onto this boat back in Smuggler's Harbor,"

Jaron told her. "I gave you both the option to leave and you both chose to come."

The archer rolled her eyes. "Spare me the freedom of choice. You knew Lorelei would want to come with you to learn how to control her magic and you played into that. Parading it as a choice was only to quell your rising guilt, wasn't it?"

Jaron gripped the wheel tighter, his knuckles white underneath his scarred skin. The archer was just as dangerous with her words as she was with her bow. He'd never met someone so infuriating.

"And pretending to understand my motives will help you believe that I am evil and cruel and all the other horrible things you dream up in your head?" He tried his best to keep from raising his voice, but he couldn't stop the growl in his tone. "You want to know what's evil and cruel, archer? Having to hold your dead sister in your arms after pirates came and pillaged your harbor. Never seeing your brother again because those pirates took him with them. Being utterly and truly alone . . . and for what? What purpose? Was the loot more important than the lives they ruined?"

The archer parted her lips, then snapped them shut again. A moment went by before she asked, "Is that why you enlisted?"

Jaron blinked, her question throwing him off. "Yes," he said. "After losing what I did, I wanted nothing more than to be on the front lines when Incendia attacked Cerulia. I wanted revenge. I wanted to find the ship with those brown sails. But now . . ."

Don't let her get into your head, Magnus whispered.

"Now what?" the archer prodded.

"Never mind it," Jaron said, turning his attention completely back to the wheel.

The archer was quiet for a moment, but her eyes were on him, trying to read him. If he could just shut her out completely, then he could rebury these confusing emotions arising in him.

"I wasn't born in Cerulia," she said. "I was born in the mountains of Ventys to a mother who didn't want me and a father who didn't know I existed."

Jaron glanced back at the archer, watching her face soften as she spoke. He thought he had recognized the etchings on the blade of her sword, but hadn't known too much about Ventys. Neither did the rest of the world, since they kept themselves hidden away behind the Frozen Gap.

"I wasn't blessed to be a frostblood and I certainly wasn't blessed with any support, so when I was eleven, I snuck out of the orphanage and stowed away on a trading ship."

She looked past him, as if she was reliving the memory.

"I didn't hide very well and they found me quickly, but I was only a child so the crew on board took me in as their own while we traveled. Feeding me well, clothing me warmly, treating me with more kindness than anyone had before. Even at the orphanage, we would have to scrap for food when our caretaker didn't have enough."

She sighed then, tucking her long black hair behind her ear. "The crew didn't even get to unload their shipment in Icehaven before Incendians attacked."

When the archer mentioned the very place that they were headed, his stomach tightened. He remembered the state of the abandoned island—the realities of what had happened there clicked together in his mind as she continued talking.

"I was hiding in a barrel, silently crying as I listened to everyone around me die. And when everything grew quiet, and I finally left that barrel, I saw the crimson sails of the *Scarlet Maiden*. The

Maidens gave me shelter, gave me training, and put a bow in my hand."

The archer glanced back at Jaron, the frost in her eyes melting. "They gave me a purpose."

Jaron was silent for a moment, taking in the archer's story. He had thought he'd known so much about the workings of the world and the people who lived in it. He'd deemed all Cerulians as vile and selfish. Perhaps he'd been wrong. Perhaps he'd been taught wrong.

You're letting the girl trick you, Magnus whispered in his head. *Is it so easy for you to turn your back on your nation over a pair of pretty eyes?*

"No," Jaron replied aloud.

"No?" The archer raised her brow at him. "I suppose that is the sort of response I should expect from you."

She turned to leave and he reached for her without thinking. His fingers delicately encircled her wrist. She stopped and turned, glancing down at his hand before looking back up at him. He quickly let go.

"Wait," he said with a sigh. "I didn't mean to say that. I am . . . sort of arguing with myself at the moment."

The archer cocked her head.

"Forget about it," Jaron spit out, trying to move on from his slipup. "So, what is it?"

"You continue to confuse me," the archer said, always so serious. Jaron had seen a glimpse of something new from her a moment ago, and he found himself wanting to see it again.

"What was the purpose they gave you?"

The smallest of smiles pulled at the corner of her mouth while she looked out at the sea. "To protect the family that I'd found."

The sea wind played with her hair, her face welcoming the glow of the rising sun. He couldn't take his sight off her, and he cursed himself for it.

"Lorelei has become a part of that family," she said without looking at him. "That's why I chose to continue on with you. Not for any other reason. Although you have been doing well with training her. Her wind was able to make us sail much faster."

The silence between them was filled with the crash of waves. He pulled his gaze away from her and out to the open water again, spying a shadow in the haze on the horizon.

Jaron cleared his throat. "We've nearly reached our destination." His heart felt oddly heavy at the thought. *It's only because you're anxious about what comes next*, he told himself. Everything would be fine. His god would ensure it.

The archer watched the growing shadow of an island with him, tension resting between them. It was as if they both wanted to say something, but neither would bend.

"I am sorry for the loss of your family," the archer said, her voice unwavering. "And I admire your determination to avenge them. I only hope that you will not destroy the lives of the innocent for it. Or yourself for that matter."

Or himself? Nothing else mattered except for Alrik and Glenna. The thought didn't feel wholly like the truth.

"Don't worry about me," he said.

"Maybe someone should," she told him. He felt her judgment back on him. "There's something off about the sword you carry."

Focusss on your mission, Magnus whispered, his tone holding a bite. *No more games.*

Jaron held his tongue even though he wanted to respond to the archer. Perhaps it was for the best.

"Fine then," the archer said, stepping away from him. "Have it your way, emberblood."

Heat rose to his fingertips. He shook his head and let go of the wheel, clenching his fists to make his rising flames recede.

"Wake Lorelei and prepare yourselves for departure," he told her. "We dock in Icehaven soon."

"Icehaven . . ." The archer's voice trailed off, concern filling her eyes before rushing off to wake Lorelei below deck. Perhaps she had remembered they were enemies.

Good. Jaron would rather her be scared of him than warm up to him. It was best for all parties involved if they continued hating each other.

—

Icehaven was warmer than when Jaron had left it a couple moons ago, but the wind still held a bite. The snow they trudged through wasn't nearly as deep, but the ground remained frozen beneath them.

As they continued up the hill to the house at the top, Jaron snuck a glance behind him. Lorelei held the furs she wore tight around her, but she was still unable to cover her cheeks and nose, red from the cold wind. The archer stayed close to her, only wearing a jacket as thick as Jaron's. The cold didn't seem to bother her at all, her concern focusing only on Lorelei. When the archer's gaze connected with his, he quickly turned back around.

He quickened his pace to the house, hoping they would keep up. The sooner this was over with, the better.

Jaron stood in front of the door to the ramshackle house, unmoving, while the stormblood and the archer crunched through the snow behind him. The home wasn't missing any more nails or wooden slats than it was before, yet he felt more uneasy now than he had then. He almost didn't want to go inside.

"What is this place?" the archer asked, their footsteps coming to a stop. When he didn't answer, she pressed further. "Who is in there waiting for us? I swear if something happens to Lorelei, I will make you regret it in this life and the next."

"It's okay," Lorelei said, looking at Jaron. "Jaron offered to help with my storm. He wouldn't bring us harm after extending his hand like that. It would be unforgivable." Either the stormblood was incredibly naive or she was firing a warning shot.

He truthfully did not want to bring the two of them any harm. He'd never lied about that, but he didn't know much about Turncoat except that Magnus trusted him. He didn't even know the entirety of the fire god's plan. For the first time, the thought twisted his stomach. He took a step back.

Where is your faith? Magnus whispered. *Remember where you come from.*

Alrik's wide eyes and charcoal hair flashed in his mind. Glenna's smile as she'd sing shanties she'd heard in the harbor. He'd never forget where he came from, even if he didn't know where he was going. He grabbed the doorknob and opened the door.

The stormblood and the archer stayed closed behind Jaron as they made their way through the aisle of lit lanterns and candles, stepping over piles of wax and discarded scrolls.

"Something feels off," Lorelei whispered to the archer. "I don't like it here."

"This will be over soon," the archer whispered back. "Don't worry. I'll protect you."

Jaron tried his best to ignore them, but his sinking guilt wouldn't let him. He took a deep breath and entered the room at the end of the hall.

Turncoat sat in the same chair, but with a different feathered hat. This time he was not alone. Two other men stood behind him, swords at their waist, their expressions holding a promise of violence.

"Ahh, you've finally returned," Turncoat said, a smile twisting beneath his mustache. "He'd told me you were nearly here." His gaze went past Jaron to the stormblood and the archer who followed in the room behind him. "And you've brought not one, but two? Magnus chose well when selecting his champion."

A gasp rose out of Lorelei. It was so sudden and sharp, Jaron spun to look at her, assuming she'd been hurt. Hate filled her shocked expression as she looked past Jaron at Turncoat. He glanced to the archer who wore the same face, only deadlier.

"You . . ." she said, her voice trailing off.

Jaron's mind couldn't keep up. How did these two know this man?

In his confusion, he didn't see the archer reach for his obsidian sword. In a single breath, she unsheathed it from his waist and pointed it at Turncoat.

"You wretched coward," she said through her teeth. "You've been hiding from us this entire time."

Jaron glanced between the two of them, trying to understand what was going on. He looked to the two men behind Turncoat, their hands at their own swords, ready to attack if necessary. Jaron focused on the archer, eyeing his obsidian sword in her hands and hoping that she didn't turn it on him.

"Think this through," Jaron told her calmly, his hands splayed in surrender. "You're outnumbered." He glanced at the stormblood, whose face had gone white. "Think of Lorelei," he said quietly.

"What are you mumbling about over there?" Turncoat said. "Give Jaron back his sword already. I swear you and Miss Storm no harm."

"You lot and your promises of no harm," the archer sneered. "If not now, it will only be a matter of time." She took a long glance at Lorelei, then sighed in defeat. She shoved the hilt of the sword into Jaron's hand and he took it.

"Don't think I've forgotten what you've done," Lorelei said, her tone dark. "I'm not that powerless girl anymore." Her eyes flickered with blue and gold, but it was gone in an instant.

"Keep calm," Jaron said close to her ear. "If you lose control here, you put everyone in danger."

"I don't care," she said under her breath. "This man murdered my mother. He plotted to have me killed. I deserve my vengeance."

Revenge. Wasn't that what he was after? It didn't feel fair that he could be allowed his vengeance and she could not, but he knew that it would tear her apart if she hurt her friend while trying to attain it.

"Even if it means hurting the archer?"

The stormblood took a deep breath through her nose and closed her eyes. He was proud of the progress she'd made in the past couple of days, letting go of her magic and filling the sails with wind and reeling it back in. It was easier and easier to her each time, and now she was able to calm her storm before it unleashed.

He wasn't sure how much longer he could control himself though. He felt like a man on a journey without a map. He wanted answers *now*.

"Who are you really?" Jaron asked, facing Turncoat. "I want the truth, not the riddles you speak in."

Turncoat settled back in his chair, his face seemingly amused. "Very well." He curled his fingers into a fist and admired the silver rings he wore. "My name is Dominic Rove. Does the name ring a bell?" He glanced at Jaron, waiting for a reaction.

Jaron remembered the parchments on the walls of the forts he'd visited over the years. The lists of wanted pirates and the captains of the fleet crews. The name Dominic Rove had always been at the top.

"You were a captain of the fleet," Jaron said. "You're Cerulian." He struggled to keep up with how fast his mind was moving. "Why would you—why does my god trust you?"

"Aye," Rove said. "I was born there, but I found my beliefs more aligned with that of the Incendian kingdom and their gods. It isn't just those privileged enough to be born into a royal blood-line who hold their godly magic. Magnus and his brother, Vulcan, bestow their blessing on those they deem worthy."

"I'm well aware of how my people are gifted their embers," Jaron said. "This still doesn't explain why you would betray your nation."

Rove smiled. "Once Magnus is finally risen, then I will be blessed as an emberblood."

"You've always been weak," the archer said with disgust. "So weak, you'd betray us all to strengthen yourself."

"And Lorelei and her mother?" Jaron asked next. "What could possibly be your reason for wanting them both dead? Have you no honor?"

Rove was undisturbed by his questions. "It was a necessary death. Both of theirs were. It was their bloodline that trapped

Magnus in the first place and once it left this world, he would've been released. Those plans were thwarted when Miss Storm couldn't stay dead."

Jaron glanced to Lorelei. Tears brimmed in her eyes. There was so much he didn't know. He'd been such a fool.

"Wouldn't you do the same?" Rove asked, leaning forward and resting his elbows on his knees. He stared at Jaron as if he knew the conflict rising inside him. "If you were promised everything you ever wanted, would you do what needed to be done?"

The question nearly yanked Jaron's boots out from under him. If he could find Alrik . . . if he could somehow bring back Glenna . . .

I can, Magnus whispered. *I can ensure you will all be together again. It'sss only right after what was taken from you.*

Rove gave Jaron a nod of understanding.

"Jaron," Lorelei said, nudging him. "Whatever you're thinking, you're not like him."

Yet he was.

He glanced at Lorelei, feeling the archer's eyes on the back of his head. "What would you do to see your mother again?"

Her chin wobbled. He knew she was thinking it over in her head.

"You would do nothing like this," the archer interrupted, pulling Lorelei's attention away from him. "Your heart is kind and gentle."

But Lorelei's expression remained unchanged.

"Why are we even here?" the archer asked Rove, ice in her tone. "What do you want from Lorelei?"

"The Storm is always the key," Rove responded, glancing at Lorelei. "And it looks like you've trained her well, Jaron. I can practically feel the storm wanting to burst out of her, yet we're all still unburnt."

"It was your plan all along?" the archer said quietly, her gaze not meeting Jaron's. "You made us believe you truly wanted to help."

"It's not what it looks like," he tried to say, but Rove clapped his hands.

"No more squabbling," he said. "We've already wasted enough time waiting for you to arrive. It's a shame we weren't able to chat further before our departure, but we might have time aboard the brig if you desire."

"I'd rather talk to the potatoes," the archer said, gaining a chuckle from Rove.

But Lorelei remained silent, her full attention locked on Rove. A dark storm brewed inside her and when she unleashed it, Jaron wasn't sure if anyone would be left standing.

CHAPTER NINETEEN
KANE

West Incendia
Late Rainrise

It had been two days since Lorelei's dot had stopped moving on the Serpent's map. They'd watched it stop momentarily in Icehaven before changing direction for West Incendia and now that it had made it there, it remained pinned. As small as the dot on the map was, Kane breathed a sigh of relief each time he saw it still on the map, unfaded.

Still alive.

The shores of West Incendia were swimming with the Incendian Navy. Brigs lined the shore, their Incendian flags waving in the wind.

"Thank Goddess we changed the flags," Arius said, his fists on his hips. He wore the dark uniform of the Incendian Navy, an emblem of flame over his heart that matched the flag that waved above them. "We'd be sunk by now if we hadn't."

"It was Flynn's idea," Csilla said, snapping her spyglass closed. "Why fight our way in when we could sneak in undetected?"

The brig they'd encountered was small, its crew full of recruits. It was sheer luck that no emberbloods or Scouts were onboard. While those Incendians remained marooned on an island strip, their uniforms and flag now served as a disguise for Kane and the crew to sneak into West Incendia.

The disguise didn't calm Kane's nerves as it did the others'. There was still too much at stake to let his guard down.

As they sailed into the harbor, the pit in Kane's stomach sank deeper. His gaze roamed over the harbor, or what was left of a harbor. The docks had been rebuilt recently since the wood was still fresh, but the ruins of what used to be remained untouched. Tents were spread throughout the rubble, Incendians crowding around fires. Behind it all was a sea of barren white trees.

And towering not much farther, a volcano with smoke pluming from its top.

Based on the map, Lorelei was inland, through the forest and near the volcano. They'd have to navigate through all the Incendians without being suspected first.

The ship came to a stop, a pair of men from Kane's *Iron Jewel* crew tying the boat to the docks. Kane gathered with the others in the center of the deck, hashing over their plan one last time before embarking. Nerves crawled up his throat and he tried to swallow them back down.

"I will not go with you, Blackwater," the Serpent said as they all prepared to leave the ship. "I cannot fight and my magic serves no purpose, so I will remain here."

"Very well," Kane said, with a nod.

"Since we are closer to the girl, it will be more difficult to track her on the map." He reached into his pocket and pulled out Lorelei's compass. "I've magicked this compass to guide you in tracking her farther."

The Serpent put the compass in Kane's hand. It didn't look any different, but it felt different somehow, warm to the touch. Kane glanced down at the compass face, watching as the arrow spun chaotically for a moment before pointing to the northwest.

"Thank you," Kane said.

"I hope you find her," the Serpent said.

"I do too," Kane said to himself, focusing out in the direction the compass pointed.

—

Kane led the group through the sea of Incendians scattered around the shoreline.

He held his compass casually, only checking it every so often to make sure he was continuing in the right direction. Incendians gathered in groups around their tents and fires, mumbling among each other. Here and there some of them would look up at the volcano as if they were waiting for something to happen.

"Is that a turkey leg?" Arius asked. "Do you think there is a market stall somewhere?"

"No," Flynn said, voice hushed. "Do you *see* a market here, Arius?"

"Well, then where did that bloke get the turkey leg? I'm nearly starved and it looks so juicy."

Kane spun on his heel, Arius nearly bumping into him from his sudden stop. "Who gives a shit about the turkey leg?" The wound in Kane's shoulder throbbed, the pain nearly buckling his knees. "We have more important things to worry about."

"Kane," Csilla whispered, grabbing his arm, her gaze fleeting over the surrounding Incendians. "You're drawing attention."

Kane immediately stood straighter and turned back around, glancing down at the compass again. He continued on and the rest of the group quickly followed.

By some goddess-given miracle, they made it through the Incendians without drawing more suspicious glances and entered the barren forest just on the outskirts of the ruins. The trees reminded Kane of bones chewed clean—only white spokes jutting out of the ground. He stopped, taking a momentary break and assessing the area.

Arius kept peeking over his shoulder, to the left and right, as restless as a squirrel. "If we all had our own personal hell," he said, his voice small, "this would be mine. What in Goddess's name happened to these trees?"

"I'm sure Borne would tell us," Flynn said, "if he were here."

"The trees are dead," Rosalina said, her voice quiet as she stepped out from behind the shadow of her twin. Her ringlets were tied at the back of her neck. "The whole forest is."

"I've never seen dead trees that looked like this," Flynn said, surveying the trees surrounding them.

"They probably didn't die of natural causes," Serafina chimed in. "There is a poison that does the same thing to a human body."

"Poison the *trees*?" Arius asked. "Who would do such a thing?"

Flynn rolled his eyes at his comrade and laughed. "I would place my bet on the same god who torched his own land to try to win a war. You do know this continent used to be the Incendian mainland, right?"

A group of voices came in from the east, catching Kane's ear.

"Look alert," Kane said, his hand going to his sword as he faced the sound of the voices.

A group of Incendian soldiers emerged from the trees. Kane didn't even have to count them all to see that his group was clearly outnumbered. The soldiers' eyes fell on Kane and the crew, the largest and most important-looking one leading the parade toward them. They stopped in front of Kane, the one in front speaking to him with a stern expression.

"Is there a reason your squad is here?" he asked, his gaze traveling over the group and the Incendian uniforms they wore.

"I told you our patrol was stretching too far," Flynn said from beside Kane, giving Kane an elbow to the ribs.

"Don't stray far from your designated patrol. When one of our brigs didn't show up yesterday, rumors started about pirates slipping in." His eyes raked over them all again. "Do be sure to keep your sights aware of any suspicious individuals."

"Will do, sir," Kane said with a nod, hoping he was able to mask his distaste for the words. "We will be on our way then."

Kane turned back the way they'd come, the rest of the crew following behind him. He glanced down at his compass, the arrow pointing in the opposite direction. They didn't have time to find a way around the Incendians.

"We have no choice," he said quietly to Csilla as they continued to walk away. "We have to go through them. We'll have to fight."

"But they outnumber us," Csilla replied. "And they looked much more experienced than those recruits we came upon."

"There is no other option." Kane grabbed the hilt of his sword as he slowed his pace. He would do whatever it took to get to Lorelei.

Kane suddenly got a whiff of mint. He stopped and turned

toward Serafina, who had slid over next to him. She stopped chewing on her mint leaves as she spoke. "What if, instead of fight them, we make them fight each other?" Her eyes gleamed mischievously.

"Have you tested the darts out yet?" Csilla asked.

"Not yet." Serafina shrugged. "But what better time than now? If they don't work, we have to fight them anyway, right?"

"Use them," Kane said decisively. "Quick, before we rouse any more suspicion." He snuck a glance over his shoulder, watching the Incendians continue to walk away.

Serafina and Rosalina got their darts ready in a snap, loading them into one of the pistols they carried at their hips.

"What in Goddess's name?" Arius's voice trailed off as he watched them work quickly and efficiently, loading the darts into the barrel of the gun. "What did you do to that gun?"

Flynn's gawk matched Arius's. "It's nearly criminal."

Serafina pointed the barrel toward the Incendians, narrowing one eye as she aimed. "Shut your traps and watch the magic, boys."

She pulled the trigger, but there was no bang. Only a *whoosh* as the dart burst out of the gun. Kane was unable to tell if she'd made her mark, until one of the Incendians at the back of the group stumbled to a stop. The men by him questioned him and he shook his head. Then all of a sudden, he unsheathed his sword and started swinging on his comrades.

"I'll be damned," Arius marveled. "What the blazes was on that dart?"

"A serum we cooked up in our father's laboratory that causes the mind to hallucinate for a certain period of time," Rosalina said as she took her own aim at the Incendian troop and shot. "This batch, specifically, we mixed in grimlock berries as an irritant."

Kane remembered one of the many times he'd surveyed a wild

island with his father. One time in particular he'd watched a man nearly die from eating too many of the grimlock berries he'd picked while trekking through the jungle. If he'd eaten a few more, the massive blood-clotting they caused would've turned him as purple as the berries. Whatever morbid concoction the twins had brewed up with those berries had the men hallucinating and attacking each other. He reminded himself to never piss off the twins.

Serafina shot one more dart. "That's all we've got," she said as she tucked her gun back into its holster. The Incendian soldiers were in a complete frenzy, not knowing who had been compromised and who was still sane. The leader who'd spoken to Kane shifted his focus from left to right, unable to protect himself from all sides and unsure who to attack. As the skirmish continued, Kane and the crew moved through the trees, remaining undetected while the soldiers remained occupied and distracted.

No one yelled after them or chased them. A weight lifted off Kane's chest, but his shoulder throbbed, the pain reaching past his ribs and up his neck. He gritted his teeth, breathing deeply through his nose as he gripped his shoulder. He checked his compass again, following the path of the arrow that pointed straight ahead. If he could just ignore the pain a little bit longer, if he could just get to her and make sure she was okay, it would all be worth it.

"Blackwater," Flynn said, his voice not holding its usual teasing tone. "Your neck. Your veins, they—"

Kane pulled his collar closer, knowing that the spreading of his wound must have been visible. He'd felt it swimming up his veins as the pain surged. The black veins probably crept up all the way to his jaw now.

"Kane," Csilla said, coming close and inspecting his neck. "What is this? What's happening to you?"

"This is from that wound, isn't it?" Flynn said, pressing the issue. "You said you had it under control."

"I did!" Kane yelled. He'd let the wound get the best of him again as he lashed out. He tried to quiet his voice, but the venom still lingered. "I *do* have it under control."

"Doesn't seem like it, mate," Arius said. "Seems like you're in denial."

Kane shook his head. "Don't start with me, Pavel."

"I'm not the one with black veins crawling up my neck."

"We don't have time for this!" Kane's fists shook at his sides. "I don't care about my wound. I don't care about whatever the Incendians are planning on this goddess-forsaken continent."

Truthfully, he didn't want any of them to care about him. He deserved whatever fate held in store for him after the acts he'd committed and the lives he'd ruined.

Caring about anything that didn't bring him strength or power was something he'd thought foolish. He'd stopped letting himself devote his heart to anything since his mother died. He hadn't thought himself worthy of caring or being cared for in a long time.

Until he'd met Lorelei.

"I care about one thing." Kane winced and took a step forward. "And she is out there." Another step. "And I will find her."

He waited for Arius to jab at him or for Flynn to say something to change the conversation as they both typically did, but instead they both walked with him. The silence in their support spoke louder than any words they could have said in that moment.

The rest of the crew followed as they made their way through the white forest with Kane's compass leading the way.

CHAPTER TWENTY

LORELEI

West Incendia

Late Rainrise

The air smelled like rotting eggs.

Jaron said it was sulfur from the volcano, but Lorelei didn't know if she believed him or anything he said anymore. He'd come down to talk to them many times during their voyage to this place, speaking to them through the bars of their cell on board the Incendian brig. He truly was one of them; if he wasn't, he would have let her and Nara out.

Nara was exceptionally cold toward him, never once looking him in the eye each time he visited. Lorelei wondered if something had happened between them that made this feel like more of a betrayal, but Nara wouldn't say much.

"There are two sides to every coin," she had said one night as they watched the candle flame flicker out in the lantern above their cell. "I thought maybe he'd realized that." When Lorelei had tried to press her further, Nara shut her down. But Lorelei knew her friend was speaking of Jaron.

Jaron stayed near them when they docked in West Incendia and during their trek through the ruined forest. Even now at their encampment at the base of the volcano, Jaron remained at their side. He was personally guarding them, making sure they didn't get away, but Lorelei had a feeling that he was also protecting them, even if he wouldn't acknowledge it.

Lorelei sat on the barren ground next to Nara, both of them tied to a post. Jaron stood a few paces away, watching as Rove's men patrolled.

Torches circled the area, their flames dancing in the wind. Rove spoke with a man in special robes ordained with symbols of flame. A priest? Nerves twisted in Lorelei's gut. A line of hooded figures stood behind him, their faces cast in shadow.

"What do you think is happening?" Lorelei whispered to Nara.

"I'm thinking they're preparing for some sort of ritual," Nara replied. "I would bet that the volcano, the priest, and Magnus are all related."

"The volcano is sacred," Jaron said, his gaze remaining forward as he spoke to them. "It was raised from the ground by Magnus and Vulcan themselves."

"For what purpose?" Nara asked. "Isn't this the very volcano that made this land barren?"

"New life will bloom here in time."

"This land has been deserted since the Old War. You continue to lie to yourself."

"Do you question my faith, archer?"

"Enough," Lorelei said, tired of their squabbling. The unease in her veins was enough to make her feel seasick. "Tell us what's going to happen to us, Jaron. We deserve to know at least. Please."

"I do not know his plans for you," Jaron said with a sigh. "Only that you will remain safe."

"Are they . . ." Lorelei swallowed and glanced to the priest and the hooded people. "Are they going to free Magnus?"

Jaron turned and faced them. He crouched down, his elbows on his knees as he clasped his hands together. Lorelei noticed he wore his gloves again, covering his scars. She hadn't realized he'd stopped wearing them around her and Nara on the ship. Was that confliction she saw in the depths of his eyes?

"That's always been the plan," he said. "Magnus never should have been locked away in the first place."

"He started a war because he was rejected," Nara said, her face tilted up at the sky as if she was uninterested in anything Jaron had to say.

Jaron shook his head. "Cerulian history is wrong."

"The only thing that you know how to do is lie."

Lorelei tried to remember her life back in Incendia and what she knew of the history she'd learned while living among the harbor-folk. Her mother's stories had always been filled with other parts of the world—krakens and ice dragons, bandits and pirates—never any bit of magic from Incendia, only how they devour like the flame they worship. The devotion to their gods, however, could be seen from miles away when the light from their flame festivals shone so brightly.

Lorelei narrowed her eyes at Jaron, trying to understand. She remembered the story that Kane had told her about the love between Magnus and the Sea Sister, Anaphine. "Magnus wanted Anaphine to leave everything behind to be with him," she now told Jaron. "He couldn't bear a life without her."

"Among other things. Magnus also wanted to change the realms, to create a new one where immortals, mortals, and all creatures could live together and prosper."

Lorelei could understand how a nation could easily rally behind a cause such as that. Many would forget the atrocities their kingdom had committed as long as their crops remained bountiful and their lives comfortable.

"I have met your god," Lorelei said, "and I promise you, he is not as holy as you believe him to be."

Jaron winced, his eyes snapping shut for a minute. It was almost like he was in pain, but then his gaze darted around the scene, never staying in one place for too long. She recognized that behavior. She'd seen it on Rhoda in the jungle when she'd tried to kill her on Crossbones.

"He's whispering to you right now," Lorelei said, making Jaron's attention snap back to her, "isn't he?"

A battle raged behind Jaron's stare.

"He's using you," Lorelei continued. "He's been using you this entire time and you haven't been able to see it. What has he promised you?"

Jaron's eyes flashed and the air surrounding her suddenly felt hotter. "You have no idea what you're talking about," he said through his teeth.

"You're scared," Nara said. "She's right and it terrifies you."

Jaron stood back up, his fingers curling into fists at his sides. "I will no longer listen to the mind games you two play."

"The time is now," Rove called to Jaron. "Come!" He turned to the men patrolling the area. "Let us witness the second coming of our god."

Lorelei's heart clawed its way up her throat. She had to do something. She had to stop this from happening. If Magnus was unleashed, nothing would be able to stop the Incendians from conquering everything. As Jaron walked away toward the gathering group, Lorelei pulled at her binds.

"It's no use," Nara said. "I've already tried."

A gust of air left Lorelei. She knocked her head against the post as if she could force an idea. *Nothing*. There was nothing she could do except watch the unthinkable happen. She sighed, willing herself not to cry.

Something brushed against her wrist and she nearly screamed until she heard a voice in her ear.

"Don't scream, it's me."

Even though it was hushed, she'd know that voice across any sea. Lorelei glanced to her left to see Nara being cut loose by Csilla. As soon as Lorelei's wrists were free, she scrambled from the post and threw herself into Kane's arms.

"You're here," she said quietly, her voice wobbly. "You're here."

She'd told Kane not to follow her, yet here he was, and she'd never been more grateful that he didn't listen to her. He'd come. And this made her feel more treasured than she ever had before. She didn't even want to let go of him, afraid that if she did, she'd never get him back again.

"We have to get out of here," Kane said, grabbing her hands and pulling her. "Before their distraction fades."

Magnus.

They couldn't leave. Not yet.

"No," Lorelei said, stopping in her tracks. "We have to stop them."

"There's too many of them," Kane said quickly, looking past her.

"They'll see us at any minute and we'll all be prisoners. Let's go."

Then Kane went still.

"Well, well, well," Rove said, his voice carrying across the distance to them. "Look what the tide's washed in."

Kane suddenly seemed like he didn't want to leave anymore. "Rove," he said, a growl in his voice.

"It's good to see you too, mate." Rove tipped his feathered hat at him. "I'm truly glad you were able to make it to the show, and you brought the whole crew with you. Including the Queen of Bones. Impeccable timing, if I might add."

"Don't do this, Rove," Kane said.

"But it's already begun," Rove said with a wicked smile.

The hooded figures and the priest behind Rove had their hands splayed and pointed up at the mountain. Flames covered their skin from wrist to fingertip, burning brightly as they recited words in a language Lorelei had never heard. Emberbloods. But what were they doing?

"You see," Rove said, "when you lot brought back Miss Storm, you failed to fully seal Limbo. I'm sure you've noticed an odd creature or two causing havoc. They were lucky enough to escape, but Magnus couldn't leave so easily. He needs a bit more . . . firepower." He chuckled at his own sick joke as he motioned to the emberbloods. "Can you believe Incendians are so devoted to their god, they're willing to give up their own magic to return his strength?"

Lorelei's hand went to her mouth, imagining what would happen once Magnus gained their sacrificed power. If they couldn't stop this, and they couldn't fight because of the numbers, then they had to at least try to get away. Perhaps they could at least survive and figure out what to do next.

"Ah," Arius said. Lorelei braced himself for whatever it was he was about to say. "But don't you have to have a vessel for Magnus? Where's that emberblood with the obsidian sword?"

Vessel?

"Vessel?" Jaron asked, looking from Arius to Rove. "What is he talking about, Rove?"

"Arius," Kane said under his breath. "For once I'm glad for your nosy trap."

"I'll take that as a compliment, Blackwater," Arius said with a smirk.

With Rove and Jaron both distracted, now was the perfect time to try to make a break for it. There had to be a way for them to cause even more confusion before they tried to slip away. If only they couldn't be seen . . .

Lorelei closed her eyes and took a deep breath through her nose, thinking about the morning fog back on her mother's farm. How the cloud would cover the land from the cottage to the wheat fields. She breathed out through her nose, imagining the mist forming with the release of her breath.

Gasps echoed around her and she slowly opened her eyes. A thick cloud covered the area.

"Lorelei," Kane said, his expression full of wonder as he looked at her. "Was that you?"

"I've learned a few things," she told him. "We have to get out of here. Now."

"Get them!" Rove yelled through the mist. "Don't let them get away! Bring me back the Storm and the Queen of Bones alive!"

The group turned and ran back toward the trees, the yells of Rove's men getting closer and closer. The fog was thick, making it hard to see, and Lorelei and Kane quickly became separated from the rest. Lorelei knew they'd reached the forest line when they nearly ran into one of the white trees.

"Kane," Lorelei said, pulling him to a stop. "Wait. Let's wait for the others first."

A gunshot echoed, followed by the clanging of steel.

"Rove's men found them first," Kane said. "Let's go."

They turned in the direction of the fight, but men emerged from the fog in front of them, their swords drawn. Kane unsheathed his own sword and blocked the first attack, knocking the man to the ground before the next one barreled in.

Lorelei took a step back, feeling useless. She wanted to be useful. She *needed* to be useful. Kane grimaced as he swung his sword each time. Something was off about him. It was almost like he was in pain.

He lifted his sword again to counter another attack, but each movement was becoming slower and slower. Another man came in from the right and his sword clashed with Kane's, the two of them standing off, their swords crossed. The man started pushing in on Kane, gaining traction. One wrong movement and Kane would be hurt.

Curling her fingers, Lorelei thought about what it was like to fill the sails of Jaron's ship. She envisioned pulling the wind into her fingers like it was as pliable as dough, gathering what she could before letting it burst from her fingertips. Her magic flooded out of her like a cork out of a bottle, making the man fly backward into the fog.

Kane turned to look at her. Shock painted his expression at first, then a smile split his lips. "Look at you," he said with approval. "You controlled your storm, I see."

Her heart swelled as she looked at him. But then she noticed the black veins creeping out past the collar of his shirt and onto his jaw. She rushed toward him, her fingers tracking the vein at his jaw.

"What happened to you?" she asked. Her voice trembled, but she couldn't hide the fear she suddenly felt deep inside.

"It's nothing," he said, shaking his head.

"Show me."

Kane sighed in defeat and yanked at the buttons of the Incendian uniform he wore. The veins webbed over his chest and disappeared under the fabric, but in the place where his chest met his shoulder was a long black gash.

"How did it get this bad?" she asked, her voice nearly failing her.

"I had more important things to worry about," he said, looking into her face.

Another attacker sprang at them from the fog and Lorelei quickly blew them back. Kane blocked another from his left, kicking the man in the chest so that he stumbled into the mist. Lorelei pummeled the men with wind each time they appeared, her wind blowing fiercer each time. Two men came in from either side and she pushed her hands out at her sides, sending their bodies flailing and disappearing into the fog. One man she launched clear into the air before slamming him back down into the ground with a gust of wind from above.

She'd never felt more *powerful*.

She could keep going and going and going.

Someone was calling her name, but she couldn't hear them over the roar of wind in her ears.

Lightning flickered at her fingertips. One little zap and she could roast these men. *Every last one of them.*

"Lorelei!" came the voice again. Hands gripped her shoulders and forced her to turn. She looked up at Kane, his gunmetal eyes swimming as he looked down at her. His hands slid up to her face, cupping her cheeks. "Lorelei. Come back to me."

"Kane?" she asked, confused. "I'm right here."

"You were gone," he said, his gaze reminding her of when she'd woken up from Limbo. "Your eyes were lightning. The gold . . . it's spread all the way up your arms now." Kane surveyed her face as if he was searching for something out of place. "And when you were fighting those men. When you hurt them. You were smiling."

"You're scared of me," she said. She'd seen it on his face that night by the fountain, same as she saw it now. Full of fear.

"Lorelei," Kane said, taking a step closer. "I'm not scared of you. I'm scared *for* you."

Her lip quivered and she swallowed down the lump in her throat. He was right. Something had happened a moment ago when she'd fully embraced the storm inside her. She'd enjoyed the power coursing through her veins, but now that she looked back on it, fear welled up inside her too.

She'd only used her storm like that to protect Kane. But what else would she do willingly if it meant protecting those she loved?

"So am I," she finally admitted to him.

Before she could say anything else, an anguished cry ripped through the air. By instinct, Lorelei took off toward the sound, unprepared for what waited beyond the mist.

CHAPTER TWENTY-ONE
CSILLA

West Incendia

Late Rainrise

Chaos descended upon them like a sea storm.

One moment they were in front of Rove and his men, the next they were running through the mist of a cloud. Her ankle throbbed as she ran, making her slower than the rest of the crew, but Flynn stayed with her, never leaving her alone.

The shouts of Rove's men continued to get closer until they started to burst through the mist behind them. Flynn turned and shot his pistol.

"Keep going!" he yelled to her. "I'll hold them off."

Csilla turned around to face the men emerging from the fog one by one. "I won't let you die for me," she said, unsheathing her sword.

Steel clanged as her blade stopped an attack. She pushed his sword away and kicked the side of his knee, making him buckle and crumble to the ground. Another man took his place. The tip of his sword pointed right at Csilla as he ran toward her. She sidestepped his attack and sliced her sword as he passed, cutting him down.

Next to her, Flynn held his pistol in one hand and his half-sword in another. After dodging an attack, he hit the man in the temple with the end of his gun, knocking him out.

Csilla peered through the cloud, hoping to see one of her allies, but only more of Rove's men emerged from the fog. There were too many of them. Without the mist to help mask them, Csilla and the crew probably would have been dead or captured quickly. She'd only wondered briefly where it came from. Lorelei must have figured out how to use her storm. But she remembered Lorelei's panic that night on the balcony. Her fearful confessions about the dark influence of her magic.

"Looks like you lot need some assistance," Arius said as he slid in next to Flynn.

"It's about time you showed up, mate," Flynn said, aiming his pistol and shooting. "Was beginning to think you'd run off."

"And miss all the action?" He put his pistol into his holster and unsheathed his sword instead. "Absolutely not."

More men barreled through the fog toward them, their swords high. Flynn shot the first one down and Arius intercepted the second with a counterattack. Csilla gripped the hilt of her sword with both hands as a man wielding an oversized axe lurched toward her. He stood taller than all three of them, his arms thick enough to be a weapon on their own. He smirked at Csilla. She glanced over at Flynn and Arius, who were both in their own duels.

"You're coming with me," he said.

"I take orders from no one," she replied. She squared up to him then, pointing her sword at him as she looked up from under her brow.

"The boss said you're needed alive, but perhaps there will be an accident." He smiled widely, exposing one of his missing teeth.

"Then stop talking and swing your axe already."

His smile was quickly replaced by a scowl as he gripped his axe tighter. Csilla was already prepared for his attack, having observed him and the way he'd held his axe while he spoke. The axe swung in hard and heavy from the right. All in one movement, Csilla dropped and rolled to the left—the axe slicing the air above her—and rolled up onto her knee. She swung downward with her sword, slicing the back of his arm.

As he stumbled back and yelled, Csilla quickly rose to her feet and went on the offensive. She swung toward his side, her blow blocked with his axe, and she swept low and he dodged, but each attack from Csilla had him falling back.

He stepped forward and reared his axe up above his head. Csilla burst forward, running full speed toward him. Her ankle protested but she gritted her teeth and barreled into him before he could swing his axe down. They both fell back and his axe clattered to the ground.

Csilla scrambled up onto her feet while he reached for his axe, but she was closer. Before his fingers could scrape the handle, Csilla stomped on them with the heel of her boot. His pain-ridden face looked up at her, the color draining from it when Csilla pointed her sword at him, the sharp tip dangerously close to his wide eyes.

"Careful now," Csilla said softly, watching as the brute held his breath. "We wouldn't want an accident now, would we?"

He looked up at her, then to his axe beyond his reach. It took him only a moment longer to decide he'd lost. He scrambled back from her and up onto his feet, not sparing a glance in her direction as he retreated back into the fog.

The clanging of others' steel continued on around her. She glanced to see Arius still dueling with the same man. But where was Flynn?

"Csilla!" came Flynn's frantic voice. "Watch out!"

She looked in his direction just a moment before he threw himself in front of her. He jerked to a stop. The clang of steel faded away. The yell from the man on the other side of Flynn was muted, like he was underwater. Like they were all underwater. Csilla only heard the shuddering sound of Flynn's breath.

The man on the other side pulled his sword back and up into the air, its tip coated in blood. Flynn leaned back into Csilla and she slid her arms under his, hugging him from behind as more of his weight fell into her. She looked over his shoulder at the man, who aimed his sword for his next strike at them.

Arius lunged in from the side, cutting the man down before he struck. He quickly turned and looked at Flynn, his face paling as his eyes traveled down to the wound Csilla hadn't seen yet.

Csilla struggled with Flynn's weight as he leaned into her farther. Arius rushed to Csilla, helping her get Flynn to the ground. She angled Flynn's head on her lap and she brushed his hair out of his face. His skin was already pale, his lips losing their color. Her gaze trailed down his body, stopping on the pool of blood spreading across his abdomen. She pushed her hand against the wound, clinging to the last bit of hope she had that if she applied some pressure, she could buy time. But time for what? Arius stood back up, swinging his sword as he warded off another attacker. He fought him off, screaming as he barreled toward the one who came next.

Flynn's blood seeped through Csilla's fingers.

Time was fickle. Just like a life.

She turned back to him, her hands shaking, tears welling in her eyes.

"Flynn," she said, her voice breaking off into a sob. "It's okay. It's okay." Tears freely streamed down her face. "Everything is going to be okay."

She couldn't lose someone else she loved. Not like this. *Not like this*. She could fix him. She could save him. If only she could—

Flynn's hand cupped her cheek, his thumb wiping away her tears. Her gaze found his, the sea of his eyes shimmering at her.

"Do you remember"—Flynn coughed, his breath short—"that night I found you in the rose garden?"

Csilla held his hand against her face, leaning into his touch. She nodded. "Of course I do." She smiled through her tears. "It's one of my favorite memories."

"Then I've won," he said, the fragility of his smile nearly causing Csilla to break even further. "If I've left you with good memories"—he paused, taking another breath—"then I've won."

Even in his final moments, he tried to paint Csilla's canvas yellow instead of gray. Every shared moment of theirs swept past her memories. From their nights together to their banter in the jungle on Crossbones. The fire in his gaze when he told her that he loved her. She'd never get lost in the sea of his eyes again.

She leaned forward, the realization making her unable to hold herself anymore. She rested her forehead against his. "Don't leave me," she pleaded. "There's still so much I have to say to you."

He nuzzled his face against hers. "Shh." It was a sound she could barely hear. "I'll find you again. Tell me then."

She nodded, biting her lips to keep from sobbing as she held his face with her hands. He closed his eyes then, his breathing shallow. She pressed her lips against his, feeling his last breath leave him.

If only she could go back to that night in the rose garden. If only she could accept his love then and there. She knew more than anyone that just like roses, all things die.

"Don't go," Csilla whimpered, pulling him up into her arms and cradling his head against her chest. "Don't go, don't go, don't go." The words all jumbled together. "I love you."

She looked up, searching for someone, *anyone*. Arius's gaze found hers. Blood was splattered across his face and he was breathing heavily, but no more men attacked. The sword fell from his hand as he dropped to his knees, his face twisting into a sob before he hit the ground. Csilla threw her head back and screamed, not recognizing the sound that came out of her.

CHAPTER TWENTY-TWO
JARON

West Incendia

Late Rainrise

As soon as the stormblood unleashed her cloud, Jaron knew they would all try to get away.

Except for the archer.

He knew that she would be coming for him amidst the chaos.

The emberbloods continued their ritual behind him, their words growing louder, the flames beginning to dim. Nearly all of Rove's men had run off into the fog, leaving only a couple back, including Rove himself. Not once did the man reach for the sword at his hip. Jaron began to think it was more of an accessory to him than a weapon he'd used, letting his men do all his dirty work for him.

With the reveal that the Turncoat was Dominic Rove and the emberbloods were sacrificing their magic, unease had taken root in Jaron, growing like a weed. Now was not the time to be doubting everything, but with the cards laid out in front of him, he didn't know what he stood for anymore. Only that he wanted to see his family again.

Movement in the mist.

Was it her?

His hand went to the hilt of his sword without a second thought. She'd snuck up on him so many times before; she could do so just as easily now, but this time there would be consequences for him.

A rushed footstep behind him.

Jaron turned just in time to dodge the archer's sword. It nicked his shirt, tearing at the fabric. He glanced down, making sure she hadn't gotten him, then back up at her.

"Caught you this time," he said, unsheathing his sword. "Are you getting reckless now, archer?"

Rove gasped. "Where did you come from?" He yelled for the few men who hadn't run off into the fog. "Get her, you fools!"

"No," Jaron said, waving them off. "I've got her."

"Busy yourselves and keep a watchful eye," Rove said to the three men. "We can't have anyone else sneaking up on us like that. The ritual is too important."

Jaron watched the archer carefully, waiting for her next move when a scream echoed through the dissipating fog. The sound clung to him, weighing him down from the pure despair in its tone. Figures moved through the fog in the distance, racing toward the scream.

"Csilla," the archer whispered. Jaron looked back at her, watching a range of emotions flicker over her face. "This has to end now." She turned toward the emberbloods, their backs completely unprotected.

He jumped forward as she raised her sword, knocking her blade aside before her swing could strike. "What are you doing?" he yelled at her.

"How many unarmed people will die when Magnus is freed?" the archer said. For a moment he thought he saw the glimmer of tears, but it was quickly replaced by a mask of pure hate. She moved to go around him and he stepped back in front of her. "How many more people will suffer?"

"But they are unarmed!" He held his sword at the ready as she angled hers once more. "Would you attack a defenseless person? I'd begun to think you all were better than that."

The archer hesitated. "You're right," she said. "Perhaps it's you that needs to die." She twirled her sword in her fingers as she stepped back, preparing to launch an attack on him.

His heart sank to his stomach.

"You are his vessel," the archer said. "What will Magnus do when you no longer exist?"

She attacked, her sword slicing low. He barely had enough time to nick her blade to prevent his thigh from getting sliced open. Her words muddled his mind and he didn't see her fist coming before it connected with his face. He stumbled back from the sudden blow and shook his head clear.

"I'm not his vessel," Jaron said. "I'm his champion. He chose me to wield this sword. *He chose me.*"

"He's using you," the archer said, repeating the words that Lorelei had said earlier. "He's been using you from the start. Can't you see that?"

She swung her sword and he countered, but she quickly attacked again, stabbed the air next to his head. His eyes followed the blade as she pulled it back.

After digging up this sword, after killing men he didn't want to kill, after everything he'd done, Jaron could not accept that he was being used. Magnus had promised him things that he would never be able to achieve on his own. When the nights were at their darkest and he was on the brink of giving up on becoming an emberblood all those years ago, it was Magnus who'd whispered to him and brought him back. It was he who had given him a purpose. His god wouldn't betray him.

He *couldn't* betray him.

Could he?

The silence in his mind was a trigger to a flame.

"You're holding back," he said to the archer. "If you want to kill me, then *do it already*!"

The two of them clashed, their swords crossing. He swiped her sword down and she came at him again, swinging high this time. Again and again she struck, her swipes and slashes becoming easy to predict. Their swords clashed in the middle once more. He made eye contact with her through their blades.

"You're still holding back," he said.

"I thought you were the chosen one," she said with a growl. "So, why haven't you killed me yet?"

Finish her, came Magnus's whisper. *You're thisss close to having what you desssire. Don't let her ssstand in your way.*

Flames danced up the obsidian blade of his sword. The archer seemed shocked at first, then her face set with determination. She lunged away, taking a new stance, daring him with her gaze to come at her.

He darted forward and their swords became a flurry of steel and flame. The archer moved just as quickly with a blade as she did with a bow, blocking each of his attacks and launching her own with ferocity. He knew that she'd be able to keep up with him, but seeing her in action like this for himself was more than he'd imagined. She didn't wield weapons. She *was* a weapon.

Their blades crossed once more, both of them pushing against the other. Her steel began to warp against the flames. The fire licked the archer's face, but she didn't pull away, continuing to push forward with all her strength.

Suddenly, she kicked his ankle out from under him, knocking him to the ground. His sword fell from his hand. She crawled on top of him and held her warped sword over his head. The side of her face was red from the flame. Her eyes filled with hate as she prepared to plunge her sword into him.

Yet, she hesitated.

Jaron used the opportunity to his advantage and rolled them both so that he was now on top of her. He reached for his sword and brought it between them as he lifted himself off her. She looked at him, her face a mixture of defeat and confusion.

"Why have you stopped?" she asked, desperation in her voice. "This is your chance. End me now and nothing is stopping you from getting what you want from Magnus."

He didn't respond. His mind was awash with so many conflicting thoughts.

"Why aren't you killing me? What's stopping you?"

He slowly lowered his sword, remembering the words she'd told him that night on the docks in Baltessa. "If I wanted you dead, you would be dead."

The archer paused for a moment, as if holding her breath. Then, like rainrise after a harsh frostfall season, her frost melted away. Her gaze softened, the harsh line of her mouth curving up into an almost smile.

He realized then that he wanted her to have more smiles. He wanted her to keep fulfilling her purpose. He wanted her to live.

The emberbloods' chanting stopped. He glanced over to them, watching as they each fell over limp to the ground.

The ritual.

"It's complete," the archer said, but he couldn't really hear her. When he glanced back at her, she wasn't looking at the ember-bloods or the volcano. Her worry was for him only.

The ground below him trembled.

At the same moment, he began to feel warm. No, *hot*. Something wasn't right. Heat radiated from his core, spreading through his veins like a wildfire, growing stronger, moving faster as the ground continued to shake.

Jaron understood then. They were *all* right. He *was* the vessel. Magnus had manipulated him specifically for this purpose and he'd been a fool. He suddenly felt sick, his face clammy. The ritual was already done. The volcano was actively rumbling. There was nothing he could do to stop what was already happening. His legs went weak, and he fell to his knees.

The archer crouched by him, putting her hands on his shoulders.

"I should have listened," he admitted, breathing raggedly. "I should have—"

The archer's hand slipped into his. She gave it a squeeze.

"I'm afraid." His voice cracked.

She looked at him softly again. "Try to stay with me. Maybe if you push Magnus aside, don't give him permission, he can't take over."

Jaron closed his eyes and tried to push the heat back, calling his own flames to him, but it was no use. Magnus was too strong. Jaron was only a mortal.

He thought of Alrik's curiosities and Glenna's smile once more. He thought of his growing fondness for the sea, and of the archer who hated him.

Jaron opened his eyes and looked at her. "Archer . . ." he said haltingly.

She gazed at him for a moment, a look of understanding passing over her face. She knew he'd lost his fight.

"Nara," she said, her voice softer than he'd ever heard it. "You can call me Nara."

Jaron nodded, swallowing back the lump in his throat. His voice was barely a whisper as her name left his lips and everything went black.

"Nara."

CHAPTER TWENTY-THREE

LORELEI

West Incendia

Late Rainrise

The earth shook under Lorelei's feet. She struggled to keep her footing and held on to Kane as they continued toward Csilla. Lorelei had known the scream had come from her, but she was afraid for what they'd find when they reached her. She'd heard a wail like that once before in her life, back in Port Barlow when a woman had found out that her husband hadn't survived a storm at sea.

As they got closer, Lorelei could see Csilla, but she was on the ground, holding something in her arms. *Someone.*

"Oh no," Kane said, as they stumbled to a stop.

Arius was on his knees in front of Csilla, both their sights on the person in Csilla's arms.

"Flynn . . ." Tears pricked at Lorelei's eyes. "He's—"

"He's gone," Csilla cried, holding him close.

The ground continued to shake, smoke billowing from the volcano's top. Lorelei glanced around; the fog was now completely gone. Serafina and Rosalina ran toward them. But where was Nara? Lorelei spotted her back by the enemy, next to someone hunched over on the ground. Past them, the hooded emberbloods lay motionless on the ground.

The ritual must have been successful.

"It's Magnus," Lorelei said. "He's coming."

The ground shook violently, causing them all to fall to the ground. An explosion ripped through the air and the quaking stopped. Lava suddenly spewed from the volcano's top.

"What is that?" Kane asked from the ground next to her.

She looked closer and watched as something flew out of the volcano. It spread its wings, lava flinging off it in all directions. A roar split the air as it stretched its neck.

"A dragon," Lorelei whispered, half-terrified, half-amazed. Her mother's stories had included ice dragons, but never any born from flame. She only knew that they were locked away in Limbo like the rest of the creatures.

But now it was free.

What else was slipping through the cracks at that moment?

"We have to go," Kane said, rising to his feet. Lorelei stood up with him. "*Now.*"

The dragon's wings completely unfurled as it made an arc, circling around toward them. Arius tried to get Csilla to stand up.

"Csilla," he pleaded, "we have to run. It's coming."

"I'm not leaving him," she said, her face as emotionless as stone.

"You'll die," Arius said, his voice pained.

"I said I'm not leaving him!"

Kane pulled at her arm to run with him, but the moment Lorelei turned, they were greeted with a wall of flame.

"Where do you think you're going?" called a familiar voice.

Lorelei slowly turned around. Jaron stood there; his hand splayed as he spread the wall of fire until it made a complete ring around the entire area. He walked toward them, motioning Rove and others to follow him down.

"You too, little archer," Jaron said with a smirk. Nara followed behind him, her eyes never leaving the back of his head. They descended down the small hill as the dragon flew toward them, steam rising off its massive wings.

Lorelei gripped Kane's arm as the dragon came closer. They were sitting ducks with nowhere to run. She held her breath as the dragon's shadow loomed over them, gusts of wind striking them as it beat its wings. Instead of attacking them, it came to a landing behind Jaron. Rove and the others scuttled out of its way, fear warping their faces. Nara ran over to them, falling to her knees beside Csilla.

But Jaron only turned and walked toward the dragon.

Its obsidian scales reflected the sunlight, and steam still rose from its body. Eyes the color of flames watched Jaron closely as he neared, his hand reaching forward and resting on the scales.

"Beautiful creature, isn't it?" Jaron asked, looking over his shoulder at them. "Wingspan longer than any ship. Scales tougher than any armor. Flames hotter than any emberblood's."

He turned around completely and clasped his hands behind his back. He still looked like Jaron with his short-cropped hair and his dark eyes. His voice still sounded like Jaron's, even and crisp. But the overconfident smirk that played on his lips was not his own. Lorelei had seen it before in Limbo.

Magnus had been successful. Jaron was now his vessel.

"Welcome to the New Realm," Magnus said. He took a deep breath, as if inhaling the scent of his burning flames surrounding them. Everyone remained silent, even Rove, who usually had plenty to say. "I am truly honored that you would travel all this way to witness my second coming."

Magnus's gaze roamed over the area, over everything, stopping over the line of sacrificed emberbloods for a moment. "I knew it would be easy, but I didn't expect it to be *this* easy. They were all given such a remarkable gift, yet so easily gave it up." He laughed. "All for the glory of serving me. Such simple mortals."

The emberbloods remained unmoving, not even a breath rising out of them. They'd not only given their magic, but their lives.

"And Jaron." Magnus raised his arms at his sides as if he was showing off new armor. "Maybe the easiest of all."

Lorelei thought about the Jaron she knew from their voyage. The one who'd never treated her cruelly despite their circumstance. The one who'd seemed to walk alone in life yet still tried to help and protect them until the last moment. In another world, in another scenario, would they have been friends?

She glanced over at Nara, who was seething while she sat with her arm around Csilla, watching Magnus parade Jaron's body around.

"He didn't ask for power or riches." Magnus chuckled. "I only had to promise a reunion with his long-lost brother. A brother who has been dead this entire time."

With his last words, Magnus flinched like something had stung him. His face paled and he swallowed, then shook his head like he was trying to get water out of his ears.

Lorelei had seen this same type of reaction from both Rhoda

and Jaron when they'd heard Magnus's whispers. There was a chance that perhaps Jaron was still in there with him. Perhaps after hearing the truth about his brother, he was fighting against him. This, however, would mean that Jaron was trapped inside him, aware of everything, but unable to move his own body.

Lorelei stood up, unable to listen any longer. "Jaron helped you!" she yelled at Magnus. "He had such faith in his god. Is this how you treat those who serve you?"

"Ah, it's the stormblood." Magnus smiled at her. He seemed pleased to see her. She wasn't sure why, considering she'd kicked his ass the last time they'd met. But this time it was different. This time he was in her realm. "I've kept my eye on you. You've made real progress since your time on Crossbones."

"I am stronger now," she said.

His smile stretched even farther. "You are. You've learned how to control the wind and I've witnessed what you can do with lightning. You've hurt people, even killed." He stopped for a moment, his eyes narrowing like he was recollecting something. "You still have much to learn, but you will be a great asset to my army."

"Army?" she spat out, the very idea leaving a terrible taste in her mouth. "Why would I join your army?"

"Think about how powerful you felt when you learned how to fill the sails with wind," he said, taking a step closer. "Think how strong and useful you felt when you fought those men with magic of your own." He continued walking toward Lorelei, focused entirely on her, his tone convincing. "I know your lightning frightens you, but imagine your power when you learn to fully control it. Imagine what it will feel like to be truly unstoppable. No one to tell you what you can and can't do. Join me and you will feel no greater power. You will never feel useless again."

Kane suddenly stepped in front of her. "This is what he does, Lorelei. You know this. He makes promises so that he can use you as his tool." He moved to withdraw his sword, but grasped at his shoulder instead. He fell to the ground, groaning in pain.

Lorelei knelt down and tried to help him back up to his feet again, but he didn't have the strength. He could barely even lift his head. The black veins crept farther, inching up his cheek to his temple. Her heart started to race faster as she watched him writhe.

"You could save him," Magnus said, pulling her attention back to him. He gazed down at Kane, lingering on the infected veins. "He doesn't have long. He was poisoned by the sword of a lost soul that escaped Limbo. The poison will soon take over and he will die."

"How?" Lorelei asked frantically. "How can I save him?" She couldn't save Flynn or Jaron from their fates, but if she could save just one person . . . If she could save Kane . . .

Kane groaned, saying something in protest, but she ignored him.

"Join me," Magnus said, simply. "Join me and I will save the pirate."

"No." Kane's voice was strained, like he couldn't get enough air. "Don't do it, Lorelei."

Lorelei had once been helpless as she'd waited under the floorboards while her mother was killed. But now she was the one with the power. She was the one who could change things. Magnus was twisted and evil and his plans for her were still unknown, but they couldn't be good. Carnage and destruction would follow his path and she would play her own role in it. Magnus had manipulated everyone else, but Lorelei was completely aware of the decision she was making. She knew the consequences that would follow.

But it would be worth it.

Her mother was gone. Friends of hers, gone. She glanced at Csilla, still holding Flynn in her arms. The life was gone from her face. Blood smeared on her hands.

Not one more person. She couldn't let one more person die.

"I'm not worth it." Kane looked up at her from the ground, his expression pleading. "I would rather die and have you be free."

"And I would rather watch you live." She straightened her back. "A world without you is not one I want to see. I would rather watch the world burn than know that I could have saved you and didn't."

"Lorelei, no!" Nara stepped forward. "Don't do this!"

Csilla snapped out of her stupor for a moment and called her name. Arius and even the twins joined in, but Lorelei drowned them out. The dragon behind Jaron growled in their direction, making them all hush again.

"I'll help you if you save Kane," Lorelei said. "You're a god, right? So, heal him."

"Of course," Magnus replied, a sly smile spreading across his lips.

"And you let all my friends leave this place alive."

He hesitated. "Anything else?"

Her attention fell back to Flynn. "Bring back Flynn."

Magnus shook his head and made a clicking sound with his mouth. "That is something I cannot do, stormblood. The boy's soul is already gone from this realm."

"Then allow us to take his body with us," Csilla said, her voice surprisingly even. Her eyes were swollen. "Let us give him a proper burial at sea."

Magnus sighed. "If that would please you, then so be it. Our partnership would be much better off as a mutual arrangement, don't you agree? Consider this a token of good intention, stormblood."

He turned away from her and looked at Kane, then pulled at the air with one hand. The black veins in Kane's skin started to recede, disappearing completely under the collar of his shirt as the color returned to his face. Kane blinked at Lorelei and stood up, fully healed from his wound, and relief flooded through her.

"Lorelei," Kane said, his eyes searching hers with a different kind of concern. "What have you done?"

Rove suddenly started to yell for his men to get in formation. "Grab any weapons and leave the dead behind. Bind the hands of the pirates behind their backs."

Lorelei spun back around on Magnus. "You said they would go free!"

He waved his finger at her. "I said they would leave. We said nothing about freedom." He looked past her toward Rove. "I did agree to them taking their dead friend though." He pointed to Kane and Arius. "Let those two carry the dead man. But watch them closely in case they try anything."

Kane took one long last look at Lorelei before joining Arius at Csilla's side. Lorelei couldn't watch as they pulled Flynn from Csilla's arms, leaving her looking down at the ground instead.

The entire land was barren, its soil brittle and dry, not a sign of green the entire time she'd been there. She glanced out at the white trees of the forest, no sign of life clinging to their dead bark—the destruction that Magnus had left behind when he'd last entered this realm.

"It's time to go, stormblood," Magnus said.

But her feet wouldn't move.

She'd done what she had to do, she told herself. Anything to keep her family safe. She took a step forward.

Jaron's question echoed in her mind, just as vivid as the day he'd asked it.

If you were promised everything you ever wanted, would you do what needed to be done?

If it meant protecting those she loved, she'd watch the world burn.

EPILOGUE

Flynn Gunnison cracked open his eyes little by little, like he was waking up from a long night with a bottle of rum. The sun was brilliant and blinding, its warmth welcoming on his skin, but it was too damned bright. He lifted his hand to shield his eyes, finally able to open them enough to see what tavern inn he'd found himself in this morning. But when his vision straightened, he realized he was in no tavern inn.

"Where the blazes am I?" he asked himself.

He lay on a beach, only the beach had the whitest sand he'd ever seen. Even whiter than the pearls Arius had found when deep diving by the coral reef in Ravana. He scooped up a handful, watching it spill through his fingers. He looked to the left and right, to the water washing in on the shore, as clear as glass, then back behind him to a row of white palm trees. It was as if someone had taken a brush and painted the whole world white.

He thought of Csilla and then everything replayed in his head. Sailing to West Incendia, fighting in the mist, jumping in front of that sword for Csilla.

Csilla. Goddess, she'd been so sad and all he'd wanted to do was make her smile again. But he couldn't.

He clutched his gut, remembering the pain, but when he looked down there was no blood. He lifted his white tunic to see no wound, no blood. Just his abs. He gave them a slap for good measure.

It was then he realized where he was. *Limbo.*

"Of course." He laughed to himself. "I guess I *am* a lost soul."

He dug his toes into the sand, the warmth feeling nice on his cool skin. He wasn't sure what he was supposed to do next. He supposed he could try to find a way to the other side to wait for Csilla one day. Maybe explore Limbo for a bit before. There was probably treasure galore hiding about this realm.

He looked up at the sky, wondering what he should do first when a shadow blotted out the sun. He blinked, taking in the silhouette of a person, then he saw an outstretched hand. His gaze traveled up the person's arm to their face, recognizing her immediately.

Her dark hair was pulled back and her expression was unreadable, even for a mastermind such as Flynn.

"I never thought I'd see you in all white," he said to her as he grabbed her hand and stood up.

"Shut up," Rhoda said. "We've got work to do."

Being your mom is the greatest blessing I've been given, even when you argue over the remote or see who can sing the loudest note for twenty minutes straight. You make every day beautiful . . . and eventful!

Mom and Dad, my gratitude for your endless support is something that I will never be able to adequately express. Thank you for always fostering my creativity as a child and making me feel like becoming an author was something that I could do and that any dream I had was reachable. When I came to you and said, "Hey, I'm going to start college with two young kids!" or "I know I'm in college and working, but I'm also writing this book!" you never once tried to caution me against taking the paths I'd chosen. Your guidance is what brought me to this destination today.

Mikayla, my sister, your inner strength inspires me and I'm so very proud of you. Laughing with you is something that always takes away any stress I have. Thank you for being there. Thank you for being you.

Francesca and Sonia, you are both amazing. You're still cheering me on, still talking out scenes and characters with me after all these years. I hope you didn't plan on getting rid of me, because you're kind of stuck with me now.

Kathleen, if it weren't for you, it would have taken me ages to get this book out of my head. You pushed me (delicately) and helped me find the words I couldn't express. Thank you so much for the time you spent supporting this journey. I am eternally grateful for you.

To the team at Wattpad, you're incredible. Regardless of how excited I was about this book, it was difficult for me to get out. You showed me such grace and patience during this time and I truly felt supported on so many levels. Austin Tobe, thank you for helping me keep my head on straight and for being the incredible supporter that you are. To Fiona Simpson, Deanna McFadden, Jen Hale, and to anyone else who had a hand in making this book an actual book, thank you, thank you, *thank you*!

Without you, this dream would've never been possible.

ABOUT THE AUTHOR

Kimberly Vale is a reader, a bit of a hopeless romantic, and started writing on Wattpad as a teen. In the years since then, she has accumulated millions of reads online. With a BA in education, Kimberly teaches remediation and dyslexia intervention in public schools and lives in Arkansas with her husband, two children, and two dogs. She also enjoys playing video games, trying new recipes, and coming up with ridiculous theories about her current TV obsessions. *Dark Tides* is the second book in the Kingdom of Bones trilogy, which began with *Crossbones*.

Turn the page for a preview of

BRIANNA JOY CRUMP

OF CAGES AND CROWNS

WATCH THE WORLD BURN.

Available November 2022,
wherever books are sold.

CHAPTER 1

Benson Homestead
Three days before Sacrit

I'd only just finished at the pump and was heading back to the house when I heard the crunch of tires on the gravel lane. *Shit.* I had enough sense to dart behind the nearest shelter—the outhouse—but as soon as I was there, my mind went blank.

I'd hidden, but now what? Where could I go with so much open space between where I stood and the main house? And it wasn't like I could really go inside either—what if whoever was in the automobile wanted to go into the house for something? They'd see me. They'd ask questions.

I needed . . . I needed to . . .

My heart plummeted, my insides doing a wicked backflip as I peered out from my hiding spot. Dust rose in a swirling cloud as an automobile headed our way. I scanned what I could of the yard, looking for my brothers.

Bad. This was bad.

Warning bells pealed; red flags waved.

What if they found me? That would almost be worse, because then they'd wonder why I'd hidden at all. Then, if they were anyone important—and they had to be, if they were driving an automobile in Varos of all places—they'd ask about my identification card. Goddess knows, they would see some pretty huge discrepancies if they did.

I was very obviously a blond, seventeen-year-old girl and not the boy my card claimed I was. And that discovery would lead to questions and those questions would lead to examinations. And if they noticed the mark on my hand . . .

The outhouse creaked as I leaned against it, careful to stay in the shadows. The rumble of the automobile's engine died out just as the front door to the house squealed open on unoiled hinges. My oldest brother, Ambrose, shouted a muffled greeting, but the words were lost in the sharp *clack* of the screen door slamming shut behind him as he exited the house.

My other brother, Kace, walked out of the barn to my far left, his brows lifted in surprise at the vehicle parked outside our ramshackle house. He headed toward Ambrose, but stopped in his tracks when he caught sight of me. For a moment we just stared at each other, both of us ensnared by curiosity and fear.

The stillness of the moment died as the man in the automobile called out, "Mr. Benson, I come with a summons."

Kace's eyes widened at the words, and he took off again. I glanced around the other side of the outhouse and then abruptly darted back into the safety of my hiding spot. *A magistrate. There was a magistrate here—on our farm. Only a few feet from me.* Bile rose in my throat and my heart became a caged bird in my chest—the pressure of each beat more valuable and more erratic as I considered every terrible thing that might involve a magistrate.

The distance enveloped the rest of the man's words as he climbed from the automobile and then began to, presumably, explain to my brothers what the hell he'd come for. I dared another look just in time to see Ambrose step forward to take a small bundle of letters from the magistrate's outstretched hand.

The magistrate cleared his throat and pulled a handkerchief from the pocket of his suit. He dabbed at his shining forehead, his voice growing loud with annoyance as he said, "Hot summer Varos is having. If the rains don't come soon, crops will suffer."

I knew exactly what he meant by that: if the crops suffered, the queen's coffers would suffer. You couldn't tithe the dead.

My throat grew tight at the implication. *More than just the crops would suffer without rain. My family could starve or lose the farm.* We relied on our crops to earn enough money to keep us alive. My mother's job as a midwife was rarely paid with coin, and my brothers' apprenticeships in town hardly even made enough to keep the livestock fed—much less put food in our bellies.

In recent years, the government hadn't been as tolerant with their collection of county tithe as they had in the past. And the tithe in Varos would come due in early fall whether we had the money or not.

"I will pray for rain," the magistrate said.

"Seems our prayers are as empty as our pockets these days." Ambrose tucked the letters into the back pocket of his trousers and fiddled with the strap of his suspenders. I winced at his boldness as he continued. "Too much rain and they drown. Too much sun and they fry. Varos always places its bets in extremes. Always too hot or too cold. Too wet or too dry. It's the people who lose every time."

Kace ran a hand through his light-brown curls and said, "Let's pray the goddess sees fit to give us both rain and shine in moderation."

I smiled to myself. The predictability of the response was enough to ease the tension in my body. Kace was nothing if not a kiss ass to government officials.

He was always so good at playing pious when it suited him, but I knew he visited brothels and did all manner of temple-forbidden things. Despite how he acted, I knew he couldn't name half of the Sanctus names or recite any of the official remembrances. But then, neither could I, so I supposed that didn't mean much.

In our defense, Mama wasn't religious at all and hadn't raised us to be. While I was fine being a little heathen, Kace had aspirations of becoming a royal guard one day—and, according to him, they were required to be pious, sanctimonious little shits. I didn't think he needed to practice that, but there he was, kissing ass like it was his job.

The magistrate tucked his handkerchief into his pocket and put his bowler hat back in place. "May the goddess be honored in your harvest."

"May the goddess be honored," Kace returned.

The man turned to leave, but he made it only two steps before Ambrose said, "Excuse me, Magistrate, sir? While I have you here: has there been any official word on when this part of Varos might be moved to higher lands? We've never had water so close to our property before. I worry that with the rains coming we will find ourselves overrun."

Whatever the magistrate said in response was covered by the rumble of the engine as he climbed into the vehicle and started it. *It's bad news.* I could tell by the way Ambrose fiddled with the rolled cuffs of his shirt; the way he seemed to hold himself back from arguing. His hands opened and closed at his sides.

Let him leave, I begged silently. *Let him get away from here before he decides to be curious.*

And what was there to say? Each year the eastern floodlands took more and more Varos territory. The sea was literally washing away our county, bit by bit. And each passing year brought the coastline closer to our farm. If we didn't get the official clearance to move, either to a higher spot in Varos or to a different county, our property would eventually be drowned, and we would be homeless. Hundreds of others had already suffered that fate and the queen had done nothing to save them.

I stayed hidden behind the outhouse as the automobile puttered its way down the path to our house and around the far tree line. Ambrose's back was to me as he watched the man drive away, but once he was gone, Kace turned and met my gaze. He looked pointedly at the letters sticking out of the back of Ambrose's trouser pocket and raised a brow.

Dread pooled in the pit of my stomach, turning my mouth to cotton and my throat into a vise. I didn't want to know what those letters said, and yet, something in me—some deep, instinctual thing—already suspected what they would say. *The Culling.*

Magistrates rarely left the county centers and markets. They weren't errand boys or lackeys. If the queen had sent a letter with this man, then it could only mean one thing: the prince had come of age, and the Culling was beginning.

It was archaic and yet a custom treasured by so many—mostly, I'd imagine, by those it would not directly affect. It was a spectator sport. Something to bring just a touch of excitement to the dreary lives of the Erydian people. The Culling promised the beginning of a new era. A new reign.

Only ten girls in all of Erydia were goddess-touched and

capable of fighting in that competition. And I was one of them.

These ten girls would be forced to fight to the death for the Crown. By the end of it there would be nine bodies and a new queen on the throne. The tradition occurred once every thirty or forty years. It was supposed to provide us with a strong queen, one who could guarantee that our country would remain safe from our enemies beyond the mountains.

Or so the temple taught. And, truly, what truth was there in what the temple said? Enough truth to make them right about one thing: the ten heirs were goddess-chosen. All ten girls would possess supernatural abilities. They always did. It was the abilities that made the temple believe that the Culling was the only way to choose a queen. It was also said to be the only way to ensure that the new queen's reign wouldn't be questioned. After all, there was no better opening statement than one coated in the blood of nine other people.

Coated in my blood.

I held my breath, my fingers numb around the handle of the water bucket, as I waited for Kace or Ambrose to call out to me. But I had been forgotten in favor of the letters. By the time the sound of the automobile had faded completely, my brothers were already walking into the house.

Their muttered conversation was turning loud and angry as I ditched my bucket and went after them. The front door was ajar, and I didn't bother to close it behind me as I stepped into the cramped kitchen. Even with the windows and doors open, the summer heat was stifling. The cotton of my dress clung to my back with sweat as I edged toward where my brothers stood by the kitchen table.

"What did he want?"

Ambrose turned toward me. "Don't you have chores to finish, Monroe?" My blood boiled at his tone. Kace opened his mouth to speak, but Ambrose cut him off. "Don't *both* of you have chores to finish?"

With two opinionated brothers and close quarters, I'd witnessed my fair share of fistfights—I'd *started* my fair share of fistfights—but the look on Ambrose's face said that it wouldn't be wise to push him today. Usually, I'd listen to those cues. We were friends, not just siblings, most days. And I had his back, especially when Kace poked at him and tried to start shit. But I didn't like being spoken to like a child. And . . . I was curious.

Kace and I exchanged a glance. *If we both push him, he'll have no choice but to cave.*

"The rains are coming; we need to prepare," Ambrose said, oblivious to our silent plotting.

"Yes, the rains are coming. But, while we wait, what are the letters about?" I asked.

"Nothing that concerns you." Ambrose nodded to the still-open door. "It's a conversation for later. There are things to be done, and the sun is leaving us."

Kace bristled. "To hell with the sun and rains. Let me see the letter."

A sudden swell of heat pushed at my skin, a warmth that had nothing to do with the stifling temperature of the house. It was a slithering sort of anxiety that I knew could turn to true flame if I willed it. My ability to conjure fire, and the cost of my goddess-given gift, was what pushed me to ask, "Is it the Culling?"

"Chores," Ambrose said. "Now. I'm not arguing with either of you about—"

"If it's the Culling, I deserve to know."

7

"One of them is addressed to me," Kace blurted. "The magistrate said there was one for each of us."

So, maybe it wasn't the Culling then. That news would probably be directed to the whole family. The government wasn't aware of who was goddess-touched. They wouldn't send a letter to each child in the family just to announce the competition and gather the girls.

Ambrose pointed to the door again. "Finish your work, Monroe. Mama will be tired enough without having to cook dinner and tend to your chores too. We aren't dealing with any of this now."

Kace held out his hand. "You aren't the damn king, Ambrose. I don't have to listen to you. Neither does Monroe. Now give me my letter."

That tight coil of power in my gut seemed to relax. The tight chains I'd used to bind it to myself—keep it contained—seemed to unwind at the realization that I might still be safe. If the letter wasn't a Culling announcement, then I had nothing to worry about. But curiosity still prevailed.

"I have plenty of time before Mama's back. I'm sure it won't take me all afternoon to read one letter." I held out my own hand. "If there's one for me, give it here."

Kace smirked, pleased to find the two of us on the same side for once. Without a word, Ambrose brushed past us and out the door.

"Good idea," Kace called after him. "Run from your problems, that's always worked before."

I caught up to Ambrose just before he got to the barn. I didn't say anything as I darted behind him and snatched the bundle of letters from his back pocket. I was already three steps away by the time he realized what I'd done.

"Good goddess, Monroe."

He came after me, but rather than grab for me, he swatted for the letters. I sidestepped him and twirled out of his reach, holding the letters in front of me. Before he could make a second lunge for them, I rotated my wrist and called fire to flesh.

He only had time to yell, "Don't—" before my entire fist was wreathed in flame.

The fire seemed to swell in my chest—pushing out every other thought until I was nothing but flame. I felt alive. Like I was my fullest self when I burned like this.

And it had been weeks. With my mother always around, I'd resorted to small actions—invisible hands to coax the flames in the stove higher, a stray candle lit, or a cup of coffee warmed. I'd learned quickly that siphoning the heat from my veins was a nearly unnoticeable action if I was clever and careful—it was something I could do without upsetting or worrying my mother.

But, goddess, I'd missed the feel of flame on my skin.

Ambrose cursed under his breath.

"They aren't burned. I won't let the fire touch them," I said, rotating the bundle so he could see that the fire was only wreathed around my wrist. "But I could."

"You wouldn't dare."

"Wouldn't I?"

My brother crossed his arms over his chest. "If you burn them, I won't tell you what they say."

"Kace heard the magistrate. He knows what they're about at the very least. He'll tell me." I swallowed. "But I'd rather hear it from you."

We stared at each other for a long moment.

"Fine. Read them then." Ambrose threw up his hands and

turned away from me. "You're bound to hear about it anyway."

My fire fizzled out as he continued into the barn without another word. The humor and teasing from earlier dissipated just as quickly.

Ambrose tended to be overprotective, especially where I was concerned, but this—the fear on his face had nothing to do with me. I looked at the letters in my hand. One for Ambrose, one for Kace, and one for me. All of them from the war office.

My stomach bottomed out. *Oh, goddess.*

"Ambrose!" I hurried after him. His back was still to me, his attention on the sacks of grain slumped against the far wall of the barn as I said, "What is this? What—"

"Read it."

I shuffled through the three letters until I found the one addressed to me. The wax of the royal seal cracked under my fingers as I tore the letter open and began scanning the words. Two lines in and I was barely processing them. The world around me faded, as if I were being sucked into a deep, dark hole in the ground.

This was a declaration of war and a call to action. Drafted. My brothers and I had been drafted. Erydia was going to war against Vayelle—again—and every able-bodied man over the age of seventeen was expected to fight.

"We've barely recovered from the last war and it's been almost twenty years," I breathed.

"I was in the market with Ellora this morning when the announcement was posted. It was all anyone could talk about. The paperboys were yelling it on every street corner. I didn't . . . I didn't think the war office would move so quickly. I figured we at least had a few weeks before we would need to report."

I read the letter again, and then a third time. "It says here we have five days— *You* have five days. You and Kace."

Not me.

Although the letter in my hand held my name, it was addressed to Monroe Benson, the boy. The letter was addressed to the lie my mother had created. I couldn't go to the war office without revealing myself.

"What . . . What will happen if I don't show up?" I asked.

Ambrose ran a hand through his blond hair, mussing the short curls. While we shared the same sun-warmed skin and brown eyes, there was a darkness in his gaze that I didn't possess, a heaviness that came from being the head of our household. It made him appear older than his twenty-three years.

"The magistrate said they'd be investigating any deserters. If you don't show, they could come looking."

"Mama . . . Mama and I will have to run. Or . . ." I swallowed.

Ambrose slipped the remaining envelopes from my hand. He turned back to the sacks of grain as he said, "Let me think on it. Go do your chores."

"Why not let Kace have his letter?"

"Because I know what he'll say. I've been listening to him gush about joining the army for as long as I can remember. I don't have the energy to listen to him talk about it. He heard the magistrate same as I did. He knows there's a war coming. He can have the letter and start planning tonight. Between the concern over you and the rains, Ellora, and Mama," he shook his head, "I have too many things to worry about. I don't have space for his happiness."

"How will we survive if you and Kace are gone and we can't hunt? What will we do about the tithe or the floods or . . . ?"

His expression fell slightly and I regretted saying anything at all. "Chores, Monroe. We'll worry about all of that later."

"But—"

His voice turned sharp. "You wanted to know what the letter said, now you do. There's nothing to be done about it. We can talk tonight. I've got to feed the chickens, and you need to finish dinner and start heating water for the baths. Mama will be home shortly. If she . . ." He sighed. "If she doesn't know about the draft yet, she will soon enough. She'll be upset and I can't— Monroe, I can't . . . I don't want you to be afraid."

"I'm not afraid."

I just want to do something. Anything. I want to crawl out of my skin, to be more than I am. There was always this unspoken assumption in our family that because I was a marked girl and had been hidden away from the world, I couldn't possibly understand or help carry our family's troubles. And it just wasn't true. I was the reason we were in this desolate county to begin with, and I never went a day without blaming myself for it.

All I wanted was to be a part of the solution, but I was once again a part of the problem.

"I'm not afraid," I said again.

His smile was sad. "Well, I'm glad one of us isn't."

I was almost outside when he called back to me. "Monroe?"

I turned, my fingers tight against the chipped paint of the door. "Yes?"

"It's going to be all right." Something in his voice told me that the words were as much for him as they were for me.

I nodded, trying to push down the tidal wave of anxious fire in my blood as I said, "Of course, it will."

CHAPTER 2

Benson Homestead
Three days before Sacrit

We were halfway through with the dishes by the time Mama finally arrived home. Ambrose and I stood at the kitchen sink, me washing, him drying. He'd been quiet through most of the evening's chores and all of dinner.

I nudged his hip with mine. "How was Ellora today?"

The corners of his lips quirked up at the mention of his fiancé. Ambrose sighed and placed a dried plate onto the stack next to him. "I was with her when I heard about the war. She . . . She didn't take the news well. I didn't expect her to, and I hate that I can't fix it. I wouldn't leave her if I didn't have to."

"I know that. I'm sure she does too."

"Her father says—"

"Twins!" Mama announced as she came through the door. Ambrose crossed the room and took her midwifery bag from her. She smiled across the room at me. "Both girls, both healthy, and both blessedly unmarked."

I was elbow-deep in dishwater, the black mark on my palm hidden beneath layers of soap, and I still felt the need to ball up my fist. The fire beneath my skin pushed insistently, reaching invisible hands toward the embers in the stove and the rising fire in the hearth.

There was no need to say that. With the prince's eighteenth birthday looming, it was assumed that all of the marked girls were already born. Already into their teens. And besides that, there was only ever one marked girl per county, and I was here in Varos—though it wasn't the county of my birth. So, it could also be assumed that there wouldn't be another goddess-touched girl born here.

But my mother hadn't said it because she'd expected any baby she delivered to be born marked, she'd said it because despite the reality of the situation, my mother relived the trauma of my birth—of my being born marked—with every child she ushered into the world. She saw me in them. Saw my mark on their skin, even when she knew that there wasn't truly one there.

The words were a reminder. And I hated that I was the root of her fear. I hated that my existence was tainted by my looming fate and her efforts to outrun it.

Ambrose caught my eye as he turned back toward the kitchen table and set Mama's bag on one of the empty chairs. "Thank the goddess for that," he said pointedly. *Don't start anything, Monroe,* he seemed to say to me.

"Yes." I sighed. "Thank the goddess."

Mama's honeysuckle-and-mint smell enveloped me as she moved past Ambrose to stand at the washbasin with me. "And thank the goddess for all of you. Seems all the chores are done. Dinner smells wonderful." She tugged at the rolled sleeve of my dress. "You know, I'd like to see you in something other than my old clothes. Maybe come spring, I'll get fabric and we can make you something new."

She must not know about the draft then.

I nodded despite myself.

Mama shrugged out of her sweater and untied her apron, each motion practiced and achingly familiar. The vision of her unlacing her shoes, washing her hands and face, tying back her graying hair, and pulling out her midwifery tools to be sanitized—all of those actions were as familiar to me as my own face.

This was my normal, my sense of peace—and watching her go through the processes of coming home to us made me realize what I was going to miss now that things might never truly be normal again.

Kace opened his mouth like he might tell her about the arrival of our draft letters, but Ambrose stopped him with a well-aimed jab to the ribs.

"There's stew left for you," I said. "And I made bread earlier."

"I doubt there's any bread left after Kace got a hold of it," Ambrose said.

Mama paused by the woodstove, lifting the lid of the pot to examine the vegetable stew warming there. "You know," she said, glancing pointedly at Kace. "Earlier today, someone mentioned to me that the magistrate was making rounds. Did he come by here?"

Ambrose sighed in defeat.

Mama set the lid aside with a soft *clack*. And smiled, tight-lipped, to herself.

Kace had always been a rule follower and if Mama asked a question, he'd answer honestly. It was nice sometimes—especially when you didn't want to be the bearer of bad news—but as siblings it was mostly a curse. Kace was nothing if not a snitch.

Mama grabbed a bowl and began filling it. Ambrose leaned his hip against the wooden kitchen counter and let out a long-suffering sigh as Kace said, "He delivered our draft letters."

My mother's posture turned stiff. "What draft?"

The bowl in her hand fell slack, nearly spilling its contents all over the floor. Ambrose pushed away from the counter and crossed the room in two steps. He took the bowl from her and pulled out one of the kitchen chairs before he guided her into it.

In that moment, she looked eighty, not barely forty-five. "When?"

"We have five days to report," Ambrose explained. "Me, Kace, *and* Monroe."

"Monroe?" Her face drained of color.

"Ambrose said that if I don't show up, they'll send people to look for me."

"It may not be a bad thing," Kace said quietly. "The prince turns eighteen this month. I know we didn't plan for her to go to the Culling, but maybe—"

"No." Mama was on her feet in an instant. "I'm not discussing that. We'll . . . We'll move. I can do my job anywhere. There are always babies to be birthed and mothers to tend to. And I still have the money Philip put away. I'm sure we can rent a place or—"

"What will you eat?" Kace said. "How will you hunt? And how will you explain where you've come from or who Monroe is?"

"I can wear gloves or wrap my mark or," I pulled my hands from the basin and grabbed a towel, "or I could just stay hidden. I've been staying away from town for years. Plus, with another war brewing against Vayelle, everyone will be too busy with their own troubles to worry about one teenage girl. I'm no one."

"You aren't just some random girl, Monroe. You're goddess-touched." Kace pulled out the chair across the table from where

I stood and sat down. "That may have worked in the past, but it won't work once the Culling is announced. Our neighbors may not care about you now—they may not question a bandage or any of your other lies—but once the Culling is in session and one girl is missing, there will be a price on your head. The Crown will come looking for their missing contestant."

"We'll deal with that when it comes," Mama said, standing up again. "For now . . . For now I can only deal with one issue at a time. We'll find a way to move. We'll make a new life. Monroe will remain hidden. If anyone asks, all of my sons are enlisted, and I have no daughters. I live alone." She grabbed her bowl from where Ambrose had placed it next to the stove and walked back to the table.

"Monroe should continue to practice her ability," Ambrose said. "She needs to work with it. She's been smart about using it so far. If she uses her judgment and doesn't lose control, she should be fine. But as things are, it wouldn't be smart for her to neglect her training. Not with so many threats hanging over her. Over both of you."

"She isn't going to the Culling," Mama said. "I didn't move all the way to this goddess-forsaken county just so that my baby— *just so Monroe*—could be taken from me. It will not have been for nothing."

"It isn't just the Culling I'm worried about," Ambrose admitted.

Kace leaned back in his chair. "When the Culling is announced and Monroe doesn't show, every abandoned and starving woman in Varos will be fighting to be the one to track down the missing goddess-touched girl. They always offer huge incentives to help track down fleeing girls—with the draft in place and most of the men gone, the stakes will be high. Someone will find you. People will turn on each other for the reward alone. They'll need it to survive. Monroe can't—"

"Then I'll get the necessary papers and go to Vayelle," I said. "They don't believe in the Culling or the goddess."

Kace laughed. "No, you won't. With the war, the border between us and Vayelle will be closed off. No one will be able to get safely through the Suri Gap. And we aren't capable of scaling those mountains. Plus, you're talking about going into enemy territory."

"Vayelle isn't my enemy. They're Erydia's enemy—and right now, that country is safer than this one. They want our land. They care nothing about us."

"You're making assumptions," he said. "You don't know what you're talking about."

Fire heated my blood. "The border isn't closed now, is it?"

"It isn't. Not yet, at least," Ambrose said. "I saw people at the train station earlier today."

"Goddess, would the two of you get your heads out of your asses?" Kace said. "It would take months to get the necessary paperwork to leave Erydia. And that's without a war starting and without a damn mark on your hand. The choice is simple enough, Monroe."

Mama put her head in her hands. "Please, don't argue about this."

"I'm not arguing," Kace said. "I'm simply trying to get the three of you to see reason. Monroe, especially."

I straightened. "What would you like me to do then?"

"I'd like you to give up on outrunning the Culling and do what's best for the family," he said. "I'd like you to stop being a coward."

Mama inhaled sharply. "Kace Benson—"

"I'm not a coward," I said. "I've stayed hidden because it's what *Mama* wanted me to do."

"Maybe the time for hiding is over," Kace said. "Maybe you need to step up and help provide for our family. Ambrose and I have always pulled our weight. We have always made sure you were safe. But that's coming to an end. What will Mama do with Ambrose and me gone, when the rains come and the floodlands expand? When the winter stretch sets in and everything freezes over for months, what will she do?"

Mama shook her head. "What happens to me isn't Monroe's responsibility."

"Yes, it is," Kace said. "It's as much her responsibility as it is mine or Ambrose's. With us gone, neither of you will be able to hunt. The laws surrounding that won't change just because there's a draft."

"There's food in the cellar," Mama argued. "And I'll get money and food from patients."

"When the rains hit and the winter stretch sets in, you won't be able to travel to births either," Kace said. "There goes your food and your income. Ambrose and I will be gone and will have no way to look after you. The money we make in service won't be enough, and you'll starve. If Monroe remains here, she'll starve too. Hell, even if she could make it across the border to Vayelle, she'd still starve. How will she support herself? What will you do if the Vaylish decide to turn you in? You're relying on rumors and naïve hope. Neither will feed you. What will you do, Monroe? Do you plan to stand on street corners and sell your flesh?"

One of the logs in the hearth snapped and sparks hissed

against the stone base of the fireplace as I said, "Whatever I plan to do is my decision, not yours."

"Enough," Ambrose said.

Kace shoved a finger in my direction. "If you go to the Culling, Mama will be taken care of. Our family would receive an allowance for as long as you're in the competition. And indefinitely if you become queen. You could save us. All of us. Imagine it, Monroe: a girl from Varos, from the slums, becoming Queen of Erydia. That's the solution, don't you see?"

"You're asking Monroe to put her life on the line," Ambrose said. "You're asking her to join a competition that could end with her death."

"Our lives are *all* on the line," Kace countered. "We're joining a war that could just as easily end in *our* deaths."

Ambrose shook his head. "You're talking as if being a soldier isn't something you've been dreaming about since you were a child. You *want* to serve the Crown."

"Good goddess, Ambrose." Kace gestured to me. "Don't you see? She could *be* the Crown. She could be queen. That mark on her hand isn't going to go away just because Mama refuses to acknowledge it."

"That's enough," Ambrose said. "You can express your opinions, but you aren't going to bully anyone into agreeing with you."

"We're arguing over a threat that doesn't even exist yet," Mama said, her voice drained. "The Culling is a bridge we'll cross when it comes. For now, we need to focus on the draft. Monroe and I can try to sell the farm and—"

Kace cut her off. "If Ambrose and I have to go to war, why shouldn't Monroe have to fight too?"

Ambrose's fist hit the table. "Because war with Vayelle isn't the same thing as a damn Culling, Kace. There will be nine other gifted girls in that arena. It's a glorified slaughter."

Kace shrugged, incredulous. "Monroe can hold her own. She isn't a child. She's seventeen years old and she's marked. She can create fire from nothing."

Even though I had no desire to fight in the competition or claim the crown, I still felt pushed to say, "Kace is right. If I had to go to the Culling, I could—I think I could survive, at least for a while—"

"But should she have to?" Ambrose demanded, not even acknowledging I'd said anything. "Should she have to fight and die for a few stray coins?"

"If it would help keep Mama alive while we're gone, then yes. She should."

The room fell silent.

"Have you seen her practicing behind the barn? It isn't like she doesn't know what she's doing. And it certainly isn't like Monroe doesn't *enjoy* using her ability." Kace nodded to me. "She only pretends to be disinterested because she knows it bothers Mama. She uses it every chance she gets. Every time Mama's back is turned, she uses it."

"Enjoying what I can do doesn't mean I want to die for it," I said.

"Listen to me," Kace said, his attention entirely on me. "You've spent years hiding from who you are and it hasn't changed anything. That mark isn't going to disappear. Your choice is to die running from it or die fighting for it. And you will never outrun the goddess."

I didn't have to look to know that Ambrose rolled his eyes. My brothers ran in different circles and held vastly different friends—and while they argued over a great many things, one of the biggest dividers in our household was the goddess and the temple.

Ambrose saw my mark as a threat.

Kace saw it as our divine deliverance.

I couldn't look at him as I said, "If the border is still open, then I'm going to try to make it to Vayelle." Kace opened his mouth to protest, but I held up a hand. "I've been saving money every birthday since I was little. I'm not sure it'll be enough to buy travel waivers, but—"

"I'll get the papers," Ambrose said. "And the train tickets. I'll get us both safely across."

Kace shook his head in disbelief. "You'll run from the draft?"

Ambrose nodded. "I'm not sending her to Vayelle alone."

Mama sighed. "I'll stay here and tell anyone who comes looking that two of my sons have run."

"You'll starve," Kace said.

She shook her head. "I'm not weak, Kace Benson. I'll remind you that I lived alone on this farm for years with three small children. I kept it running. I kept the three of you clothed and fed. I survived those years on my own and I can survive whatever else is to come. I lost my husband to the last war and I will not lose my children to another. I certainly will not lose my daughter to the Culling. Not if it's within my power to stop it."